Fire in the Bones

By

Irma Ned Bailey

Panther Creek Press

Spring, Texas

Published by Panther Creek Press
116 Tree Crest
P.O. Box 130233 Panther Creek Station
Spring, Texas 77393-0233

Cover photo copyright © 1978 Robert Neal Quinn
Conroe, Texas
Cover design by Adam Murphy
The Woodlands, Texas
Manufactured in the United States of America
Printed and bound in Houston, Texas

1 2 3 4 5 6 7 8 9 10

Library of Congress Cataloguing in Publication Data

Bailey, Irma Ned
    Fire in the bones

     I. Fiction   II. Texana   III. Burkburnett   IV. Oil Boom

ISBN 0-9747839-3-5

Acknowledgments

I would like to thank the Burkburnett Public Library for helping me locate
tapes of local oral histories and the Kemp Public Library in Wichita Falls
for sending the *Wichita Daily Times* from 1918 - 1919 on microfilm. I
thank the San Antonio College Library, my colleagues in the English
Department, and the English Department staff for their continuing help
and support; Jeff Landrum, Mattie Dell Aulds, and Lowell Woods for their
useful suggestions about the oil field; and the Rev. James Price and Mrs.
Willa May Price for information on farming. Any errors are mine, not
theirs. I am especially grateful to Cynthia Massey and Hillary Stevens for
their care in editing the manuscript, and to Judy Lampert, Judith Infante,
Linda Shuler, Janice Clayton, Marjorie Wells, Jennifer Endsley and Betty
Bell for their careful reading. Last, I am grateful to my children–Hillary,
Samuel, and Daniel Stevens–for their encouragement, suggestions, and,
not least, patience.

In Memory of Roger Blackwell Bailey (1939-2001)
and
Daniel Wesley Stevens (1982-2003)

His word was in mine heart as a burning fire
shut up in my bones.
(Jer. 20: 9)

1

"Let me help you." A soldier limped toward Margaret from the now empty train car. His red hair was set off by his olive uniform. He stooped to pick up her suitcase.

"Wait." She peered out the window one last time. Below her the platform seethed with roughnecks speckled with oil and dust. But she couldn't spot Dutch. Just like a man. She'd sent him a telegram, traveled two days in this God-awful heat all the way from Shreveport, spent the night in that smelly hotel in Fort Worth, and he was nowhere in sight. The air reeked of oil, tobacco, and sweat. She heard the racket of drilling rigs and steam boilers, the crashes of oilfield equipment and pine logs unloaded from the train and reloaded onto wagons. Underneath it all, hundreds of men's voices buzzed with optimism.

So this was a north Texas boomtown. Three weeks ago she hadn't dreamed such a place existed. Standing here for the first time, she felt doubt. Maybe Dutch's mother was right, calling her too bullheaded for her own good. Maybe, but her mother-in-law didn't know Margaret well.

His green eyes on her, the doughboy straightened his long frame. My, he was a beanpole, so thin that Margaret's mother would've insisted he was peaked and offered him squirrel and dumplings.

Margaret shifted Beth to her other hip. "Really, I can manage." She had to holler over all the noise.

But even limping and carrying her suitcase, he had already maneuvered himself off the train. With Beth on her left arm, pocketbook on her right, she trudged to the top of the steps, feeling unsteady on the high heels of her lace-up boots. He held out his hand. She felt bewildered. She needed three hands: one to clutch Beth, one to lean on the handrail, and one to hold up her skirt so she wouldn't trip and fall headfirst into that mob. She stood paralyzed. He set down the suitcase. Grinning, he reached for Beth who, brown eyes wide, went to him with no protest. Even though his wool uniform must scratch her chin, Beth looked around with interest. That was a surprise. What was he, an expert on babies? Beth usually kicked up a row with a stranger. All day long she'd fretted if Margaret so much as laid her down on the seat. Babies could sense what their mamas felt inside.

Margaret scanned the crowd once more. Still no Dutch. She stepped onto the platform, her hair sticky with sweat beneath the rose-covered hat, her silk dress smudged with the dust that crusted everything around her and made the sun a fuzzy blob.

She took Beth from the soldier and placed the baby against her shoulder. The soldier pushed through a crowd more unruly than the one in Wichita Falls. She raised her chin and followed his uniform. Strange to see a soldier here, and he wasn't the only one. Against the overalls and khaki pants and shirts of the roughnecks, occasional olive drab uniforms stood out. Why weren't these doughboys fighting in France?

"It's chaos, ma'am." He looked around the platform and motioned toward an empty space against the station, a small red wooden building. "Is someone meeting you?"

"I sent a telegram." He must think she had no sense at all. Aware of the soldier's eyes, she pushed up her hair, which was escaping from under the hat, and felt herself blush. "The train was late."

He frowned. "A lady and a baby shouldn't be here alone. It's dangerous, Ma'am."

"I can take care of myself." She couldn't remember how many times Mama had taken the hairbrush to her behind for sassing. And her smart mouth had caused friction with Dutch and recently with his mother. To make amends, Margaret tried to smile at the soldier, but her lips were so dry that they stuck together, and all she managed was a smirk.

Around them men clamored to board the train. For some folks travel must be a way of beginning again, a way of being granted a second chance at life. Perhaps Dutch had felt that way after their last argument. He'd realized she was bound to have trouble staying with his parents on the farm in Louisiana, but she didn't want to be dependent on her own folks while he was in Texas.

The crowd surged, someone shoved, and she fell backward. As

Beth started to slip from her grasp, Margaret screamed. In this crowd they would be trampled, and Dutch would never know. She caught Beth and clutched her tightly.

The doughboy pulled her up with a hand as soft as her own. Strange, strength without hardness. Dutch's hands had been calloused as long as she'd known him. Unlike the men around her, the soldier looked freshly shaved and even smelled clean.

"Would you like me to hold the baby?" he asked.

"No, I was scared for a minute. That's all."

"May I take you somewhere?" He ran a freckled hand through his hair, which shone in the sun. "This is not a safe place for a lady."

Margaret had to admit she was frightened. She reminded herself that she'd been through worse fixes than this, like when she was lost in the piney woods at home. She hadn't panicked and had discovered the way out. She bit her lip. "I'm quite all right."

"If you're sure—" The soldier hesitated and then dissolved in the crowd. Margaret smoothed her dress, as inappropriate in this dingy mob as her pink-flowered hat. Dutch would ask why she was so gussied up. Of course she wanted to look her best—she had come to meet him. She sat on her suitcase. She didn't want to risk its being stolen. But perhaps Dutch couldn't spot her with all those bodies milling around. She covered her nose with her handkerchief, doused with lavender water before she left Fort Worth. Up before five to catch the first train, she'd found the hotel lobby already swarming with men, many touching a gilded statue of a derrick for good luck. She should've touched the statue too.

Margaret held Beth against her hip. "Help me find Papa." Beth still looked alert, but she'd be hungry soon.

The train left, and the crowd scattered. Margaret counted the forest of wooden derricks surrounding the station, reaching ninety before she gave up.

"Ma'am?"

Margaret jumped.

An elderly man with a drooping mustache and glasses thicker than Dutch's appeared, the lenses so strong that they made his eyes huge gray saucers. "Sorry to startle you. Why don't you stand on that suitcase? You could see better." He laid it down for her and steadied her elbow. "You're not from here?"

"We live on Caddo Lake."

He looked blank.

"In north Louisiana. Near Shreveport."

"Who're you waiting for, Ma'am?"

"My husband. He'll be here anytime." She searched the crowd, smaller but still milling around. "Perhaps you've met him? Dutch Sanders?"

"Don't know as I have. I hear tell there are maybe twenty thousand people right in Nesterville. Forty thousand in this area near Wichita Falls." He frowned at her dress and hat. "I don't know as how your husband would cotton to you being here by yourself. There aren't many ladies, and they don't come downtown without their husbands."

She half expected him to sniff in disapproval like Dutch's mother. She shaded her eyes with her hand. "He'll be here."

"If it gets later, Ma'am, you ought to find a room. There are too many carryings-on for it to be safe."

Margaret nodded. The man hobbled back to a bench of three old-timers down the platform. They raised their hats to her in unison while the man with the walrus mustache conveyed his information. They looked dismayed. She'd no doubt done it again: insulted the kind soldier and now the elderly man. She wiped her forehead. Beth whimpered, hungry.

Through the dust the sun was setting, a red disk pasted on the sky. Wisps of clouds stained orange and pink grew luminous. The sunsets weren't like this at home. Fewer men crowded the street, and fewer wagons raised dust. The clouds faded to gray. She couldn't wait here for Dutch all night. She lugged her suitcase inside the empty station, stopping every few steps to rest.

Behind her came the slap of running footsteps. She turned, exuberant, about to say "Dutch!" A hand shoved her so hard that she fell back onto the floor as a man grabbed her suitcase and then her pocketbook. She screamed. Beth howled. Even as she fell, Margaret clutched the baby to her with one hand. and grabbed his trouser leg with the other. Cursing, the man tried to shake her off, but she clung to him, hollering.

He bent down and punched the side of her head, but she held on to his pants leg. He dragged her toward the exit and finally wrenched his leg free. The three old men and the walrus man appeared in the doorway, staring as the thief ran toward them. He pushed them aside with her suitcase as if they weighed no more than she. Sitting up, she watched them call "Help!" and follow him onto the platform.

Trembling, she sat gripping Beth until she heard the sounds of the world above the thumping of her heart. She pressed Beth to her, comforted by the baby's warmth. "It's all right now. He's gone." But Beth kept gasping, shaking with sobs. Margaret stood, rank from tobacco stains and oil. She peered out the door but couldn't spot the hijacker, whom she could describe only as a pudgy man in overalls. Some help to the police she'd be. Her head throbbed as she paced, jiggling Beth, who wouldn't be consoled. "Stop that racket. Mama's got to think."

Without warning she heard a cough. "Ma'am?" Beside her stood the old man with the thick glasses and walrus mustache and behind him the three oldtimers. "We couldn't catch him." He paused, breathing hard. The three men nodded in agreement before, touching their hats, they shuffled out. The walrus man said, "It's getting dark. You shouldn't stay here."

Where else would she go?

He touched the ends of his mustache and nodded east. "The nicest rooming house is Miz Butler's. It's on my way home." His face was still flushed from the exertion of the chase. What if he had a heart attack?

Margaret sighed.

"We've howdied, but we haven't shook. Bob Johnson. I own the feed store by the train station."

She wiped her grimy palm on her sleeve—too late to worry about impressing Dutch now—and her sweaty hand was enclosed in his damp handshake.

She mustn't panic. True, she'd lost everything; all their savings were in the pocketbook, but she had to be strong until Dutch found her.

"Theft's bad here." Mr. Johnson sounded disapproving.

Was she supposed to know that? "Call the police."

"No law in town, ma'am. Sometimes a Texas Ranger." He stepped to the door and turned. "They wouldn't bother about a little thing like a suitcase and a pocketbook."

A little thing? She frowned. "You don't understand. I don't know what to do. My husband didn't meet me, and I have nothing: no money, no clothes. Nothing."

"I'll take you to Eve's, ma'am. She'll help."

She shrugged. What choice did she have? "I'd be beholden."

Men, who seemed to be mainly in their forties, barely too old for the draft, sauntered along the street, apparently with nothing to do, nowhere or no one to go home to. Where had they all been when her suitcase and pocketbook were stolen? Once she thought she glimpsed the red-headed doughboy.

On Main Street they passed stores found in any small town: groceries, dry goods, barber shops, a laundry, picture shows featuring Houdini and Charlie Chaplin. But on the side streets, interspersed with houses and derricks, Margaret also glimpsed boomtown businesses: canvas-covered dance halls next to stock offices, brokerage houses, and oilfield supply stores. In the doorways, Margaret searched for both Dutch and her suitcase, dropping her eyes when the men stared. Some tipped their hats and murmured, "Evening, Ma'am, Bob."

Mr. Johnson squeezed her arm. She pulled away. Something wasn't right. He smiled. She must have misunderstood. Maybe.

They were on a raised wooden walkway a few inches above dust that looked at least ankle deep. Margaret's dress and boots were coated with grit. She wiped Beth's face with the handkerchief, and Beth whimpered. She mustn't become discouraged; she had, after all, chosen to come here. Margaret marched in silence.

Above them, scattered through the commercial and residential areas, rose wooden derricks, crisscrosses of scaffolding above raised platforms crammed so close together that Margaret thought she could walk from the floor of one platform to another without touching the ground. With all the derricks, Nesterville looked like a pincushion around her.

After three blocks of the business section, they turned the corner and passed tar paper shanties, shacks made from box cars, and rows of tents, some Army style with wooden walls up to three feet, others with makeshift frames covered with canvas or tar paper. Through open doors stretched lines of cots. She hoped this boarding house was a bona fide building. Everywhere she sensed haste and flimsiness. She felt she was walking but not moving forward, her body little more than perspiration and dirt.

Mr. Johnson pointed at a two-story white frame building ahead, permanent looking among all the temporary shelters. "I hope we can catch Eve."

Margaret glanced at him.

"She plays the piano at the Red Onion. A saloon."

What next? Maybe this woman was a madam, this rooming house a brothel.

A giant of a woman slammed the screen door and strode toward them. About thirty years old, she must have been fifty pounds heavier than Margaret and at least a head taller than Margaret's five-foot-seven. Her thick auburn hair was twisted around her head in two braids. Margaret expected her to pull out a Viking sword.

"Eve, hold your horses. I've brought you a roomer. Her suitcase and pocketbook were stolen."

The Viking woman turned. "I'm full up." Her eyes fell on Beth, and her voice softened. She shrugged. "Give her the room by the back stairs. Used to be a storeroom, but it's better than nothing. Bob, get some biscuits from the kitchen. Also some rags for diapers." She addressed Margaret. "I've got to run. See you in the morning." Then she was gone, her long skirt swishing around the corner.

Margaret felt numb. Mr. Johnson opened the door for her.

"Don't trip," he warned.

His arm encircled her waist. She shoved her elbow into his soft stomach. "What are you doing?"

"I thought you stumbled."

"I didn't stumble." Dirty old man.

Red-faced, he indicated a room under the stairs. She stepped inside, keeping her back to the wall. Not meeting her eyes, he said, "I'll fetch you some grits."

The tiny room was bare except for a cot, an oak dresser with the top scarred by cigarette burns, and a rocking chair pushed up against a small window that looked onto a side street. Margaret dropped into the rocking chair, Beth on her lap, barely able to remember the enthusiasm she'd felt twelve hours before.

Mr. Johnson returned with two biscuits, a glass of buttermilk, and a pan of murky water with a film of oil on top. "This is all I could get. Here's some rags for diapers." In an instant he'd metamorphosed from lecher to kindly grandfather. Who was he really?

She pursed her lips. "This is the room she wanted me to have?"

"Lucky to get it. Most people rent cots in tents or space on porches."

He left with a cheerful "See y'all later," but she didn't trust him. She waited until she heard the front screen slam. Then she scooted the dresser over to block the door. That should keep her safe. She bathed Beth, who lay on her back and waved her arms and legs. Margaret bent over her, blowing and saying "Boo." Her dark eyes on Margaret, Beth laughed. It didn't take much to satisfy a baby.

Sitting in the rocking chair, she unbuttoned the top of her dress, relaxing so the milk would come. Beth flailed her arms until she found Margaret's breast with her mouth and both hands. Exhausted, her head aching, Margaret leaned against the back of the chair.

It had taken the packed train almost all morning to go the hundred miles from Fort Worth to "Witch-ta" Falls, as the conductor said, and then fifteen miles on another train to Nesterville, men crammed into every seat and stuffed in the aisles. As the train had inched farther north to the base of the Texas Panhandle, the landscape had flattened, the grass died, and the trees became sparser and more stunted until only an occasional mesquite, delicate leaves shining, protruded above the plains. Margaret yawned. Beth hung heavy in her arms, stirring only once when Margaret laid her on the cot.

Margaret washed in the oily water, but she still felt dirty. The stale air smelled of tobacco and the sweat of the previous occupant, and the room felt as if all the heat of the day had been trapped inside it. Dare she open the window? If it was a choice of being assaulted and robbed or suffocating, she'd choose not to suffocate. She opened the window a few inches and placed herself on the narrow bed, adjusting her bruises, careful not to jostle Beth. All night long, pumps and boilers chugged, chanting, "Foolish, foolish, foolish."

2

Margaret dreamed she sat on the porch at home, smelling the honeysuckle and wild roses and feeling the evening breeze off Caddo Lake. They were all bunched together—Rachel and Ida by Mama and Mr. Graham, she and Brother Aut on the steps petting Shep—while Mama read her poem about the mosquito so big it carried off a horse. Her mother laughed loudly, the strong laugh that always surprised Margaret. In the dream Dutch walked out of the pine trees and touched her hair, but she was too young to have met Dutch. Puzzled, she woke, returning to the cacophony of the wells, men's voices in the adjoining rooms, and the clatter of dishes. She lay still while the world came back and with it her hopes. She would find Dutch today.

Beth was asleep in her favorite position, on her stomach with her left cheek against the sheet, knees bent and bottom up. Through the open window Margaret saw wagons and men already trampling the streets, dust clouding the cool air of dawn.

Outside the window a dark form rose, transforming into the head of a man with a long beard and a cowboy hat. Margaret pulled the sheet up while the man gazed into the room as if memorizing every detail. Raising his hat, he pronounced, "You're fired," as solemnly as if intoning a prayer in church. With dignity he turned and marched across the street, ignoring the taunts of the wagoners and drivers. Good heavens, below the cowboy hat he wore nothing but beat-up hunting boots. She grabbed her dress, hearing at the same time a knock and a loud woman's voice.

"Come on, Girl, before I throw out your grits. Time to get cracking." Margaret smoothed her wrinkled dress and picked up Beth before that crazy man returned.

Outside her room on the other side of the stairs, four long tables were littered with debris in the biggest dining room she'd ever seen. The Viking woman, braids to her waist, wore a cotton dress sprigged with purple flowers. "I salvaged you some oatmeal." She stared at Margaret's bare feet and tangled hair.

Margaret burst out, "A man with no clothes—just a hat and boots. By my window. He said I was fired."

Eve waved a work-hardened hand. "Jerry? He's harmless. Lives in the church. I'll tell Brother Pound."

"What's wrong with him?"

"Nothing, really. Just slow."

"I can't believe he runs around loose." Thieves, an old lecher, now a lunatic. Some mess she'd got herself into. "I can't pay you until my husband finds me. He should be here today." She tried to ignore Eve's skeptical glance. "Mr. Johnson said Dutch would know to look for me here."

Eve shrugged. "Maybe."

She would overlook that. "Mr. Johnson made me very uncomfortable. He kept cozying up to me. What a lecher! When I protested, he acted innocent."

"Ignore it. He'll leave you alone now that he knows you're respectable. Deep down, he's good-hearted."

"I hope so." Margaret voiced her real concern. "What about Dutch? He was supposed to meet me. I wonder if you know him?"

"I haven't met anyone called Dutch." Eve patted her hair. She had biceps that would be impressive on a man. She poured coffee, placed a bowl of oatmeal in front of Margaret, and spread a calico quilt on the floor. "Put the baby here. It's clean." Beth pushed herself up on her arms and stared at the colors. "My mother made it for my hope chest. Some hope. You can have it."

"I couldn't."

"Why not? I'm not using it." Eve set down her cup. "What are your plans? That is, if your husband doesn't show up today?"

She spoke as if Dutch were a rabbit that might materialize from a magician's top hat. Margaret gazed at the abandoned plates smeared with leftovers. "I'll look for Dutch, and I'll write my folks so they'll know where I am—if Dutch writes them, I mean, and then—" She swallowed. "By then I'll have found him. He's got to be somewhere. I'll look everywhere downtown. I'll get a job so I can pay you—if we can stay here, I mean—while I look for Dutch. It might be hard with Beth. I used to teach school before I married." Her voice trailed off, and she sighed. "I don't know what to do about my suitcase and my pocketbook."

"Nothing you can do. What's left?"

"Just these clothes."

"I can lend you some." Eve twisted her lips. "I've got a few things that might fit the baby too."

"I didn't realize you had a baby."

"I don't." Eve left the room, calling over her shoulder, "Let's see what we can find."

Margaret followed her into a spacious bedroom across the hall. Lace curtains covered two large windows, dark oak floors shone, and on the double bed a crocheted spread over a maroon satin quilt spelled out the Lord's Prayer.

"What a beautiful room!" Margaret hadn't expected such luxury. She checked her feet for dirt.

"It used to be my parents' room. My mother and grandmother made all this."

Eve pulled out a drawer in a mahogany bureau. "Here are some sit-upons." She opened the door of a matching wardrobe to reveal black skirts, white blouses, and two dresses, one purple satin and the other aqua taffeta. She selected a skirt and blouse. "These should do for now. This afternoon I can make you something better."

"You can make something in one day?"

Eve raised her eyebrows. "Can't you?"

"My mother showed me how to sew, but I was a failure. Nothing fit." She felt immature next to this woman who looked as if she could accomplish almost anything.

"One of my many talents." Eve pushed aside hatboxes on the top shelf of the closet and brought out a carton. "Let's see." She held embroidered shirts and smocked dresses up to Beth. "Try these."

"I can't accept them. They're too valuable. All this handwork."

"Nonsense. They're not getting any use."

"Why do you have all these?"

Eve kept her eyes on the clothes. "Once I thought I wanted a baby, and I made them for fun, like making doll clothes when I was little." Eve paused. "Now you and Beth might want a bath."

"I'd like to help you clean up first. To pay for my room and board."

"There'll be plenty to do later on." Eve heated water on the wood-burning stove and then filled a tub. Margaret hadn't been waited on so much since Dutch left. She missed his pampering.

"Nobody will be back for a few hours. You're safe," Eve said.

"This is so kind—"

"Happy to do what I can. But I could use some help around here."

"I'd like to look for Dutch also."

"We can try." Eve didn't sound very optimistic. "Now I've got to sweep the dining room."

Margaret stepped into the warm water and lay back, her eyes closed. She wished Dutch were here to wash her back. She'd find him. They'd be happy again. She scrubbed her hair, the grit loosening and washing away, but still a buzzing in her head distracted her, her worries spreading like ripples on a lake: what if he didn't want to be found? Ridiculous. Why wouldn't he be happy to see her? True, she'd gone against his wishes and angered his parents by leaving. His mother had surely written to tell him she'd run off. That's what she'd call it: run off. But married folks should stay together. That's what her mother had told her, and she ought to know.

Dripping, Margaret climbed out of the tub and picked up Beth, who was rocking back and forth on her hands and knees. She'd be crawling any day. Back in the tub, Margaret held Beth, squirming and splashing, on her knees. Margaret hadn't expected much of motherhood. In fact, it took her until she was six months pregnant even to accept the idea. What a surprise, the joy she'd felt when she first saw Beth, as amazing as the intensity of her feelings for Dutch.

Still damp, Margaret dressed. With the waistband of Eve's skirt and the sleeves of her blouse rolled up, she felt like a child playing in her mother's old clothes, but she didn't care. She was clean.

She dressed Beth in a white batiste shirt with pink embroidery. She hoped Eve's baby, if she'd had one, hadn't died. She could hear her practical sister Ida admonish her not to compose histories out of airy nothings. She ought not to question Eve's far-fetched story about making the clothes for fun and accept the baby clothes with gratitude. Ida would probably also say Margaret shouldn't have up and come without more notice. What if Dutch hadn't received her telegram? That was Ida, scrutinizing every possibility, chewing a subject to extinction. Thank goodness she wasn't like Ida, although perhaps she should have waited to hear from Dutch, but at least until now, her instincts had guided her right, as straight as furrows in cotton fields. Anyway, she was in Texas, and it was useless to say "should." She spread the towel on the back steps to dry and opened the door into the dining room.

"Look at you. Like you've lived here for years." Eve leaned on her broom.

"Is this a good time to look for Dutch?"

"It won't hurt to try, I guess."

They walked to town, retracing Margaret's steps from the previous evening. As Eve greeted many of the men on the street, Margaret felt their eyes and realized she was blushing only when Eve interrupted her running commentary on the town to dart an amused look at her.

Eve lectured like a teacher. "The rigs operate day and night. Some shifts run from noon to midnight and midnight to noon, so businesses are open twenty-four hours." Men rented space on porches and the church and the funeral home to sleep. Sometimes one cot would be rented to three different men in twenty-four hours.

Margaret's mind drifted. She didn't care how many people slept on how many porches. All she wanted was one single man. Was that too much to ask?

"Are you even listening?"

"Of course." Margaret pulled herself back to the dusty street and noticed how everyone seemed exhilarated: fortunes were waiting. They passed clumps of men exchanging money and signing papers. Margaret didn't understand.

"What's all this?" she asked.

"The awl bidness doesn't wait for anybody."

Awl? Oh, oil.

"They're forming companies."

"On the street?"

"No more office space."

Margaret watched as a kid called "Clean spring water, ten cents a dipperful." He looked about six years old, the two buckets he carried dwarfing him. A man pulled a wad of bills from his hip pocket searching for change. She and Eve lined up. She lifted the dipper. My, that water was good, cool and fresh as a breeze off the lake, so different from Eve's water with its surface layer of oil.

Margaret pulled on Eve's sleeve. "Wait. I'll tell that Texas Ranger about my suitcase and my pocketbook."

"Don't bother. They've got worse crimes to worry about. Another hijacking and murder last night. You were lucky. Too much money too quick for their own good. Oil fever. You and your husband should make what you can and get out."

"Why do you stay?"

"Nowhere else to go. This is home." Eve shrugged. "My family came here before I was born. Lived in dugouts and caves in the hills near the riverbed." Dugouts? Hills? Everything around here was flat.

Eve glanced at the sun climbing the derricks. "I need to start dinner. I'm expecting at least twenty."

"You cook for twenty people?"

"Me and a kid who quit last week. You could help and make some money."

"I'd be glad to, unless of course Dutch comes today."

"Sure." Eve sounded so skeptical Margaret didn't challenge her.

3

A soft, round woman sat on Eve's porch swing. Her silver hair was pulled back in a knot, and her dress was sprigged with purple flowers exactly like Eve's. "Heavens," Eve whispered. "I'll wager anything she'll fan herself like crazy when she sees I made my dress from the same flour sacks she made hers from. Watch."

The woman fanned herself with a plump hand and called in an exaggerated drawl, "Hey, you gadabouts."

"I told you," Eve hissed in Margaret's ear.

The woman extended puffy arms to Beth, who favored her with a grin as wide as her face. "What a darling baby. Bring it out of the sun. Babies shouldn't be in this heat. Let me hold it. Babies love me." She patted the swing beside her. "Sit a spell. I'm Eula May Johnson. And you're the new girl in town. Robert told me you didn't find your husband yesterday." Mrs. Johnson sounded pleased. For her, everything must be a source of gossip.

Margaret bit her bottom lip. "I'm very grateful for Mr. Johnson's help. I'm sure my husband will come today. He should have received the telegram several days ago." Her depression, buried under the luxury of a bath and the novelty of the town, crept back like a cloud inching over the sun.

"I declare, I hope he hasn't left you," Mrs. Johnson said.

"What do you mean?" Margaret raised her eyebrows. The nerve of this stranger.

Mrs. Johnson touched her cheek. "Nothing, dear, of course. But sometimes men do. Go to a new place. Start a new life. But I'm sure your husband wouldn't be up to anything like that. He couldn't leave such a sweetums baby." She fanned Beth with her handkerchief and peered at Margaret through small glasses with silver rims. "What does your husband do?"

"He's a roughneck. He cleans and changes the drill bits and helps the driller, Paul, the man he came with." She was proud of Dutch, so young with such a responsible job. But she wouldn't tell this gossipy woman their dream of one day owning a drilling rig with Paul and drilling for themselves. Dutch's mother had scoffed when Margaret confided in her, sparking the quarrel that made Margaret leave. She shouldn't let herself be baited. She should be quiet and take it, like Dutch's dad, but she couldn't.

"Have you been married long?"

"Three years." Surely Mrs. Johnson had something to think about besides Margaret's history.

"Quite a spell for one so young."

"I'm twenty-five." Margaret glanced at Eve, who stood behind Mrs. Johnson rolling her eyes.

"You need a sunbonnet. You're already burned." Mrs. Johnson touched her own face, as white as a China doll's. "And this poor baby needs a hat, don't you, Little One?" Mrs. Johnson tickled Beth under the chin. Beth beamed, loving the attention. Nothing spoiled about this child.

Eve stretched. "I've got to start dinner."

"I'll help." Margaret reached for Beth, delighted to escape.

"I'll keep the baby here," Mrs. Johnson said. "It's cooler in the shade."

In the kitchen, Eve laughed. "Don't mind her. She means well."

Margaret scowled. "What a nosy woman!"

"She's good-hearted really." Exactly what Eve had said to excuse Mr. Johnson's lechery. The most good-hearted one around was Eve. "Mrs. Johnson doesn't have enough to occupy her. Her son's grown. She helps her husband at the feed store and works in the church. It's hard for a woman with a lot of energy."

"Is Beth safe with her?"

"Certainly she is."

Margaret wrinkled her nose, trying to dismiss Mrs. Johnson, and glanced around. "What can I do?"

"Peel the potatoes."

"All these?" Margaret looked at the full bushel basket. It could take hours.

"We're feeding twenty or maybe more, remember?" Eve started cutting up a pile of chickens, already plucked and singed, Margaret was relieved to see.

"You're pretty brave, you know," Eve said.

"Why is that?"

"To come here by yourself. Especially with a baby. How old is she anyway? Eight months?"

"Eight and a half." Margaret looked up, amazed. "How can you tell?"

"Easy. She's almost crawling and waving."

"You don't see many babies around here, do you?"

"A few. Sometimes at church. You might like to come."

"I would." Margaret wiped the perspiration off her forehead with her sleeve and attacked the potatoes. If she was going to do this, she'd better be a good sport. She might need a job for a spell. Eve had, after all, taken her in and lent her these clothes. She was still curious about the baby clothes.

Margaret began on the first potato, trying to peel off the skin evenly, digging for the bad spots. "Do you live by yourself?"

"Why?"

"This is a lot of work for one person."

"Not everybody has the luxury of a husband." Eve sounded bitter, but she was concentrating on thwacking the chicken leg at the joint. Mama said she could tell if somebody was a good cook by how well she cut up a chicken. "My mother died last year and my pa just after her. So I took over the boarding house. My folks would be amazed."

"What do you mean?"

"Before July, there were fewer than five hundred families here. And more arriving every day."

"Mr. Johnson said maybe twenty thousand people live here now."

"They'll go away eventually." Eve sighed. "In the meantime folks have to make a living." She brought the cleaver down smack on the joint between the drumstick and the thigh.

"How did this all begin, the boom, I mean? Dutch wrote something about a Fowler's Folly?"

"The well that started it? Folks say it's making between five and seven thousand barrels a day." Eve brightened. "Miz Fowler thought they should drill. She kept noticing oil on top of the water from their well. Some people say she had a dream about where to drill, and others say the rig broke down on the way to the site, and Mr. Fowler said to drill where they were." Eve washed the pile of chickens and put them into a kettle of water on the stove. She opened the window above the sink, and the heat poured in. "It's lasted for three years. People say it can't go on. The drouth."

Drouth? Margaret said the word to herself. Texas speech would take getting used to.

"Don't you get lonesome, living by yourself? I'd die without my husband to talk to."

"You're lucky to have somebody. I never have." Eve brushed away a fly. "Have you known your husband—Dutch?— long?"

"Since I was ten."

"Every time I meet a man, something goes wrong."

"Always?"

"So far. But I met a man a few weeks ago." Eve smiled.

"What's he like?"

"I can talk to him. And he accepts me as I am. It's hard to find men I don't run off."

"Why would you?"

Eve turned to face her. "I'm tall as most men and weigh more than some. I have a business, and I play the piano at a saloon. Men get scared off." She shrugged.

"And this man isn't frightened? He sounds perfect."

"We'll see." Eve's lips set in a straight line. "You can put out glasses for iced tea."

Mrs. Johnson appeared at the door with Beth asleep against her shoulder. "Poor little baby's worn out with all this gallivanting around town."

"I'll put her down for a nap. Thank you."

"It was a privilege. We don't see many babies around here."

The boarders started coming into the dining room at noon. When they saw Margaret, they raised their caps.

Eve brought in a platter of chicken. "Forget it, Mr. Willis," Eve told the bird-like man nearest her. "She's married."

Mr. Willis grinned as he ran an oil-stained hand over his overalls as if to shake hands, inspected his palms with the engrained dirt, and decided to wave at Margaret. "Nice to have a good-humored woman around here for a change."

Margaret liked him right away. She watched Eve bantering with the men and envied that ease. Eve's life seemed simple, although it couldn't be, what with the loss of both her parents and the mystery about the baby clothes.

As they cleared the table, Eve asked, "So what do you think?"

"The men? They seemed nice. Embarrassed, innocent somehow."

"They've been away from home so long they don't know how to act around a respectable woman. You should see them at the Red Onion. Mr. Willis—the frail one—could drink all the rest of them under the table and never show it. Goes right back to work the next morning."

"I feel sorry for his wife if he's like that at home."

"Probably not. Men are different when they're by themselves."

"What about that thin man with the big nose? He kept trembling. He almost couldn't get his fork to his mouth."

"That's Bucky. Shell-shocked in April in France, Seichprey, I think—I can't twist my tongue around those French words—so bad they had to ship him home. He's from Houston, but his old job was taken over by a woman, so he came here."

"Can he work shaking like that?"

"Some days are worse than others. He still has nightmares. If you hear hollering, it's Bucky."

Margaret was weary of this war.

"We're already seeing more wounded doughboys. Some worse than he is. Amputees. I don't know how on God's green earth they hope to make it here, rough as it is." Eve started back to the kitchen with a loaded tray. "Now the dishes."

Exhausted, Margaret wiped her forehead with her apron. The excitement of the previous two days, the hope of finding Dutch had buoyed her up, but now she felt flat. Washing all these dishes seemed more than she could do. She promised herself that when she finished, she and Beth would sleep and sleep. When she woke, perhaps Dutch would bend over her and touch her cheek as he used to when he came in from the garden early, smiling and saying, "Sleeping Beauty, I thought you were never going to wake up."

4

Despite the heat of their closet room, despite the chugs of the engines and the hum of men's voices, Margaret did sleep the rest of that day and through the night, and the next morning she woke rested. She stretched, hearing Eve in the kitchen, even though the sky was only just lightening. She left Beth asleep and tiptoed out, feeling her way through the dark dining room into the kitchen.

"What can I do?"

Bent over the stove, Eve jumped. She had circles under her eyes, and her hair was tangled.

"What's wrong?" Margaret had not seen Eve discombobulated before.

Eve pushed her hair back over her shoulder. "Why?"

"You look tired."

"I play the piano late. Sometimes it's hard to sleep." She passed a hand through her hair, and her face assumed its usual confidence. "Glad you're up. I checked on you before I went to the Red Onion. Both of you sound asleep." She gestured toward a cabinet. "You can set out the bowls." She quoted Mr. Hoover's slogan: "Don't let your horse be more patriotic than you are—eat a dish of oatmeal."

At the beginning of the war effort, deciding what to cook had been a challenge on flourless days. And meatless days too, although chicken and fish didn't count, so it had been easy for Margaret's parents on the farm. Now it seemed normal not to use much wheat flour or pork or beef.

Margaret liked helping with the war effort but hadn't talked about it with Dutch, who felt useless because he couldn't join the army. His weak eyes were the answer to her prayer, but she'd never told him, keeping that a secret between her and God. Paul, who already had children, was their only friend left in Oil City. As all the rest signed up, including her brother Arthur and Dutch's brother Earl, Dutch's frustration grew. When Paul heard about the boom and suggested they go to Texas, Dutch was eager. "Everybody else is in France," he had said. "It's all folks talk about. All I see in the paper." He'd thrust under her nose a front page proclaiming the

German offensive halted, announcing the French counteroffensive at Marne. "Maybe in the oilfield there'll be something else to talk about."

"What about Beth? Or me? Won't you miss us?" They'd never been apart for one single night since they'd married.

In his enthusiasm he ignored her misgivings. "Don't you see, Margaret? This is our chance. I'll be making good money. I'll send for you."

"When?"

"As soon as I save enough. It won't be long. Who knows? Paul and I may buy our own rig yet."

She had pouted. Five minutes later, she was annoyed with herself for acting like a spoiled brat, her mother's most damning epithet. How could she have been so insensitive, puncturing Dutch's dream, fueling his desire to escape to Texas? What he said was true. In Oil City, the war news, pasted on the front page of each newspaper, seemed real, whereas in Nesterville, the war seemed distant, despite the casualty lists and letters from local boys at the front. Here, the headlines of the Nesterville weekly and the Wichita Falls daily papers announced the latest gusher, while she had to turn to the second or third page to find even the optimistic recent war stories like the successful AEF offensive early in August.

Margaret put out pitchers of molasses, which she was becoming accustomed to instead of sugar. Then she went to the bedroom to check on Beth. Grinning, Beth pushed up on her arms. Margaret lifted her above her head, Beth laughing the whole time. Margaret's heart tightened. Dutch had already missed a month of watching Beth grow. She could pull herself up on furniture now.

In the dining room the boarders took to the baby right away. Beth crowed and held out her arms for Mr. Willis, who wanted to give her a little oatmeal. She grabbed the spoon.

Mr. Smith, the ruddy, bald boarder, touched Beth's hair as he walked by, and Beth grasped his finger. "Y'all make us feel to home," he laughed. Margaret liked him too.

And the men, unlike most of Dutch's family, took to Margaret. Dutch's pa was the only reason she'd stayed with them for three weeks after Dutch had gone. His pa used to smile at her and raise his eyebrows whenever Dutch's ma or sisters accused her of not working hard enough in the cotton fields, as if to say, Don't mind them. She'd wished Pa Sanders would shout at them to leave her alone, but he never intervened. That wasn't his way; he worked long hours by himself in the fields and later smoked his pipe alone on the porch. Although he and his wife occupied the same house, they were seldom together. Dutch didn't want their marriage to be like that, and neither did she. She'd observed Mama's and Mr. Graham's companionship since he had married Margaret's mother, a widow with four children. Such ease didn't come of itself but required, Margaret already realized, attention as constant as Mr. Graham's garden, which he worked in daily.

After breakfast Eve dampened the broom and swept while Margaret fed Beth.

Margaret couldn't stop sneezing. "I don't know what's wrong."

"It's the dust. People get used to it."

"I don't see why you bother to sweep."

Eve laughed. "I've experimented. It's worse, believe me. Let's go downtown."

When they picked up the mail, the day felt as hot as the previous one, the air so suffused with dust that the sky looked blurred.

Men crowded around the depot.

"Why is everybody staring?" Margaret felt her face flush.

"Two women and a baby alone. You'll have to get used to it. But something's different." Eve turned to the nearest roughneck. "What's the excitement?"

"You know about the freight embargo?" he said.

Eve nodded, explaining to Margaret how everything had to be shipped in by rail—food, hay, coal oil, lumber, machinery. So all the trains came to Nesterville, but there wasn't much freight to carry out, and there was no place to park the extra freight cars. Now anything shipped by freight had to have a permit, and that took quite a spell to get.

The roughneck pointed at the train. "See that? Somebody needed it so bad to drill that he had it shipped express on the passenger train."

Between the steam engine and the wooden passenger cars,

Margaret saw a bull-wheel on a flat car, like a giant spool of thread perched in majestic isolation. She wished she could tell Dutch about it.

Eve laughed. "If that doesn't beat all. No telling how much that cost to ship express."

"All the way from Pennsylvania. I heard the shipping cost as much as the bull-wheel did to start with," the roughneck said.

The air of exhilaration was contagious. Margaret could almost understand why Eve didn't leave the town. People could be addicted to hope, just like gambling.

At the post office, they lined up for Eve's mail. Margaret fidgeted, but Eve, like everyone else, stood patiently.

"What's your hurry?" Eve said.

"I want to look for Dutch."

"Hold your horses. This line isn't long. I usually wait over an hour." She glanced around. "Sometimes I can find a young fella who'll let me have his place for a quarter, but I don't see him today. You have to get used to lining up for everything."

As they left, Eve sorted through her mail, mumbling "I don't know why I still bother." When she noticed Margaret's stare, she asked, "Did you check for your telegram?"

"Where?"

"See that pole? There are so many they post them up there."

Margaret shielded her eyes from the sun. "One's addressed to Dutch. I bet it's mine." She stretched up for it. "I can't reach it."

Eve handed it to her. "Probably something else."

"It's mine, all right. So he never got it." Margaret felt the blood drain from her face, and she clutched Eve's arm as she remembered Mrs. Johnson's suggestion about his deserting her. "What if—something's happened?"

"Don't get in a lather. With so many people around, he hasn't seen it yet. He'll find you." Eve reached up to replace the telegram in a prominent place and glanced at the sun. "Let's start dinner."

"We just finished breakfast." Margaret was frantic to keep searching. "How can I ever find him if we're always cooking?"

"Do you want a job or not?" Ignoring the whistles and calls, Eve marched ahead, the men separating to make room for her the way water parts for a ship.

5

At lunchtime as she carried two pitchers of tea for refills, Margaret stumbled. She watched one pitcher fall onto Bucky's head and tea splash all over his hair and shoulders. He screamed like a terrified rabbit, jumped up, upsetting his chair, and wailed, his entire body shaking. From her high chair Beth cried out.

"What's going on?" Eve ran in from the kitchen. She glared at Margaret.

"I'll clean it up." Margaret leaned over to sop up the tea.

It took Eve and Mr. Smith a while to calm Bucky down. If this was what war did to folks, Margaret was even more thankful Dutch hadn't gone. She scrubbed the table and the floor with determination and then set Beth in her lap, crooning.

"Don't blame yourself." Mr. Willis passed a pan of biscuits. "Have one. They're delicious. Nobody makes them like Eve. I could eat her biscuits every day."

Eve smiled from across the table, where she stood patting Bucky's shoulder as his sobs diminished, his head in his hands. Nobody but Margaret seemed bothered by his crying. "None of your sweet talk, Mr. Willis," Eve said. I took the food pledge. Tomorrow's a wheatless Wednesday."

"Fine with me. I'll take rice pudding any day."

"With sugar rationed? Tell me how, and I'll do it."

Their joking continued, but Margaret still glanced around the table every time she heard an unexpected noise.

After dinner, heat waves radiated around them as they walked to the nearest grocery store, thrown up in the last month, tar paper tacked over a wooden frame.

Mr. Boyd greeted them in a high-pitched voice. He was balding, and under his nose grew a mole with a hair sprouting out of it. Margaret tried not to stare. How did he breathe? He smiled. "I'll hold the baby. You can look around." Folks were always glad to see Beth.

Beth screamed as he extended his arms for her.

"She's at the age where she doesn't like to go to people she doesn't know," Margaret said.

"I understand. Five of my own. All grown now." Mr. Boyd beamed, pulling at the hair growing from the mole and rocking back on his heels.

Margaret turned away. She bumped smack into Mrs. Johnson, who must have been eavesdropping.

Mrs. Johnson nodded to Eve with a pained grimace that was perhaps supposed to pass for a smile.

Outside, Margaret said, "She's as sweet as green persimmons."

Eve laughed. "She's not worth your notice when she acts like that. If anything, you should feel pity. Her husband and their boy, Jimmy, come to the saloon every whipstitch. Mr. Johnson is so drunk by the time he leaves that it's a good thing Jimmy's there to help his pa find his way home."

After they shopped, Margaret helped prepare for breakfast the next morning, setting the table and laying the fire in the wood stove. Margaret was amazed at Eve's stamina. By six o'clock, they had finished for the day, and she and Beth lay sweating in their room. Margaret fanned Beth with a newspaper until she fell asleep. For supper they ate leftovers from dinner; she was thankful Eve didn't feed the boarders at night. Margaret didn't think she'd have the energy.

Of an evening, when it was cooler, Margaret sat with Eve on the front porch, moving the swing with her bare feet, holding Beth in her lap. Despite all the hubbub in Nesterville, she liked living by herself. It wouldn't take long for her to establish a rhythm of days here. She already had two dollars in her purse from working. Dutch would be proud of her. Her eyes automatically scanned the sidewalks, still crowded in the dusk. Perhaps something had happened to him: he'd fallen off a derrick like the man she'd heard about at lunch or had been hijacked or murdered. Or he'd walked out on her. Maybe, like her, he had discovered he liked independence; maybe he even preferred it to marriage. If she concentrated hard enough, any minute she might spot him, at least a foot taller than most of the men, striding toward her, pushing out of his eyes the dark hair that by now would need a good trim.

A tall silhouette left the crowd. She jumped up, almost dropping Beth: Dutch.

Eve sounded alarmed. "What is it?"

The figure was limping. Dutch was hurt. No glasses. Lost. She gasped. Not Dutch. The doughboy. She plopped down on the swing.

The soldier stood with one leg on the bottom step, peering up at them, hesitant. "Evening." His head was turned toward Eve, but he spoke to Margaret. "Glad you found a place to stay. Did you find who you were looking for?"

"My husband? No."

"You were waiting for your husband?" He sounded surprised.

"Right." What kind of idiot was this? Who besides her husband would she go through such trouble to meet? "He didn't get my telegram."

"I thought I saw you today." He stared at his foot. "Maybe he's in Springtown."

"What's that?"

"A new field west of Nesterville." He nodded in the direction of the train station. "A gusher came in yesterday."

"Should I go look?"

"There's no point, would you say, Eve? Most roughnecks stay in Nesterville and take jitneys or walk there."

"Right. It's rough, Jimmy Johnson told me last night. Nothing but tents from one end to the other. You're better off here."

Margaret didn't believe that for a minute. If Dutch was in Springtown, wherever it was, that's where she should be. If he didn't show up soon, she'd go there. She hadn't come hundreds of miles to miss him because he was one mile out of town. Rough indeed. She frowned at the soldier, but it was too dark for him to see her expression, so she sat up straight, willing him to sense her annoyance.

"I'm glad you found a place—" He raised his right hand as if to salute or to raise his hat but waved instead. "See you later, I hope." He moved away.

Eve turned to Margaret. In the dusk Margaret couldn't see her face but could hear her laughter. "What's that all about?"

"What's what all about?"

"Your new admirer. You've rendered practically speechless the most eligible bachelor around," Eve said.

"What are you talking about?"

"You don't know who that is?"

"The soldier who helped me off the train."

"Indeed? He's the new doctor in town. He was shipped back from France early like Bucky. Hurt his leg at a place called Château-Thierry in June. You didn't see the newspaper article last week? Also, apparently severe shell shock. He couldn't help the wounded, so he was sent home. Came here about the time you did. I know of at least three women who'd love to land him. A little too tame for me."

"How do you know all this?"

Eve considered. "I'm interested in the war. The local news comes from Mrs. Johnson, of course. Who else? And her son's just like her."

The thin figure of the soldier/doctor materialized again on the porch steps. Eve whispered, "Shhh."

"I didn't mean to disturb you." His voice—that was it. His slow, soft voice. Since she'd met him on the train, something had nagged at her. Now she knew; he sounded like her brother Aut. "I wondered if you ever serve people who aren't boarders."

Eve's voice became brisk. "Anytime. A dollar a meal, breakfast and dinner. No supper."

"I'll see you then." He turned without so much as a word to Margaret, who, recognizing Aut's gentle tone, yearned to delay him, to keep him talking. She extended her arm and started to call out, but noticing Eve's stare, she pulled it back.

6

"Have you seen a man named Dutch Sanders? Over six foot, large build, curly black hair, twenty-eight years old?" For the next three weeks, Margaret repeated these questions in every store, saloon, tent, and rooming house in Nesterville and came to expect a puzzled "No, ma'am."

Sometimes she thought that if she heard one more "no," she'd give up. She missed Mama, the lake, the pine trees so bad in this desert, but she missed Dutch worse, so much she felt hollow. He'd taken her hunting and taught her to wait hidden at the edge of a slough until sunrise, to blow into the caller that squawked to attract ducks, and to rub together the lid and base of a wooden box to call geese. Once she shot a goose while he killed only one scrawny mallard. Laughing so hard he couldn't hold his box camera still, he took her picture as she stood grinning, both birds tied to the barrel of her shotgun. And he taught her to love. "Why do you want to marry?" the minister asked. She answered, "Because I can't live without him," which was true, but she'd been too self-conscious to say, "Because he makes me feel like poetry." That's how she felt three years ago, and despite their quarrel before he left, she still felt that same tightening of her heart whenever his image floated into her mind. She'd do everything she could to locate him, if indeed he wanted to be located.

Holding her breath, she read the Wichita Falls and Nesterville papers about accidents happening to roughnecks every day, of murders committed every night in the oil patch, but Dutch wasn't mentioned. Relieved, she put the papers aside until the next day, but she kept reading. At least that way she'd know. Not knowing was worse.

Her decision was simple. As she and Eve washed dishes, she stared at the water, murky with grease, and realized she couldn't stand the suspense. "I've got to go to that new tent town. Wasn't there another gusher a few days ago?"

Eve frowned. "Springtown? It's rough. Makes Nesterville look like the center of civilization. You could try. But there's no post office there, so he'll come here for his mail, and when he does he's bound to find your telegram."

Margaret didn't believe that for a minute. "Why? He hasn't found it yet."

"If I were you, I'd stay put."

Perhaps Eve was reluctant to lose her new employee and Beth, whom Eve had taken quite a shine to. "I don't mean move there. Just go for the day. I can't give up my job here." Margaret swabbed her forehead. "Is it far?"

"You could walk, but I'd take a jitney if I were you. Tell you what. I'll go with you when we finish these dishes."

Her doubts about Eve dissolved. How could she have found anyone kinder?

They paid a jitney five dollars to go west on a dusty road with potholes so deep Margaret thought the Model-T would break down any second. Once they got stuck, and she and Eve helped the driver try to move the car. Even together they couldn't lift it out until the driver of a wagon helped, though he cursed the whole time. Margaret's face streamed with perspiration, and her dress stuck to her. All this effort would probably produce nothing.

But once they started again and felt the breeze–hot air but moving nevertheless—she looked around with pleasure. She hadn't been out of the town, so she was surprised, just as on the train, by the stark beauty of the landscape, punctuated by the delicate green mesquites and the gray sagebrush.

"Look!" She pointed to a small tan-colored animal on its back legs atop a mound. As they neared, it whistled, dropped to all fours, and popped up again, up and down. Other identical animals scurried between mounds.

The jitney driver frowned and spoke around the plug of tobacco in his lower lip. "Them's parara dogs." Margaret puzzled out the word: "Prairie dogs." They resembled squirrels more than dogs. The driver continued, his tobacco intact. "Horses trip in the holes. Break their legs. Have to shoot the horses." He spat, and Margaret jerked out of the way. "There's a power of them hereabouts. Coyotes too." He nodded in the direction of the fence beside the dirt road. As far as they could see, nailed by their bushy tails to fence posts, were carcasses that looked like medium-sized dogs with light brown and reddish fur. "Nothing but nuisances. Kill the chickens. The calves. There's a bounty on them. I wisht we could get shut of every dang one. You ever hear the yipping early, just before daybreak?"

"I think so. It's hard to hear anything over the wells."

"Them's coyotes."

Coyotes and prairie dogs. Margaret wanted to store up all this newness and pour it out to Dutch like a gift if—no, when—she found him. Around them grew Indian blankets, small maroon and yellow flowers shaped like daisies, and sunflowers almost as tall as she. "I bet Dutch loves all this. He won't mind the heat or the dust or the wind. He'll plant a victory garden. Eve, you should see the one we had at home." Dutch had used half of their back yard for his tomatoes, beans, and potatoes and the other half for her favorite flowers. Camellias and azaleas wouldn't grow in this heat, but maybe roses would.

"You miss him, don't you?" Eve said.

The jitney bounced to a stop. "Here you are, Ladies. Springtown. You want me to wait? It's rough for two ladies and a baby."

"We're all right." Eve dismissed him with a wave, and he chugged off in first gear, shaking his head and frowning no doubt at their foolishness. Margaret didn't care. She pulled Beth's bonnet over her eyes and looked around. She could believe that until a week ago, Springtown had been nothing but cotton fields and Johnson grass. The downtown was composed almost entirely of tents, with a tent mission church at one end and a tent cathouse at the other. Between them, rows of tents to eat and sleep in bordered the dusty street. Men sauntered along both sides, and loiterers outside the tents shielded their eyes from the sun and stared.

"What shall we do, each of us take one side?" Eve asked.

Margaret paused outside a tent with hand-lettered signs proclaiming "Saloon" and "Bucket of Blood." She felt afraid. "Let's go together."

Inside, the canvas tent trapped the heat along with the familiar stench of sweat and oil. Beth coughed. Feeling the gazes of the men, curious, speculative, Margaret dropped her eyes. Eve, undaunted, pushed Margaret ahead on the packed earth floor up to the bar, planks on top of sawhorses. Her face burning, Margaret recited her spiel to the bartender. Like everyone she'd spoken to in Nesterville, he didn't know anything. What was new? Maybe they should forget this fruitless quest. But what if Dutch were in this very room and they missed him because he was sitting with his back toward her? On her way out, Margaret forced herself to meet each stare and inspect each face. She repeated the routine in the next tent, which was labeled "Café" and smelled of chili, but there was no information.

They continued along the street, Margaret's doubts growing with each thoughtful scratch of a stubbled chin, each puzzled shake of a head, each hungry stare of narrowed eyes. She sneezed, pulled Beth tighter until she wriggled to get down, and then hushed her, "Not in this filth." Her arms ached, Beth's body made her sweat even more, and her skirt was covered with dust. Eve's face was smudged with dirt and perspiration.

"Let's forget it," Margaret said.

"We've started this; let's finish. You want to be sure, don't you?"

Margaret swabbed Beth's forehead, embarrassed that Eve, not she, wanted to persevere, although they were searching for her husband.

They stopped in front of the tent at the end of the street. The canvas flap that served as a door was draped open, and three young women, hair down, stared at them. "I'm not taking Beth in there."

"Just ask." For the first time Eve sounded impatient. "Never mind. I will." She stepped up to the open tent flap. "Is Blondie here?"

"She's sleeping."

"We're looking for this woman's husband."

"There's nobody here now." The woman's eyes softened when she noticed Beth.

A small animal darted in front of Margaret. She jumped. "What was that?"

"Where?"

Margaret pointed. "Right there. Like a tiny dragon. See?"

One of the women bent and picked up an animal somewhat like a lizard. It was about four inches long with a flat oval body, gray skin with darker speckles, and stumpy legs ending in delicate feet. Its head and body were punctuated with short spikes. "Horny toad. It won't hurt you."

A toad? "See, Beth?"

Beth reached for it, but the woman said, "Don't let the baby get too close. It spits blood."

Margaret pulled Beth away, and Beth started crying.

"Poor little baby, out in this heat." Heavens, she sounded like Eula May Johnson. Wouldn't Mrs. Johnson be shocked?

"Tell Blondie Eve was here."

"Who's Blondie?" Margaret asked as they walked away.

"A friend from school."

Margaret had never known a lady of the night before. That's what Mama had called them. "They look so ordinary."

"What did you expect?" Eve sounded short.

"I don't know." The only whores--she hated that word, but it's what Aut called them—she'd seen were the ones in Oil City who'd ruined Aut. Over ten years ago. They'd looked like any other young women when they were leaving town.

Eve glanced at the sun. "We've done all we can do. Let's go home."

Margaret nodded. It had been crazy to come. Dutch could be working now, so they'd missed him even if he were here. Beth felt limp in her arms, slippery with perspiration.

As they looked for a jitney, a soft voice called, "Eve, Mrs. Sanders." They turned. The limping former doughboy, Dr. Miller, caught up with them, his black bag hitting against his leg. "What are you doing here?"

"Looking for my husband." What else would they be doing talking to prostitutes?

"Need some help?" He sounded so eager. Where had he been the last three hours?

"We're going home." Had she said that? "Back to Eve's, I mean."

"Let me take you," he said.

Eve said, "We're beholden to you, Doc."

He helped them into a wagon. Margaret wiped her sweaty palms on her skirt. He apologized. "This isn't too comfortable, but it beats walking. I had to get here in a hurry, and this is all I could find. No jitneys. Everybody's busy."

Eve asked, "Where's your uniform?"

"I had to make a little money before I bought a suit."

Eve chuckled. "That wool must have been pretty scratchy in this heat."

As they drove to Nesterville, the land glowed in the evening sun, the sharp corners of the afternoon softened. The hazy light smoothed the landscape and hid the coyote carcasses on the fence. Driving to Springtown, Margaret had felt light with anticipation, just as when she'd first arrived in Nesterville a month ago, but now as the darkness approached, she felt a weight settle on her heart, heavier than before.

7

Dutch and Paul went to Springtown at the beginning of August. Not having written Margaret that he was leaving Nesterville, Dutch felt slightly guilty, but this was an opportunity he couldn't miss. The other thing he felt guilty about was his strong attraction to Eve. He had to leave.

Paul gestured toward the tents lining both sides of a dirt road. "Nothing but pasture a few days ago. Now it's a tent city. Makes Nesterville look like Fort Worth."

As always, Paul chuckled at his own joke. When Dutch was ten and Paul was eighteen, Paul's jokes were funny. Dutch had admired Paul so much that he'd taken up basketball in hopes of being just like him. Once Paul and some of the other big boys found an alligator nest on the slough. They sold the babies, but Paul knew Dutch didn't have the money, so he gave Dutch one, binding Dutch to him. But now Paul's jokes seemed silly, maybe because Dutch was exhausted, working twelve hours a day and worrying about Margaret.

"What did I tell you? They're paying more here," Paul said. "Five dollars a day for a roughneck."

Dutch frowned. "I'm still not sure we should have left Nesterville."

"Why? Eve? She's a looker all right." Paul elbowed Dutch. "Watch out, boy. You'll find yourself in a pickle. You're better off here away from Eve."

"Mind your own business. I know what I'm doing."

Paul held up his hands. "Of course. Why do you think I work with you?"

"Don't worry about my marriage. Just remember that the more money we save, the faster we can buy that rig and drill for ourselves." Dutch slapped his hands together in enthusiasm.

"Big dreams for a country boy," Paul said.

Paul was thirty-six, his light brown hair already thinning and receding, wrinkles creasing his forehead and crinkling the skin beside his eyes. Age and a family weighed a man down, made him cautious. Dutch would be sure that didn't happen to him. He didn't want three children like Paul either. "You're not backing out, are you? We agreed it was a long shot, but—"

"I'm not backing out. I know it's a gamble, Dutch."

Drillers and roughnecks were still in demand but becoming more plentiful. Dutch had heard that water wells here had always had a film of oil on top and that there had been oil wells in Nesterville for over ten years, but they were shallow and didn't produce anywhere near what the Fowler did. No wonder everybody was pouring in. The richness of this field caught the big companies by surprise; they hadn't even had scouts here when the Fowler came in last month. So the little men like Paul and him stood a chance, maybe their only chance.

As usual, after their shift, Dutch went to the Red Onion, located between Nesterville and Springtown. Eve's face brightened when she saw him, and her playing got more glittery, the notes sparkling up through the bluish, smoke-laden air. He carried her a beer, and when she took a break she moved to the table where they normally sat.

"A roughneck got caught in some loose cable today. The doctor had to amputate." She reached for Dutch's hand.

He felt a shock as he always did when she touched him. He stretched out his arms. "Both still here."

"Another roughneck got blown off a derrick by the wind. He broke his neck. I hate to think about you out there, Frank."

Dutch was still startled when someone called him by his real name. He didn't know why he'd started using it here. Maybe he wanted a fresh start.

"You're a bundle of cheer." He raised his glass. "To good health."

"And to not falling off derricks—" That was one thing he liked about Eve. She knew the dangers of the oilfield and understood his fear of accidents, like being hit in the head by a joint of pipe, mishaps that no amount of care could forestall. But her glass was still raised; she hadn't finished her toast. She paused, scarlet lips curling with the teasing smile he liked, issuing a challenge. "And to us, Frank, you and me."

His eyes slid away. "I'd better be going."

"So soon? I thought you might take me home dreckly."

"I'm going back to Springtown with Paul."

"Springtown?" She stared, widening blue eyes surrounded by dark lashes.

"Don't get blubbery. A fella's got to make a living. It's not that far. Less than a mile."

She tossed back her hair, which smelled of gardenias. She laughed, but as he stood she looked teary eyed.

"Paul's here. I've got to go." When he glanced back from the door, she sat staring at the table as if it was the most interesting sight she'd ever laid eyes on. He felt a twinge of guilt; he was well out of this complication.

In Springtown as the crew tripped the bits, changing them as they grew dull cutting through the rock, Dutch almost forgot Eve's lips and began to anticipate Margaret's reply to his last letter. He'd had enough batching. He pictured her by the mailbox in Oil City, waiting for the postman. She'd hug that letter to her and twirl around like a girl. She'd write him. He'd hear any day.

8

"**Y**ou know what you need?" Eve sat on the porch swing lacing her boots. They looked strange below her satin dress, but because of the ankle-deep dust people wore boots with everything.

Margaret stopped the swing, her head resting against Beth's. The baby's hair had somehow retained its fresh smell in the heat.

"What?"

"You need to get out. Have some fun. Go with me tonight?"

"I couldn't do that," Margaret said.

"Why not?"

"What about Beth?"

"Bring her. Just for a little while. It'll do you good."

"I don't feel right about it." Margaret frowned. She wasn't a temperance nut. She wasn't going to kneel and pray outside the Red Onion, as Eve had told her some women did. But a saloon wasn't a proper place for Beth. "I'd better not. Dutch might not like it." She changed the subject. "What about that new man? The one you met before I came? Won't you see him there?"

"He went to Springtown." Eve shrugged. "I haven't seen him since."

"I'm sorry." Maybe that explained why Eve stayed longer at night at the Red Onion now. She was lonely.

"Somebody else will come along. They always do." Eve stood. "You're sure you don't want to get out?"

"Maybe when Dutch gets here."

Eve sounded short. "Suit yourself. You're missing a good time." She clumped down the steps and joined the crowd on the sidewalk.

Pushing the swing with her feet, Margaret considered. She should have known it couldn't last, that first exuberance inspired by the town and fed by her native optimism, which caught her up and buoyed her along for quite a spell. But after a month these props could no longer support her hopes. She had to face the possibility that something had happened to Dutch, and she had to decide what to do. She usually enjoyed the routine at Eve's. These days she started the stove, made the bread, and prepared breakfast on the mornings after Eve played at the Red Onion. However, she was starting to think she and Eve spent too much time together. Eve seemed moody and restless lately. At home, when Margaret needed to be alone, she walked in the woods, sinking into the carpet of pine needles, breathing in the pine scent, until she felt at peace again. Maybe she needed something else to do. She yearned more than anything to hold on to Dutch's and her dream of owning their own leases, but she had to accept reality. She knew that neither her family nor his had heard from him lately. If Dutch didn't show up soon, she'd be forced to create a new life, here or in Louisiana.

The next morning, Margaret still felt uncomfortable about how Eve had left in a huff the evening before. As she swept the kitchen with a damp broom after breakfast, she heard a knock: Dutch—just when she'd given up hope. Her hair was down. She brushed it back with her hands and smoothed the top. She sneezed.

"Sneeze to the truth." Dr. Miller strolled in, smiling.

She covered her initial disappointment and then realized, surprised, that she was glad to see him.

"I talked with the principal of the school. It's bursting with students. They even hold classes on the school grounds. Not enough teachers." He studied the floor with such concentration that he might be searching for his most valuable possession. She turned her gaze onto the floor too: nothing there but dust. "The principal asked if I knew somebody for the little ones. I thought of you. If you plan on staying a while, that is."

"Why wouldn't I?" What was there about this man that, despite his voice so like Aut's, nevertheless brought out her antagonism? Until she spoke, she hadn't realized that she thought of herself as a resident, not a visitor. Of course she'd stay. She'd find Dutch. She stared into his green eyes. "I'd love to return to teaching. I hate housekeeping. It never ends." She gestured around with the broom, scattering dust, sneezing again. "But married women aren't allowed to teach."

"You're not exactly married." He raised his eyebrows.

"Of course I'm married. Exactly." What nerve. "See this ring?"

She thrust out her left hand and jabbed her right forefinger toward the gold band that had belonged to Dutch's grandmother for sixty years. At the exact moment he proposed, Dutch's grandmother related, "A star fell out of the sky." It must have been a meteor, but Dutch's family considered it a good omen. Not married indeed.

He reached for her hand and placed his beneath it as he studied her wedding band. Underneath his freckles his face flushed, and he dropped her hand. "I just meant that your husband is out of pocket. I asked the principal about that rule. They're making exceptions because of the teacher shortage."

She pushed back her hair again. "I'd like to, but I'll have to talk to Eve. She can't do all this herself. It's a chore, even with two of us." She looked at the floor, which despite her efforts, never seemed clean. "I mean, of course, I'm very grateful to Eve for taking me in."

"So, do you want the position?" He sounded abrupt.

"If they want me." She took a deep breath. "Yes, I do."

"You're to see Mr. Morris then in the morning at the school. Three dollars a day. Good luck." He turned. The screen door crashed shut so loudly she could hear it over the engines outside. There was no need for him to be angry. She hadn't asked him to come to see her.

She'd tell Eve about the job first thing when she got up. It must have been a raucous night for her to sleep late. Eve might be irritated when Margaret proposed this change to their routine. But she could still help with meals in the mornings, evenings, and weekends, and anyway, there was plenty of outside help available. Young girls were always asking for work. Their families needed the easy money. Easy, sure.

Her eye fell on Beth, who sat by the table fitting pots together. Who would watch her while Margaret was at school?

Eve came into the kitchen. "What's all the racket?"

A little door slamming was a "racket"? Eve must be exhausted.

"Doctor Miller was here, and he said they need teachers." As Margaret explained about taking the job, Eve's face lightened.

"I'd do it. It'll get you out of the house. That's why I play the piano." Eve's gaze wandered away, and her face lost its momentary brightness. The lines between her eyebrows returned. Margaret wanted to smooth out the worry, to reassure her that they would be all right, but she wasn't sure what "all right" meant.

"What about Beth?" Eve said.

"It's only till two."

Eve nodded. "You might ask one of those girls who came by looking for work. And I might ask one of them to help in the kitchen. Or there's Mrs. Johnson."

Margaret wrinkled her nose. "I wouldn't want her taking care of Beth. She'd always find fault."

"She's dependable at least. Or I could myself. It would give me a reason to get up."

"Would you? Beth loves you, and if you had some help in the kitchen, it wouldn't be too hard."

"Let's try. But first you have to get the job."

"What can I wear?"

Eve placed her index finger on her chin. "Even in high school Earl Morris was a stickler for decorum." She raised her finger. "A black skirt and a high-necked white blouse."

"My entire wardrobe."

"Perfect." Eve's laugh rang out. She was herself again.

9

The next morning Margaret realized that her clean skirt and boots would be splotched with dust after two steps outside and her blouse stuck to her with sweat by the time she walked four blocks to school. But still she dressed carefully.

She kissed Beth, surprised that she felt only a twinge of guilt, and set her on the floor. Beth reached up, sobbing, as Margaret opened the door.

"What do I do? She's crying." Eve sounded panicked.

Margaret pushed down her frustration. Eve hadn't taken care of Beth by herself before. "She'll stop in a minute. Hand her the doll." She paused, reconsidering. She didn't really want to leave Beth, but Mr. Morris expected her. She sighed and stepped outside, Beth's sobs fading among the street noises.

She felt lighter as she walked down the makeshift sidewalk of cartons outside the businesses and then along the dusty path that led to school.

At the edge of the schoolyard, she adjusted her bonnet and tried to brush off the dust. She ended up with a left hand sticky with dirt, leaving the right one ready for Mr. Morris, if school teachers shook hands in this desert.

The pupils were lined up outside the brick two-story building. She waved at the nearest adult, a bony man with receding dark hair and a frown etched between bushy eyebrows. His solemn expression didn't change as she walked over to him.

His deep voice, however, was amiable and his handshake strong. She was glad she'd kept her right hand clean. "Earl Morris. I need help in the mornings with the young ones." He gestured toward the herd of small children fidgeting in line. "Also, how's your Latin?"

"Three years."

"Good. You can take the Latin class too. Can you start tomorrow?"

She nodded.

"When the weather's fine, you can meet out here." Margaret

glanced around the bare playground, the dirt packed down by years of play, an environment hardly conducive to learning. He stared with what might be distaste at her dusty boots and skirt.

The familiar smells of chalk and sweaty child bodies struck her as she walked inside. With rows of benches and tables, a wood stove, windows on two sides, coat hooks at the back, and a big scarred oak desk at the front, it could have been the school in Oil City, except that in Louisiana the pines marched clear up to the windows. Here only a few scraggly mulberries and sycamores struggled to live in a corner of the school yard.

The students poked one another, grunted, and snickered.

Mr. Morris cleared his throat. "This is Mrs. Sanders. She'll start tomorrow with the primary school."

"Good morning. I'm glad to be here." Margaret was aware of stares, not hostile, just interested, evaluating.

"Hey, Teach, you're new, aren't you?"

"You don't sound like you're from around here."

"Was it your husband that got killed?"

She gasped. Her hands flew to cover her mouth.

Mr. Morris raised his voice again. "Children, 'Mrs. Sanders,' not 'Teach.'" He scowled. "Get out your slates for arithmetic." He turned to Margaret, softening his voice. "I'm sorry about your husband."

"It wasn't my husband. I came to meet him a month ago, but I haven't found him." The students tittered. Frowning, Mr. Morris faced the class. He might or might not be much of a teacher, but he was a disciplinarian.

Glancing her direction, he said, "See you tomorrow." She felt dismissed.

She thanked him, though she wasn't sure why. In his black suit he looked so authoritarian she had to restrain herself from saying "Sir" and curtsying whenever she addressed him.

As she left, she looked back at the school. The acrid scent of trash and burning leaves tinged the air. A plume of smoke rose into the bright sky. She felt lifted up for the first time in weeks. She had a purpose.

"Mrs. Sanders, wait." She turned. Dr. Miller's hair shone as he hurried toward her, black bag knocking against his knee with each step, suit coat billowing around his scarecrow frame. She was surprised that with his limp he could walk so fast.

She smiled into his eyes, her words tumbling out. "I'm so glad you told me about the position. I'm going to teach the little ones and Latin too."

He chuckled. "Latin to the little ones? That sounds intriguing."

She remembered the warmth of his hand yesterday and cut off her babbling. She looked down. "It was all right. Thank you."

"Have coffee with me."

"I have to get home to Beth." Home? "To Eve's."

"It won't take long. Tell me about school."

"I don't have the time."

He said, "I want to apologize."

"What for? I really—"

"I want to talk to you about Dutch."

"What?" She clutched his arm.

"You misunderstand. I just want to talk."

Her shoulders slumped, but she didn't care because she felt so let down. She allowed him to steer her along Main Street to Tom's Café, where only a few oldtimers and loafers lingered over coffee. The doctor pulled out a chair at a table by the door, propped open for fresh air that diluted the odor of smoke and dust.

"I've never been here." She looked around with interest.

"It's not bad in the daytime. You wouldn't want to come at night."

"Why not?"

"Another shooting here yesterday."

"Why do you, then?" She watched a fly approach and waved it away.

"I have to eat somewhere."

"You should come to Eve's. I—we—thought you were, but we've seen you only—what?—three or four times?"

"You'd like me to?" His eyes widened in what looked like genuine surprise.

"Sure. The food's better." She sat expectant, while the coffee arrived tepid and weak. She tried it and set down her cup. They should have gone to Eve's, but maybe Eve wouldn't want them to mess up her kitchen. She'd gotten persnickety lately, as if everything wore her down: the crowds, the lines, the scarcity of food and water. Margaret hoped it wasn't something she or Beth had done. Beth—she needed to get back.

She drummed her fingers on the table. "You wanted to talk about Dutch?"

The doctor glanced around as if searching for words that would pop unbidden from the dingy walls. "Dutch? He isn't back?"

"You know he isn't. You said you wanted to talk to me about him. Do you know something?"

"No, I–"

"I have to pick up Beth. Do you have any news or not?"

"I wanted to see you. And that was the only way I could think of. I'm sorry." He put his head in his hands.

"Of all the nerve." What was wrong with this man? She was up and turning away before he stood.

"Let me walk you."

She said, "You're close to your office."

"I have time."

"You haven't finished your coffee, Dr. Miller."

"It's cold."

Margaret heard guffaws from a table of four loafers near the back. Squinting into the dimness, she saw three men point at the fourth, who was sputtering and choking. "It's that strange man. What are they doing?"

"Jerry? It's not our business, Mrs. Sanders." He moved to take her elbow, but she continued to watch them.

"They're tormenting him. Go stop them."

"They're having fun. They dare him to drink hot coffee, and he does. He doesn't mind."

"Wouldn't you mind?"

He glanced around. "Let's go. Around here, people get shot for interfering."

"You won't stop them, Dr. Miller?"

He shrugged. "Nothing I can do."

"If you can't, I can." She stalked toward the men, her courage oozing away as she neared their table. The men looked up, curious. She inhaled and plunged ahead. "I find it interesting that your mothers failed to teach you any compassion." She took Jerry's hand. "It's time to go."

Jerry greeted Dr. Miller with a cough and then a hearty "You're fired." Together, they walked without another word down Fourth Street to the church, where Jerry left them with another "You're fired." At Eve's she didn't invite Dr. Miller in and cut off his apologies.

She sat in the porch swing to sort through everything that had happened that morning. She thought she would like the school, despite the unruly students and the condescending principal. It would be an adventure. But she was troubled that Dr. Miller continued to seek her out even though he knew she was married. She wasn't happy with herself for liking his attention, even while missing Dutch so badly. It would be easy to gaze up under her eyelashes as she used to do with Dutch five years ago, to know she had the power to transform his world from misery to bliss with one word. And Dr. Miller's voice sounded so much like Aut's. She regretted criticizing him for his refusal to help Jerry. He understood the codes of behavior here, where force often prevailed over principles. She was fortunate they'd been too amazed at a woman's interference to do more than stare when she approached them.

Inside, she took off her bonnet and called. When Eve didn't answer, she walked through the empty front room, dining room, and kitchen. Eve and Beth sat on the back steps, enjoying the shade as Eve tried to show Beth how to make a design with string. It would be some time before she learned. Relieved, Margaret felt her world fall back into place. With Dr. Miller she had walked along a perilous narrow ridge, and with Beth's reappearance she had descended into a safe, familiar valley.

Margaret sat on the steps. Beth climbed into her lap, touched her face, and said "Mama" as plain as could be. Margaret hugged Beth to her. Tears filled her eyes. Dutch wasn't here to share her joy, to hear Beth, only nine months old, say her first real word. It wasn't fair. She patted Beth as her eyes traveled around Eve's back yard, a jumble of dead weeds except for the packed red earth that led to the privy and on to the clothesline.

Eve turned. "How'd it go?"

"School? It was swell. How was Beth?"

"She was fine. She played while I did the dishes."

They were silent a few minutes. "Now that you're back, I'll sweep." Eve stood and went into the kitchen.

What a strange non-conversation. It sounded like the first day of a foreign language class. Margaret felt deflated. She pressed Beth to her. She could have told Eve about school, coffee with Dr. Miller, intervening with Jerry, or Beth's first word. Eve could have told her more of what had happened with Beth while Margaret was away. But something held them back.

10

The next morning Margaret woke as soon as she heard Eve in the kitchen. For a second she couldn't remember why a clean skirt and blouse lay on the rocker. School. She stretched, smiling.

She helped Eve with the grits. "Your Louisiana influence," Eve said. "You can start the red-eye gravy, but don't splatter your clothes." Eve handed her an apron, which was way too large for her. "It belonged to my mother. She was bigger than I am."

"Mama's my height. Also Ida. My sister. We used to trade clothes. But my oldest sister Rachel was too short. You don't have brothers and sisters?"

"Just me. My folks both had big families. Pa had twelve brothers and sisters, and Mama had six. They wanted a quieter life." Eve looked at Margaret. "Do you want any other children besides Beth?"

"Maybe three." She sighed. Where was Dutch? "What about you?"

"Taking care of Beth yesterday for some reason made me think about the past. I've never told you, have I, why I work so much?" Tears filled Eve's eyes.

What was that about?

Eve fixed her gaze on the sycamore out the window, its leaves already falling. "I work to forget what happened and to pay back people who helped me when I was down. I told you about Harry?"

"Your fiancé, the jerk who married a French girl?"

"Right. After he left for the Army, I found out I was in a family way. I never let him know. I told you I made those baby clothes for amusement. That's only half true. I didn't have anyone to talk to. My mother had just died. I found out about an orphanage that would take me in, and I told people here I was visiting kinfolks. I had a baby girl and put her up for adoption. The folks who ran the orphanage took care of me. Best people I've ever known."

"You had a baby?" Margaret stared at Eve. "How could you give her up?"

"It was the hardest thing I've ever done. But how could I raise a baby here in this one-horse town—it was a small town a year ago. You've seen how people talk. Mrs. Johnson isn't the worst gossip. What kind of life would my baby have? I don't know whether it was right, but I did the best I could." Eve's voice took on a plaintive tone that Margaret had never heard before, pleading for understanding. She wiped her eyes and glared at Margaret. "I shouldn't have told you."

"Why not?" Margaret squeezed Eve's calloused hand. "Anybody would do what you did. I can see how petty people are and how hard it would be to raise a child by yourself."

"Now you know why I love Beth so much—my baby is just a little older than she is." Eve took a deep breath and squared her shoulders. "You'd better get to school. Here I've been talking your ear off. You don't want to be late."

Margaret didn't know what to say. She patted Eve's hand and then hugged her hard. "You made the right decision." It had taken courage. What would she have done?

She tiptoed into her cubbyhole room to check on Beth, who had gone to sleep after she'd nursed. It was impossible now to imagine her existence without Beth.

"See you this afternoon. I won't be late," she said. Eve had washed her face and, her jaw set, was serving breakfasts. Margaret nodded to the boarders congregating in the dining room.

On her way to school, three children passed her and smiled when they recognized her as the new teacher. But they let her walk alone, and she was glad to arrange her thoughts. Sadness for Eve enveloped her. The town looked drearier than the day before.

Trying to shake off her despondency, she glanced to see if a light was on in Dr. Miller's office. She stared ahead as she passed Tom's Café, speculating about the greasy breakfast he would have there.

At school Mr. Morris told her to begin with reading. She arranged the students around her. They opened their McGuffey readers, the same as she'd had in Louisiana, but they didn't want to read. Four hands shot up.

"Where are you from?"

"Louisiana."

"What's that?"

One boy punched another. "It's a state, stupid."

Mr. Morris intervened. "Pay attention to Mrs. Sanders, or it will be licks."

Margaret noticed the wooden paddle on his desk. She'd hated the spankings at the school in Oil City, though Dutch and Aut hadn't minded. They stuffed books down their pants so they couldn't feel the licks. Dutch laughed at the teacher who tried without success to make him cry his first day. When Margaret taught before, there'd been no paddlings.

"I don't mind telling them about myself, Mr. Morris." The children quieted down, their eyes reappraising her. "I'm from a small town on Caddo Lake in north Louisiana. My little girl and I came here last month."

"Why isn't she in school?"

"She's less than a year old. Open your readers now."

The morning passed quickly. At recess, the girls jumped rope and played jacks, and the boys threw a softball and played mumblety-peg. She stood in the shade of the building wondering about Eve's daughter until the students lined up to go in for arithmetic and spelling.

Then there was lunch. Bringing out her biscuit, she felt as if she were back in school, except she didn't have any jam her mother made from their dewberries. Sometimes her shoes or her dresses were too small, but Mama always saved her some jam.

After lunch she had only Latin. The older students were respectful, but like the younger ones, they wanted to know about her. Linda Sue, one of the most forward girls, asked where Margaret had gone to school.

"About a mile through the woods to Oil City. The school didn't go to the last grade, so one year I stayed with my sister in Shreveport and went to a Catholic school."

"What about your family?"

"I went home on the train on weekends." That's when she met Dutch again. She was fifteen. What a difference five years made. He hardly recognized her with her long skirt and her hair piled on her head. He had changed too. Now he was a foot taller than she, and Rachel, who'd been able to beat him up when he got into a fight with Aut, wouldn't stand a chance any longer.

After Latin, exhilarated, she started home, delighted to be teaching again.

"Carry your books, Schoolgirl?" Dr. Miller appeared. He must have been waiting for her. "How was your first day?"

"Fun. The children were rambunctious at first. Two started fighting. Mr. Morris threatened them. Then they settled down." She smiled, glad to see him.

"Do you have time for coffee, or would you rather go on home?"

"Home. But you don't need to walk with me. What about your patients?"

"What about them? I've set two broken arms and a leg. That's enough for now."

"If you have the time." She glanced up just as he looked down.

He laughed, sounding as carefree as she felt, and took her books. He made her feel as if she had nothing whatsoever to do except saunter along this wooden sidewalk. She felt so light that if she lifted her arms, she might soar over the derricks. She crossed her arms across her chest to remind herself to stay on the ground.

Dr. Miller looked down. "Are you cold? It's breezy today."

"I'm fine, really. This is fun."

"What's fun?"

"Just walking. Being alive." She wished they were at home walking in the oak and sweet gum leaves that would be ankle deep by now. She could run and shuffle through the leaves as red as his hair.

"Is it?"

"Is what?" she said.

"Is it fun walking here? With me?"

"Of course. I could walk all day."

"Why don't we?"

"I have work." And a daughter and a husband.

At supper she asked Eve, "Did you run all the time and never walk when you were a kid?"

"I was the fastest one in my class. I could outrun the boys."

"I could run faster than all of them except Dutch and Aut. My brother." Margaret watched Beth pull herself up on the table leg. Aut should have known Beth; it wasn't right that he wouldn't. He'd have taught her to recognize the trees and the flowers in the woods, to find where the deer liked to bed down. She roused herself. "It won't be long till Beth's running around. If we concentrated as hard as she does, no telling what we could do." Hearing her name, Beth looked up at her mother, a smile covering her face. Margaret lifted her into her lap, but Beth squirmed down.

Eve asked, "By the way, what about Dr. Miller? He hasn't been by for a spell."

"I guess he's busy."

"Or else he's given up on you."

"Come on, Eve. I'm married. I love my husband." She banished the doctor's piercing gaze from her mind. She was too worried about Dutch for Eve's teasing to be funny.

11

Margaret read *Alice in Wonderland* to her class, but they fidgeted. Giggling, the girls passed notes. Harold Falk laid his head on the desk, snoring so loudly the other students stared at him and then back at her, testing. Pete Thompson poked the sleeping boy, who raised up, blinking. "We'll read another day," she said. Later, two boys refused to be on the same team for a spelling bee. They shoved each other, so she separated them. Mr. Morris's hawk eyes, speculative, lingered on her. The children were wild and would no doubt remain so. Her efforts to educate them seemed fruitless lately when all they witnessed was greed for the black gold that led to nothing but drinking and gambling away every cent made the previous week. If their parents could hold on to one-tenth of what they'd made, they'd be rich and could leave this barbaric spot. Most people here were petty, caught up in their own concerns. But wasn't everyone? She was too, worrying about Dutch. She yearned for school to end.

The day did not improve. During Latin, Harold Falk wanted to argue. "Rome came before Greece."

Pete Thompson, who considered himself superior to Harold in intellect if not in brawn, blurted, "Shut up. No, it didn't."

Harold punched Pete in the ribs. Pete yelped. "Isn't that right, Mrs. Sanders?"

The others crowded close anticipating a fight or a paddling at least. Margaret noticed Mr. Morris's glare. "Greece preceded the Roman Empire."

Pete preened. Harold sulked.

"Sit down, both of you." She sighed.

Five minutes later the Zimmerman brat interrupted. "Mrs. Sanders, wait. Doesn't 'Amo' mean 'I love'?"

"Of course. Why?"

"You said 'I hate.' "

"I guess I wasn't paying attention."

Miss Priss Zimmerman rolled her eyes. The others giggled. Mr. Morris, ever vigilant, frowned.

With relief, Margaret gathered up her books after school. The day had seemed interminable.

Mr. Morris called, "Mrs. Sanders, I'd like a word with you": exactly what her mother said when she caught Margaret eating cookies before supper or riding her father's horse without permission. Reminding herself to keep her chin up, her shoulders back, she approached; she was a teacher, not a misbehaving child. Mr. Morris had on the same black suit he wore every day or its duplicate, the chalk smudges identical to those of the day before.

"Is the Latin class too much? The boys need a firmer hand."

She shrugged. "They're all right." He'd forgotten what it was like to be a kid, cooped up in a hot room while autumn breezes called. Perhaps he was looking for a way to dismiss her. She waited, meeting his glare with what she hoped was professional assurance, asking with what she hoped was coolness, "Is there anything else?"

"Not today." No doubt he'd continue to watch for any excuse to pounce. He waved a long arm in his customary dismissal and turned to his desk to shuffle piles of papers that never diminished. Margaret felt like an ill-behaved student who had been let off only because of the teacher's leniency. His disapproval didn't make sense. He needed her. It must be her imagination.

Margaret closed the door of the school. The sun had broken through the few high clouds that hinted at rain, and the brilliant blue above the derricks made her squint. She took off her sunbonnet and smoothed her bun, ignoring the escaping hairs. She'd take Beth for a walk. Eve said people found arrowheads in the riverbed.

Behind her, Doctor Miller called, "Wait up." Her determination to go straight home drifted away like the smoke from the burning trash she was passing. She wanted to twirl around laughing in response to the beauty of the day and, she couldn't deny it, the pleasure of seeing him.

But he sounded urgent, his voice as taut as the students' rope in their tug of war games. "I have to see you."

She gasped. "Something's happened to Dutch? Or Beth?"

"Not that I know of. I have to talk."

"So, talk." If he could be curt, so could she.

"Not here. I want to show you something."

"I don't have time, Dr. Miller. I have to get home."

"This won't take long." He glanced sideways at her, his voice strained. "Can't you spare me a few minutes?"

His face was contorted, his bottom lip twisted. She walked without speaking. Something awful must have happened. Somebody in his family had died, or he had some incurable disease.

At the corner Margaret turned toward her house, but he touched her elbow. "Go straight."

"I need to get home. What happened?"

"Nothing. I want to show you something, and the weather's perfect." His voice pleaded. "It's not far."

She shrugged, curious despite herself.

In a few minutes they came to a hill that descended into the riverbed. Far to the left sprawled the tents and few buildings in Bridgetown, the newest oilfield settlement. Ahead lay Red River, a thin ribbon of blue reflecting the still sky, but as they descended, the brown water looked sluggish with mud. Halfway down, when Dr. Miller steered her to the left, she felt the warmth of his hand through her sleeve. She moved away. A sandy path led down to an extension footbridge about twenty feet high that stretched across the riverbed. She folded her arms.

"I'm not going on that bridge, Dr. Miller. Heights scare me." What had she gotten herself into? His eyes wide, he looked manic.

"We're not going on the bridge. But it's safe. Pumpers use it all the time." He sighed. "We're almost there."

He guided her to a nook protected by a bank and an enormous cottonwood tree. Only a few of its leaves still hung tan against the rich blue of the sky. Discarded leaves crunched beneath her feet.

"This is my favorite place. I come here to read. I wanted to bring you here. You said you miss the trees at home, and this is the most impressive tree around." He gestured. "You should see the riverbed in the summer, with pink salt cedar blooms and bluebells all over."

She tried to picture it green, but now it looked dead. "It's nice."

"Nice?" He frowned.

She tried again. "It's very nice. I mean, it's pretty."

"I didn't bring you here just for the view." He looked dejected. He reached in his jacket pocket and pulled out a small package wrapped in flowered paper. "Here." He shoved it toward her.

"I can't accept a present from you, Dr. Miller, although it's very kind, certainly."

"Open it." His voice was still tense.

She unfolded the paper to reveal a book bound in green leather. "Longfellow. I love 'Hiawatha.' Mama read it to us when we were little." They had sat on the front porch of an evening, listening to Mama's quiet voice roll out the slow rhythm. Aut had memorized portions to recite to her. "It's beautiful, but I can't accept it. It's too much."

"Sit here." He pointed to a log beneath the cottonwood. His words tumbled out. "Let me read to you, at least. Ever since I met you, Margaret, I've thought of you as Evangeline. You were from Louisiana, and you were so intent, as if you were on a quest."

Evangeline? "I really have to go, Dr. Miller."

"Can't you even call me Anthony? Or give me five minutes?"

She settled herself on the log, her back straight, her arms folded against her chest. He could be as crazy as a peach orchard pear. If he acted any stranger, she'd leave.

His voice so resembled Aut's that she again saw Aut's face: "This is the forest primeval, the murmuring pines." Despite her annoyance, she was caught up in the stately verse, forgetting that the poem was set in Canada and seeing instead the woods at home. She wished she lived in Arcadia, where, unlike Nesterville, there would be no murders, no hijackings, no wishy-washiness.

The sun would set soon. "How did it get so late? I lost track of time." She picked up her textbooks.

Smiling, Dr. Miller closed the book. "Do you like it?"

"It's wonderful. I forgot all about everything."

"Shall I read to you tomorrow?"

She hesitated, looking at the river, turgid but still flowing. By tomorrow this water might be in Shreveport, where the river was wider, though still calm, and the day after that in the Gulf of Mexico. "I have schoolwork, Dr. Miller."

"I'll be waiting."

The presumption of this man. She'd said she had work. By the time they reached Fourth Street, it was dusk, and he looked worried. "It's late. I should walk home with you."

"Please don't bother, Dr. Miller."

"You're far from a bother. Surely you know that." His voice was strained.

"I'd rather be by myself." There: that was clear enough. She needed time to understand what was happening.

On the way home, she peered through the dimming light to see whether anyone was watching. But she'd done nothing wrong. She clutched her books. They were dependable. They wouldn't change, unlike her feelings, which were all jumbled. Who was she anyway? A lover of poetry or Mrs. Sanders or Margaret or Mama? Or all the above? She felt like a walking multiple-choice test she'd given in Latin: "I love" or "I hate"? "I love Dutch" or— Don't make jokes, Margaret. She pulled herself up short as she would rein in a horse trotting too fast. She and Dutch had quarreled. She hadn't heard from him. When she arrived, she was still angry but preferred to patch up her marriage rather than stay with his parents. Now, almost two months since he'd left Louisiana, she was attracted despite herself to this soldier/doctor, who, compared to Dutch, seemed educated, sophisticated, and not least, like Aut, a wonderful reader of poetry. What more could she want?

"Is everything all right?" Eve, who had moved Beth's high chair onto the porch to catch the breeze, jumped up from the swing.

Beth cooed and held out her arms. Margaret felt remorse. Instead of looking for her husband or tending to her baby, she'd been cavorting with a strange man. "Cavorting": Mama's favorite word.

"I ran into Anthony—Dr. Miller."

"So it's Anthony now? About time."

"Why do you say that? Don't you think Dutch will find me soon?" She frowned.

"How should I know?" Eve snapped. "It's late, and I didn't know where you were. If something had happened to Dutch, you would've read it in the paper. He's probably in Springtown making money just for you."

Margaret felt worse. Rudeness to thy host, betrayal of thy husband: thy name is Margaret.

"Mama." Beth banged her spoon on the high chair tray with glee. Ready to get down, she stiffened her body, spilling her cup of milk. Didn't Eve remember that Beth still nursed in the evening?

Margaret kissed Beth's soft hair. "Wait, I need to clean up the milk. Then Mama wants supper."

"I saved you some stew. Mr. Johnson brought by a rabbit. It's on the stove."

The kitchen felt closed in after the riverbed. She held Beth on her lap with one hand and ate the lukewarm stew with the other, avoiding the pieces of meat. Eating them would be like eating her pet, Bunny-Bunny. Perhaps she would see Dr. Miller tomorrow. If she did, she would not allow him to read to her. Reading poetry could be dangerous.

12

The students were inattentive, snickering about nothing, or maybe Margaret was distracted. She listened to their half-hearted attempts to recite in a sing-song cadence the poetry they were supposed to have memorized: "In Flanders fields / The poppies grow / Between the crosses / row on row." The war seemed far away, as did that day in August two months ago when she'd arrived. It was impossible now to think of Dr. Miller as the red-headed lanky doughboy who'd carried her suitcase off the train.

Exhausted after school, she gathered her books when the students left: no cleaning up, no organizing lessons for the next day. Mr. Morris scowled, but she didn't care. She closed the door without a good-bye.

Outside, she glanced around. No Dr. Miller. And he wasn't waiting at the corner. She felt relieved but at the same time disappointed. She marched home and, a model mother, sat on the back steps with Beth, but she kept thinking of the pressure of Dr. Miller's hand on her elbow as he'd guided her toward the cottonwood and of his quiet voice reading about Evangeline's thirty-year search for her fiancé. Thirty years. Would she wait for Dutch that long? What was she thinking? Of course she would. She hoped—she guessed—she'd find him soon and end this confusion.

After supper she and Beth sat on the back steps and watched the stars come out, the "forget-me-nots of the angels," Longfellow called them. She wished she could tell Dutch.

The next day, Margaret loitered after school despite her intentions to go straight home. If she stayed late enough, Dr. Miller would realize that she wanted nothing else to do with Longfellow or with him.

He was waiting. She started to protest, but it would be only a token objection. She shrugged and handed him her books, drawn to him despite the opposing voice of duty. Laughing, he called her "Schoolgirl," and she felt free. Why shouldn't she enjoy herself? She worked hard. She deserved some fun.

"Is Margaret your real name?" he asked on the way to the river.

"Why?"

"It means 'Daisy.'" He pointed out some late blooming purple asters. "It also means 'Pearl.' Did you know that?"

Something else she'd store up to tell Dutch. Maybe not.

"What's wrong?"

"I shouldn't be here." She stopped.

"Why?"

"I'm married."

"You've done nothing wrong." He frowned. "Do you want to go back to Eve's?"

"I guess not." She didn't know.

The afternoon readings continued all week. She didn't question him about his afternoon patients but found herself looking forward to sitting on the log under the giant lone cottonwood and hearing the story of Evangeline's search. As she listened to his voice against the murmur of the river, felt the coolness of the September breeze, and gazed into the clear sky, she lost herself in the story. This was the only time she could be without responsibilities. She dreaded the end of the poem.

"Come with me." Dr. Miller hustled her to the log and read the conclusion. After years of barely missing Gabriel, Evangeline found him in a hospital, dying from some "pestilence," as Longfellow called it. Margaret felt tears about to spill over. She lowered her head and, looking away so he wouldn't notice, wiped her eyes. But she couldn't keep the tears back as Dr. Miller read of Evangeline's dying beside her true love. It was easy for Evangeline. She had one love. She wasn't torn apart by conflict and guilt.

No telling how long they'd sat there, the book open on Dr. Miller's knee, when the weeds rustled behind her. Turning, she stared into the yellow eyes of a coyote six feet away. The coyote froze, its forepaw raised. They'd been still for such a spell that the animal must have mistaken them for permanent fixtures. The coyote's gaze slid away, and it loped up the hill. Dr. Miller carefully laid the book of poetry down. He touched her arm to indicate a jackrabbit, larger and leaner than the cottontails she'd had as pets, hunkered down in the dead grass, its long ears flattened. What courage that rabbit had to remain motionless with the coyote a few feet away. She could never have that much courage or self-control in a million years. Her sobs began again. Life was too difficult.

"Don't cry about the poem. It's just a story." Dr. Miller turned her face to his and touched her cheek. She knew her nose was red and swollen. His lips brushed her eyes and then her cheeks and then, very gently, touched her lips. She tasted the salt of her tears as he kissed her. "I can't help myself, Margaret. I love you as I've never loved anyone else. I've loved you since I saw you on the train. I think of you as the pearl of great price that the man in the Bible sold everything for. I'd do anything for you. Do you realize that?"

She sat immobile, her gaze fixed on the river as Dr. Miller told her about a society girl in Dallas. "Before I went to France, I thought I loved her. I tried to talk her into marrying me before I left. A lot of soldiers did that. But she wouldn't. I thought she wanted to be free while I was gone. We argued. But she was right. We didn't belong together. I realized that in the hospital after my first battle. So much blood and torn flesh. We operated for two solid days. I can't forget it." He looked at Margaret. "I realized that I didn't really love her—Amy—that if I died right there, I would never have known what love was. But since I met you—"

She raised her hand. She didn't want to hear any more. How could she have allowed herself to be in this situation?

"Let me finish. Now, since I know you, I understand what love is. And, heaven help me—I'm not proud of this, but I hope your husband is dead." He shifted his gaze to the log. "Think of me however you will, I had to tell you how I feel."

Appalled, she saw herself as if for the first time. What was she doing, betraying her husband like this? She stood. The rabbit darted away, leaving a hollow in the grass. Nauseated, she struggled up the bank, her feet sinking into the loose sand that collapsed under her, pulling her back. Dr. Miller called, but she plowed through the sand, which worked its way into her boots and with every step cut into her ankles. When she reached the dirt road, she didn't glance back but fled, pursued by her own guilt, toward Beth, her safety and her refuge.

13

Margaret ran all the way to the hill, her skirt wrapped around her arm so she wouldn't trip; if she looked back, if she paused, she might turn around—that's what "repent" meant, the preacher said—turn around and be healed. But she wasn't sure she wanted to be healed of this pain in her heart that commenced burning whenever she thought of Dutch or now, heaven help her, the other pain that started when she thought of Dr. Miller. The two hurts twisted together to form a whip that kept her struggling up the hill, huffing, until the pains merged with the hurt in her lungs, and she could continue no farther. She stopped, bending over, gasping, still crying. But she wouldn't look back, wouldn't risk being turned into a pillar of salt like Lot's wife, whose heart had also yearned for the forbidden. Then, near the top of the hill, she did glance back. The river continued its sluggish flow, and in the lengthening shadow of the cottonwood, she could barely distinguish Dr. Miller sitting on the log, his head bent. She trudged up the hill, placing one foot into the sinking sand, then the other, hugging her chest, her ragged breath roaring in her ears and the voices of her mind repeating that adultery was a sin, a sin, and yet and yet, she hadn't done anything. She knew she was reasoning like a Jesuit. Adultery of the heart was a sin.

As she neared the crest of the hill, she sensed a drumming that she thought at first was her heart, but it grew louder, and then a rider on horseback loomed above her. She smoothed her hair and wiped her eyes. Now, on top of all that had happened and all that hadn't happened, she'd have to "brace up," as her mother used to say. She'd hated that expression as a child, and she still did. The man reined to a stop amid a swirl of yellow dust. He wore a hat jammed down over his head, and the lower half of his face was covered with a bandanna, so that only a fringe of dark hair was visible around his hat. He held a lumpy flour sack in one hand and in the other a pistol so big that she could only stare, mesmerized.

"Not a sound."

As he shifted the sack under his arm, leaned down through the haze, and shoved the pistol into her face, his bandanna slipped. She had no time to do anything but gasp.

His face reddened. "Now I'm gonna have to take you with me."

Without dismounting, he reached down and pulled her up in front of him on the horse. For a moment she hung gasping, dangling in the air like a fish while the horse, wide-eyed, pranced and side-stepped. Margaret grabbed the saddle horn. She smelled liquor and sweat as he muttered in her ear, "If you're nice, you might get out of this alive." The bandit glanced back, yanked the reins, and kicked the horse's sides as it started down the steep hill so fast they'd surely end up dead in a prickly pear. God help me, she prayed as she struggled. She jabbed him with her elbows while she searched for a place to jump off and then yelled as Dr. Miller, head raised, astonished, flashed by.

The man spoke into her ear, his breath foul. "Don't make another sound. I swear, I'll shoot if you do. I've shot one. What difference will one more make?" He looked over his shoulder again, cursed, spurred the horse, and leaned forward, heading toward the footbridge, which rose about twenty feet over the river.

Still clutching the bag and the pistol, the man jumped off the horse, dragging Margaret with him.

"I won't go up on that bridge," she said. "Shoot me right here." She planted her feet in the sand to brace herself.

As if she hadn't spoken, he continued toward the bridge, shoving her in front of him. She felt the barrel of a pistol poke into the small of her back. She hoped the safety was on. He stopped at the ladder. "Up."

"I can't. I'm afraid—" She gasped as he pushed her against the wooden rungs.

"Get a move on," he said.

She was shoved upward and willed herself to climb, looking at the darkening sky, feeling for each rung with her foot as her abductor prodded her. Don't look down, she thought. Halfway up, she tripped on her skirt and couldn't move, but he ripped the caught fabric as easily as a spider web, and they continued. Before she went any farther, she'd push herself backward, fall to the ground, and then she'd be free. Never mind that she'd break a limb or fall on her head, and Beth would grow up with neither parent. No, she'd push him off the ladder, and he'd fall. Willing herself to act, she counted to three and then kicked backward and down. He only laughed. "Getting cute, are we?" Demoralized, she felt that she had no will or energy of her own. She kept inching upward prompted by that cold, disembodied voice that muttered "Go!" whenever she paused.

From the ground a man's voice—Dutch—no, Dr. Miller—called, "Stop!" A shot exploded below her. For a moment she heard nothing except a ringing. Then the quiet splash of the river returned. Perhaps the bandit had missed. She heard nothing else. She craned her head around. No, not Anthony.

Again that hard voice mumbled "Go," as unconcerned as if he hadn't killed the only person on God's green earth who knew where she was.

At the top came what was for her the worst part: leaving the ladder. The man paused. His shoulder jabbed into her back as he looked down, and then he shoved her onto the bridge. She gasped and, grabbing the cable that served as a handrail, placed each foot in front of the other. She stared at the twelve-inch-wide boards laid end to end in a single row at least a mile across the river. She willed herself not to look at the water, turgid with mud. It was the height she feared, not the water, not here. Hadn't she climbed those cypress trees in Caddo Lake and leapt toward the water stained brown with tannin? She'd been terrified, but Aut and Rachel had urged her on until she had come to love jumping as much as they; later she even taught Dutch how. Once when she surfaced beside a water moccasin and couldn't move, Dutch jumped in and pulled her to shore. She knew her terror of heights stemmed from that snake. After that time, not even Dutch could persuade her to jump. She knew when to stop.

Toward the middle of the bridge, without warning the hijacker paused. "Oklahoma's across the river. I don't need you any more."

He maneuvered around her, and she sprawled face down, both arms hugging the board, which swayed with his steps. In a few minutes the movement stopped. She heard only the roar of the ever-present wind and the murmur of the river.

The sun descended behind the derricks of Bridgetown, igniting the west with iridescent oranges and pinks. Swallows swooped over the river. She was free. Sobs of relief shook her, and she fought the rising nausea. She tried to sit up, but the current mesmerized her, and she couldn't move. She remained face down, fascinated. She could jump. All she had to do was raise herself to a sitting position and give a shove, nothing more than pushing herself off the cypress tree, pretending Rachel and Dutch were below to catch her. And Aut, dead in June in Belleau Wood somewhere in France, would save her, and they'd soar up from this petty, confused existence.

The bridge swayed again, this time in jerks as if some wounded animal limped toward her. She gasped. What if the bandit was returning? Raising her head, she saw nothing in front of her. The movement came from the Texas side. The bridge swayed and stopped and then swayed again. She didn't dare turn to look.

"Margaret! Don't move!" The wind carried the voice to her. Dr. Miller was alive.

Still clutching the board beneath her, she maneuvered around as Dr. Miller forced himself up the ladder rung by rung in what must be a painful ascent. At the top of the ladder, he pulled his good leg up and then the injured one. He paused as if considering, lowered himself to his hands and knees, and crawled toward her. After about three feet, he worked his hands up the cables supporting the bridge, latched onto the horizontal cable, and raised himself to his knees. "Don't look down, Margaret. Look straight ahead." His face was so pale he should be lecturing himself. His voice came to her as weakly as if he were ill. Grasping the cable with each hand, he stood; jerking forward and then stopping, he eased toward Margaret, who still hadn't moved. Recovered from her fright, she felt annoyed at her rescuer. Surely his limp couldn't account for all his hesitation.

"Margaret, are you all right?"

She nodded.

"He's gone. You're safe."

Margaret gripped the cables and pulled up to her feet. She took his hand, cold and sweaty like hers. Together, at arm's length like some awkward four-legged creature, he crept backward and she forward as they inched toward the Texas side. The moon had risen, and Dr. Miller's face looked blanched beneath his freckles.

Margaret shivered. When they reached the ladder, he asked, "Can you get down?"

"I'll try." Her voice quivered, though she had thought she was all right. He descended awkwardly, trying not to put weight on his right leg. She realized he'd been shot in his good leg but had helped her anyway. Grateful, she turned, reached with her foot for the rung of the ladder, and descended after him.

At the bottom they clutched each other for support. This was between them now, his bravery despite his pain; nobody could share their terror or their relief. Shivering, he pressed her hands to his face. "Margaret, I have to tell you. On that bridge, it all came back, that bridge at Château-Thierry. We were short on medics. I volunteered to go out. That's what started the trouble in my head. Guns, the big ones—150 and 210 mm.—pounding everywhere. All around me men shot. When the bombardment stopped, I couldn't hear. The battled ended, but I didn't help our men. I couldn't move. I huddled on the bridge, shot in the thigh and shell-shocked, I was told. But I know the truth. I'm a coward. My limp is a reminder. Ever since then, when I'm even near a bridge, my heart starts pounding, I sweat, and I lose my hearing."

"But you went on this rickety bridge anyway. You helped me." Margaret put her arms around his trembling shoulders to comfort him as she did Beth. How thin his shoulders felt. How selfish she'd been, thinking only of herself. She wanted to say, I'll protect you. She raised her face toward his.

She heard shouts, hoofbeats, and horns. A group of riders followed by two Model-T's descended the hill.

"You're lucky to be alive." A tall Texas Ranger gestured over the bridge. "That bandit killed a man at the bank. We think he robbed the bank in Wichita last week. We almost caught him this time."

Margaret nodded. She felt as inert as her dress.

She rode to town with a portly ruddy-faced man, the president of the bank that had been robbed. Looking back, she saw Dr. Miller in the second car. Expansive, the bank president said, "You're plucky, I'll say that. The doc's a brave man. Crime's getting worse. Last week I heard about somebody stealing a tank. Imagine that. And pipe is stolen all the time."

At Eve's house, he and the Texas Ranger came in with her.

Frowning, Eve met them at the door. "What happened? It's eight o'clock."

The bank president held up a hand, pontificating. "She's a hero, Eve. Relax. A man held up the bank and escaped. We lost him. He took Miz Sanders hostage. She's a brave little woman. He took her halfway across that footbridge—the suspension bridge—and left her there. He shot the doc too and then went over to Oklahoma."

The ranger turned to Margaret. "Would you recognize him, Miz Sanders?"

"Maybe." She didn't know. It all seemed so long ago, as if her existence had begun only after she and Dr. Miller had descended from the bridge. "He was tall." Almost as tall as Dutch, but she was no longer sure how tall Dutch was. "His face was red."

"That's all you remember?"

She nodded.

The ranger left, his lips clenched, but she was too exhausted to think. Eve bustled around, steeping tea, asking questions. "Are you all right, Margaret? He didn't harm you?"

"No, but I was so afraid, Eve. I didn't know what he was going to do. Now I'm cold." She couldn't stop shaking.

"Where were you?"

"At the riverbed with Dr. Miller. Then I left. The man grabbed me on that big hill by the footbridge." She placed her hands around the cup for warmth.

"Why would Dr. Miller let you walk back alone? He knows it's dangerous." Eve frowned. "Why were you there with him anyway? Why didn't you come home after school?"

"I'm not sure why I was there." She felt numb. "Now I want to sleep." Eve looked puzzled. Margaret was puzzled too.

She tiptoed into their closet room. Beth lay on her stomach in Eve's cradle, arms bent at the elbow on either side of her head, one cheek against the sheet. Margaret touched Beth's forehead and smoothed her dark hair, starting to curl like Dutch's.

She longed for sleep, but first she had to take off her clothes and prepare for school tomorrow—no, tomorrow was Saturday. Her mind a muddle, she lay on the bed, narrow as her life, watching Beth's back rise and fall. She thought of Dutch and Dr. Miller—

how selfish she'd been not to recognize the pain the doctor had endured helping her. She slipped into sleep, black and formless, that lasted well into the morning. All night the engines that powered the drilling rigs banged and clanked, but she slept on, so accustomed to the sounds that she noticed them no more than the rhythm of Beth's breathing.

14

It was confusing. The next time Dutch went to Nesterville to pick up the mail, he received a letter from Margaret that she had written a month before. She mentioned nothing about his invitation to come to Texas. Maybe she hadn't received that letter. He'd write again. Frowning, he opened another letter, postmarked after Margaret's, addressed in pencil in a scrawling hand he dreaded reading. Ma wrote, "Son, you should know that Margaret's gone. Run off. She got her nose bent out of joint about working on the farm. I didn't ask her to do anything your sisters don't do. But she's always looked peaked. I don't know why you had to up and marry her. I don't know what's become of her and your poor little baby."

He struck his fist on the closest object, the hitching post outside the post office, and then swore and rubbed his skinned knuckles. Margaret had probably gone back to her folks, and her letter to him hadn't arrived yet. He could count on Ma to muddle everything. She used to threaten to leave Pa, at least once a month packing her flour sack dresses in Dutch's red wagon, marching down the street as if she knew where she was heading. All of them, even Pa, followed her, crying, begging. What a spectacle! They hadn't figured out she'd never leave. Where would she go?

He swabbed his forehead, considering. He could telegraph her folks, but he didn't want to worry them. Maybe she had pulled up stakes in Oil City and was on her way here now. He wouldn't put it past her. That wouldn't be bad. He'd better settle matters with Eve, but what was there to settle? Life did get complicated.

In the jitney on their way back to Springtown, Paul asked, "Say, what was your telegram about?"

"What telegram?"

"How could you miss it? On the pole by the post office."

It had never occurred to him that Margaret might telegraph because she always wrote letters. "Turn around." Dutch gripped the dashboard.

"We're due at work," Paul said.

The driver stopped his Model-T; the dust overtook them. Dutch coughed. The driver looked from one to the other, his jaw full of tobacco. He spit. "Do we go or not?"

A wagoner following their jitney ran up. "What's the holdup?"

Their driver frowned at them. "Make up your mind."

"I've got to go back to Nesterville," Dutch said.

"Don't get your tail over the dashboard. You've got a job. I'm here to see you do it." Paul signaled to the driver. "Keep going." The gears ground as the driver put the car into first.

Dutch growled at Paul, "I thought you were a friend." He opened the door of the jitney.

"I don't want you to lose your job." Paul grabbed his arm. "The telegram might not be from Margaret. Ever think of that?"

Dutch paused, one foot out of the jitney. Maybe Paul was right. He needed the job, and—he had to face it—he needed time to think. He eased his foot inside. The driver spat out the window and drove on. Margaret in Louisiana was one thing; Margaret here, now, was another. At least he hadn't been to the Red Onion lately. He had to plan what to say to Margaret. No doubt about it: he'd miss his freedom. He'd have to assert himself right away. As the jitney bumped toward Springtown, he stared at his hands, clenched hard on his knees.

The next two weeks he and Paul worked twelve hours every day on a rig in Springtown. Whether they were changing the bit, running the drill pipe, or watching the rotary table turn, he thought about Margaret, and by the time he went into Nesterville again, he was no longer pestered with doubt. He wanted to see his wife. Before he ate or shaved or washed, he went straight to the post office. Sure enough, on the pole with telegrams tacked to it, directly above his head was a faded yellow paper addressed to him. How could he have missed it? He ripped it down: "Will arrive August 15." Over a month ago. She must have been here—where?—all this time. What if she'd gone home already?

He elbowed through the crowd around the post office, jostling roughnecks who he hoped were not in the mood for a fight, and pushed his way to the drug store. If there was any information, Mr. Kelly would know it.

"Have you seen anybody new? A blonde young woman, pretty, and a baby girl?"

The druggist scoffed. "Anybody new? Who else do I see every day?"

"It's important. My wife and baby are here."

Mr. Kelly rubbed his head innocent of all hair except for a fringe behind his ears. "Wait. A young woman and a baby have been going around with the Johnsons, Bob Johnson, you know, with the feed store and the livery stable. And also with Eve."

"Eve?" Surely not, out of the thousands of people here.

"If it's your wife, she's at Eve's rooming house."

The druggist called "Good luck," as Dutch ducked out the door.

What had Margaret told Eve? What had Eve told Margaret? Dutch shoved through the crowd on Main Street and, wondering what he was about to find, slowed as he reached Fourth Street. He passed the familiar rows of tents and then the Methodist Church. Two blocks later, there on the porch of the boarding house, in the swing right where he had sat, were Eve and an elderly couple, the woman holding a baby who looked like Beth but who was so big he couldn't be sure. And there was Margaret, thinner but beautiful. All his doubts disappeared as fast as a covey of quail fly up in front of a hunter. He yelled, "Margaret!" Eve's face registered pleasure at seeing him and astonishment as Margaret screamed his name and ran toward him. Then all he saw was Margaret.

Dodging a wagon, she ran across the street, dust flying around her, and met him halfway, and he picked her up and spun her around, laughing. When he put her down at the edge of the road, she clutched him around the neck as if he were about to disappear. He kissed her hard, smelling her scent of lavender, even here in this desert. Then he tipped back her solemn face and traced his finger over her dry lips, upturned nose, and worried dark eyes.

"I thought you'd never come, Dutch."

"How could I not?" He touched her pinned-up hair. One strand had slipped down in front of her ear. She leaned against him, quivering. Compared to Eve, Margaret seemed fragile. Over Margaret's head he sought Eve's eye, pleading for forgiveness. Eve stared at him, her eyes narrowed. Then she raised her chin and turned away.

15

Avoiding Eve's stare, Dutch bent to pick up Beth from the woman with the silver hair. Beth pouted, drawing down her lips the way Dutch found appealing. The woman smirked. "She's at the age where she doesn't like to go to a stranger." Stranger?

Margaret, laughing, lifted Beth toward him. "Here's Papa, Bethie. He's home."

He took Beth and shook hands with the Johnsons. Beth must weigh close to twenty pounds. Sitting by Margaret on the swing, he held Beth lying in front of him the way she loved, her head cradled in his hand. "Margaret, she's so much longer." For a minute Beth grinned up at him, her eyes fixed on his. He tickled her. She giggled. Then she squirmed, and he almost dropped her. "What does she want?" His own child, but he felt awkward with her.

"Try against your shoulder. She still likes that," Margaret said.

"I came straight from work. I'm filthy."

"She won't care." Margaret laughed. "You know she won't break."

When Beth was first born, he'd been terrified to pick her up. She'd seemed so fragile, a seven-pound miniature human. Margaret placed Beth against his shoulder, her legs extending to his lap. How could she have grown so much since July, not even three months ago? Content, Beth touched his hair, which needed a trim, and his oily shirt. Even the stubble on his cheeks didn't bother her. He pressed his lips to her soft, sweet-smelling hair. He'd almost forgotten her baby scent and the feel of that silky little head.

As talk swirled around him, he pushed the swing with his foot, feeling Beth's warmth on his shoulder and Margaret's against his side. He had not forgotten that at any rate. He always slept pressed against her. She radiated heat like a stove. Now Margaret's leg touched his. He pulled her closer to him, his arm around her shoulder. In the dusk Eve stared at the floor.

"I've lived here over sixty years." Mr. Johnson's voice broke through Dutch's reverie. "I've seen some changes. Why, last year, we had fewer than five hundred families. Now look at it." He gestured toward the street, still packed with roughnecks. "But it's good for business. So I won't beef. We run the feed store, me and my boy Jimmy. I'm thankful he didn't have to join up. Flat feet. One good thing I gave him." Mr. Johnson laughed.

Mr. Johnson's quiet strength suggested what Dutch's father might have become if he hadn't been married forty years to such a nag as Ma. But Mrs. Johnson appeared domineering too—she talked so fast that Dutch barely listened, playing with Beth and feeling Margaret's warmth. As Mrs. Johnson chattered, Mr. Johnson smoked his pipe and stared into the growing darkness. Mrs. Johnson prattled about the First Army victory at Saint-Mihiel—she didn't stumble on the French names—and then went on about the price of food, which had doubled since the start of the war, never mind how much prices had soared since the boom. Dutch yawned. When she ran down, nobody spoke for a spell. Her voice reverberated inside Dutch's head. He wished they'd leave.

Margaret stood, thank heavens. "Beth's tired. I've got to put her down."

Mr. Johnson shook hands with Dutch and drifted with his wife onto the still-crowded street.

"Goodnight, Eve." Margaret kissed her. "Thank you again for all you've done. Are you coming in yet?"

"I'm playing tonight. Better be on my way," Eve said.

Never once had Eve glanced at him, and her lips remained clenched tight in a straight line. He didn't think Margaret had noticed anything strange she was so happy to see him.

"Dutch, can you stay here tonight?" Margaret said.

"Are you kidding?" He wanted Margaret to himself, now, and waited impatiently, remembering how soft and smooth her skin felt, while she nursed Beth, chattering about her new job teaching school, her new friends. Margaret seemed more self-confident. She'd established a life here. He was proud of her, but he'd have to rethink his plan to lecture her on his need for independence. The new Margaret would probably agree with no hesitation.

Hesitation: that was what he'd noticed, not as if she was hiding anything from him, of course, yet they had been apart near about three months. And if the truth be told, he had some things to hide himself. Margaret laid Beth in the cradle that he had noticed before on Eve's back porch. Margaret wanted him to pat Beth's back until she slept, as he'd done in Louisiana, but Beth kept sitting up and staring at him until Margaret told her to go to sleep, and Beth, whining only a minute, did.

At last, Margaret turned her back so that he could remove her blouse, fumbling over the buttons, and then her skirt, her petticoat, her camisole, and her unmentionables—so many clothes. He kissed the hollow in her throat and the nape of her neck the way she liked. Finally she lay smiling and rosy, beneath him, above him, and around him on the narrow bed until the darkness began to lighten.

Before he left for work, Dutch started opening the dresser drawers. Half asleep, he heard Margaret ask, "What's going on?"

"Why are you whispering?" He frowned.

"Thin walls."

Alerted to the small sounds beneath the noises of the wells, Dutch whispered too. "Hear that?" He inclined his head toward the next room.

"Mr. Smith. The thin walls didn't bother you last night, I must say." She turned onto her back, her arms behind her head, her golden hair tangled, her face glowing, a satisfied woman if he'd ever seen one.

Then she looked puzzled. "What are you doing with the drawers?"

"I thought I'd bring over my clothes from Springtown. Where can I put them? It's really crowded here."

"Do you have to worry about your clothes right now?" She patted the bed.

"We need a house."

"I'd love that." She stretched. "But nothing's available."

"Half a house would do. I saw some down the block." He gestured around the room. "There's not much space, you have to admit."

"Or privacy either." Margaret's arm, smooth and pale, lay outside the sheet. How did she keep her skin so white? His face and arms were burned dark. He sat on the bed, careful not to jostle Beth's cradle. Margaret's leg was outlined under the sheet. He traced his finger along its curve. "I've missed your body." He uncovered her foot and bent to kiss her ankle, as smooth as he'd remembered. "Maybe I won't go to work yet."

Margaret slid toward the window, making room for him on the cot. He pushed his face into her hair, as soft as Beth's, only half-hearing her murmur, "I don't want to leave here. I'm so grateful to Eve for taking me in and giving me a job. Let's wait before we move. Maybe Eve has a bigger room." Margaret scootched against him. She was still a perfect fit. "Eve's been a really good friend. I admire her. She does so much by herself."

"I guess so. You have to around here." Every time she said "Eve," he felt guilty. He wished Margaret would stop chattering. "Can't you forget about her for a minute?"

In the rooms around them, rhythmic snorts and whistles were replaced by throat clearing and nose blowing. "Does everybody have a cold?" Dutch said.

Against his chest Margaret giggled, her breath warm. "It's the dust." She stirred. "Time to get up, or Mr. Smith will beat me to the privy. I'm sorry, Dutch. Later. All right?"

"Later when? You'll be teaching or cooking or washing dishes or taking care of Beth," Dutch said.

Margaret smiled, raising herself on her elbow. "I swear, you're jealous, Dutch." She sounded pleased.

"That's silly." Maybe this new independence of Margaret's wasn't altogether a blessing. He'd been crazy with longing and lonesomeness, but now putting their lives back together as one family, somehow different—he couldn't figure out how—seemed like a difficult prospect. It had been easier before. He'd gone to work, and Margaret had been glad to see him when he'd returned home. "You came to see me, remember, not Mr. Smith, not Eve."

"You're right. I came to see you." She turned toward him and stroked his hair, her voice muffled against his neck, her lips soft.

Before long, Beth flounced around like a puppy, making sighs and moans Dutch wished he could understand. He reached down and dragged a finger over the side of the bed. Beth pulled it toward her mouth. "No, Bethie."

"Mama?"

Dutch stared, amazed. "Margaret, did you hear that? Beth

talked."

Margaret stirred. "What's wrong?"

"Nothing's wrong. Beth called you Mama."

"I forgot to tell you. She's talking."

Something else had happened: Beth could sit up, talk.

"What else haven't you told me?" He couldn't keep the irritation out of his voice.

"What do you mean?" Her voice had an edge he'd not heard before.

What was going on? He felt like a stranger with his own wife and daughter. "I mean, what else has Beth learned since I've seen her?"

Margaret considered. "She crawls."

Dutch sneezed again. "I hate for Beth to be exposed to all the dust. What if she gets sick?"

Margaret picked her up. "You're not peaked, are you, Beth?" Scrunching against Dutch, who was pressed against the wall, Margaret laid Beth on the bed. "You're right. We need more room."

"I'm fixing to get up." Dutch looked at the brightening sky, sunlight filtering through the sycamore tree outside their window, hot air tinged with the scent of dust. The aroma of bacon permeated the room. "It's late." He popped Margaret's bottom with a calloused palm.

Margaret grabbed his hand, so engrained with grime that his twice-daily washing couldn't clean it. "You smell of oil. But I love you, dirt and all." She smiled up at him, letting go of his hand.

He extricated himself. "Did you bring me any socks?" He looked around. "Where's your suitcase?"

"Stolen from the station. My pocketbook too. While I was waiting for you." She frowned. Did he hear blame?

"That's a fine how-do-you-do." He rubbed his forehead. "But I've saved most of my salary. So we have over three hundred dollars."

"And I made three dollar a days at school and a dollar a day plus room and board helping Eve. Dutch, I cannot tell you how kind Eve's been to Beth and me."

"Where did I put my boots?" He felt uncomfortable when

Margaret praised Eve. He didn't much mind the loss of the suitcase, but Margaret was still rubbing her forehead and frowning.

"The thing is, I had some stuff in the bag besides clothes," she said.

"Like what?" He looked under the bed for his boots.

"My grandmother's pearls for one thing."

"I'm sorry, Margaret. I know you loved them." Dutch put his arm around her shoulder.

"I feel awful. How can I tell Mama? She said my grandfather gave them to my grandmother when they married." She wiped her nose. "It's not just that, though."

"What? It can't be that bad. You look like somebody died."

"Your baseball glove was in the suitcase too."

"Why would you bring it? I wanted you to take care of it for me."

"I didn't want to leave it with your folks. Your ma might take a notion to throw it out. You can't tell with her." Margaret sounded almost as shrill as Dutch's ma. He knew the glove was beat up and way too small for his hand, but it was the only present his dad had ever given him.

"Why do you care so much about an old glove? It doesn't even fit," she said.

He sighed. "I thought I'd told you that story. You've seen how my folks are, how Ma rules the roost. Once, just once in my whole life, Pa stood up to her. About that glove. She said it cost too much. He said if I wanted it so bad I could have it."

Margaret started crying. Beth looked from one parent to the other and wailed. Margaret, glaring, picked her up and bounced her, but Dutch refused to feel guilty. To hope for understanding was too much. He sat there, biting his bottom lip, a bad habit he'd picked up from Margaret, but it was the only way to keep himself silent. He wouldn't yell. He wouldn't let Margaret have the satisfaction of saying he'd inherited his ma's temper.

Margaret's face was mottled. "It was my fault, I suppose, I got robbed. What if I'd gotten hurt? Or Beth?" The old Margaret wouldn't have lashed out. But what she said was true. It was just a baseball glove. She and Beth were safe. He tried to keep things in perspective.

He pulled on his boots. "Don't worry about it." Afraid he still sounded curt, he bent and kissed her. "See you tonight." His wife and baby were here. That's what he'd wanted. He should be happy. Wasn't he ever satisfied?

Paul greeted him at the rig in Springtown with a grin. "Did you find your pretty wife?"

Dutch grunted.

But as the day passed, Dutch found himself thinking about Margaret. He'd been too hasty, that was for sure. He'd make it up to her. He'd take her away from Eve's boarding house. Living there could only cause conflict, regardless of how much Margaret knew. He remembered a "For Rent" sign he'd seen.

After work Dutch went by himself to the Red Onion. It was safe: Eve wasn't there yet with her recriminations. Yet he couldn't picture her snapping at him as Margaret had. Why not? Eve was much more independent than Margaret.

He had a drink. When Mr. Westfield came up to the bar, Dutch remembered that he handled rental property.

"You don't know of any places to rent, do you? My wife and baby are here." Dutch was surprised to hear pride in his voice as he told Mr. Westfield about Margaret's teaching school. He'd forgotten all about their argument. After he and the realtor made an appointment to see a house, the thought of Margaret's pleasure restored his good humor. He'd swoop her and Beth away from that cramped room and from Eve, too.

16

Where was Margaret? Dutch shrugged off his disappointment that she wasn't waiting for him on the porch after work, but he had to admit he felt relieved too. He wasn't ready to face Eve and Margaret together. Margaret must be in that closet room. He washed his face and hands at the pump in the back yard. Even the water smelled of oil. That didn't surprise him.

He opened the door to their room and found it bare, stripped of their few possessions. Nothing on the nails or in the drawers, not Beth's or Margaret's clothes. Had they been robbed? Had Margaret been injured protecting their few possessions after he'd gotten his tail over the dashboard about the lost suitcase? Or had she run away?

"Margaret, where are you? We've been robbed!" Doors opened, and the boarders murmured about how theft was all too common.

Margaret, giggling, skipped out of the kitchen. "Surprise! Guess what?"

Dutch scowled. "What's going on? Where's Beth?"

She patted his shoulder. "Beth's fine. She's with Eve. Come upstairs." She placed her fingers over his mouth and laughed. "We weren't robbed. It's a surprise. You'll like it."

Surely she remembered he hated surprises. "Margaret, wait. I understand. We weren't robbed. But I have news." He stopped at the foot of the stairs and held both of her hands. Anticipating her pleasure, he had forgotten all about his irritation that morning.

"Tell me." She was still beaming.

"You notice I'm late?"

"I was worried."

"I did something important. For all three of us."

"What?"

He stroked her hair. "I got us a house."

"A house? Why?" She composed her face.

"Half a house actually. It's hard to find whole houses."

"Half a house?"

"To rent. And we have the option to buy."

"A house to rent?"

"Why are you echoing me? Don't you want to see it?"

"A house? Now? That's what I wanted to show you, Dutch. Eve and I fixed a room upstairs. You'll like it."

"I'm sure I would. If we were going to stay. But let's look at the house."

"First look at the room." She pulled him up the stairs.

"We have to hurry. Houses go fast here. I told Mr. Westfield we could probably move in tomorrow."

Margaret stopped outside the bedroom door. "Tomorrow?"

"We don't have much stuff. It won't take long to move." Why was she balking?

Margaret frowned. "You decided that without me? It's a big decision."

"I knew you'd like it." Why was she objecting? "I did something nice for you and Beth, and all you can do is ask questions."

She turned the crystal doorknob and ushered him into the bedroom.

Green-tinted light streamed into the windows, and the sycamore cast shadows that moved with the wind, making patterns on the dark wood of the cradle. The room looked peaceful. But he saw too much of Eve's influence. One of her rag rugs lay on the polished floor, and a Log Cabin quilt from her room covered the double bed.

"I'm sorry to spoil your surprise." Dutch cupped her chin in his hand and kissed her nose. "It's just that I was excited about the house. I want you to see it." Margaret looked so disappointed that he tried again. "This is nice, really, but I want us to be by ourselves."

"I truly do not understand, Dutch. I worked so hard to make this room pretty, and I don't see why you're acting so strange. Don't you like Eve? Look at all she's done for me, and you hardly know her." Margaret's face was red, and she was about to cry. He hoped Mr. Westfield wouldn't rent the house to somebody who might happen by before they arrived. "You weren't here. I had nothing. What would I have done without her?"

"I'm sorry I didn't meet you," he said.

"And you know I was abducted by the bank robber? I was

terrified. I could've been killed. Then I thought I heard your voice, and I was so disappointed that it wasn't you. Why weren't you here to help me?"

He took her soft hands and kissed them. "That's behind us. We can start again."

She glanced around the room. Then she nodded. "We can look at the house, I guess. I'll get Beth." She smoothed her hair. "Do I look a sight?"

"You're beautiful." Dutch, relieved, smiled. They could be at the house in five minutes.

"Maybe Eve can go too."

Dutch sighed. "I'd rather we go by ourselves." The less he saw of Eve, the better. His guilt kept rising and staring at him with round eyes as brown as Margaret's.

"I don't want to hurt Eve's feelings after all she's done for me, for us really." Margaret dragged down the stairs, her hand trailing along the oak bannister. Before Eve's parents had bought the rooming house ten years ago, it was the home of an early settler, Eve had told him, built after he'd become successful. Maybe someday he and Margaret would be that prosperous. Maybe the half-house would have oak bannisters.

Shoulders sagging, Margaret opened the door to the kitchen. He heard Eve ask, "Did Dutch like the room?"

"He didn't say." Margaret sighed. "He wants to show me a house for rent."

"Then you should look at it." Eve sounded curt. Just as well they were leaving. He'd tell Mr. Westfield they wanted that house, whatever it looked like.

Dutch carried Beth, who had gained several pounds since July. They walked east away from town, past shotgun frame houses thrown up at the beginning of the boom, three rooms straight in a row, some homes detached, some pushed together. Her lips turned down, Margaret wasn't talking. He'd make it up to her. Someday they could live anywhere she chose.

Just before the houses ended, Dutch stopped at a double house that looked like all the rest. He gestured with pride. "There it is."

Margaret raised her eyebrows.

Dutch shrugged. "It isn't what we had at home, but it'll give us some privacy."

Mr. Westfield, beaming, met them at the door. "This here's the living room, and here's the bedroom." They walked through the first two empty rooms with uneven wooden floors and walls in need of paint. "And here's the kitchen." They entered the smallest room in the back. "You're the last house on the block with electricity." He indicated a bare bulb in the center of the room. "There's a pump in the sink. A kerosene stove. Coal Oil Johnny comes around on his wagon every week. The iceman Joe Bob too." He motioned to the oak icebox. "The privy's out there." He opened the screen door into the backyard. "Nice view." He motioned east toward the sand dunes in the riverbed. "You're on a rise so it'll never flood, but you're close enough to the river for a breeze."

Margaret stepped outside and gazed at a wide expanse of sand and grass burrs. "But there are no trees." She'd loved their yard in Louisiana covered with pines.

Mr. Westfield pointed toward the distance. "Two cottonwood. Three salt cedar. Pink blooms. Some mesquites."

"Bushes, not trees." Margaret frowned.

"This is the plains, Miz Sanders. You can plant some mulberry trees. They grow fast if you water them."

Mr. Westfield must have been a real estate agent quite a spell; he could make everything sound like an advantage. Dutch wanted the house. He didn't care what Mr. Westfield said if he could persuade Margaret.

Margaret picked up her skirt to avoid the burrs, some growing on bushes as high as her knees. She jumped. "Something stung me. What's that?"

"Cockle burr. Ever seen them before? I reckon not." Mr. Westfield laughed. "They won't hurt you."

Biting her lip, Margaret pulled out the fingernail-sized brown burr shaped like a pine cone and surrounded by curved claws. Other tiny flat round burrs with small prickles around the edges clung to the hem of her skirt.

"Beggar lice." Mr. Westfield saw her horrified expression and raised a hand. "Not animals. Plants. It's a struggle to survive here, so everything has to be hardy or prickly. Sticking to things is the way the plant spreads. The burrs are the seeds."

Dutch looked interested, inspecting the beggar lice—what a name—covering his pant legs. "Are there many cactus?"

"Quite a few. Prickly pear. Big yellow blooms in the spring and purple fruit. And blue bells like a carpet in the riverbed every summer. They love the sand." He cleared his throat. "You mentioned water, Miz Sanders. It's scarce now, but we're due rain."

Dutch raised his eyes to check for clouds and for the first time noticed the river, a brown ribbon a half-mile away. Above the dry landscape stretched the deep blue, cloudless sky. Margaret would go for the view. He touched her arm to attract her attention as she dislodged beggar lice. "Margaret, look."

She drew in a breath of amazement. "I've never seen anything so open."

Dutch put his arm around her. "I thought you'd like it."

Mr. Westfield smiled with a proprietary interest. "Gets to you sometimes, the plains. That's the Red River. And that's Oklahoma yonder on the other side."

Margaret might decide there were compensations for the absence of trees. Away from most of the derricks, the air was so clear Dutch could see sage-covered sand dunes on the far side of the river.

They turned toward the house. Margaret wrinkled her nose in disgust. "What's that? And that?" Patches of hardened oil were splotched around the yard.

Dutch glanced at Mr. Westfield, who as Dutch had expected, dismissed her concern. "Just some oil. You haven't been here long, have you?"

"Why is it all over the place?" His wife would not be distracted.

"There must've been a gusher nearby, and oil ran over the slush pit because it flowed so fast. Cover it with dirt, and it'll be fine." Mr. Westfield swabbed his forehead. He kept talking faster. Dutch had better watch himself with this man. Maybe Margaret's doubts were reasonable.

"I don't think—" The earth opened in front of Margaret. She jumped back. With a whoosh a hole two feet in diameter appeared where she had been about to step.

Mr. Westfield yelled, "Watch out!" Dutch grabbed her.

Clasping Beth, she teetered on the edge. They stood astonished as sand trickled into the hole.

Mr. Westfield coughed. "Actually, it's safe. Used to be a well there, and when it quit flowing, it was abandoned without being capped. The hole caved in." He wiped his forehead on his sleeve. "Happens all the time."

Margaret frowned. "Beth and I could've fallen in that and died. We can't live here, Frank."

Dutch started at her use of his real name. For an instant she sounded like Eve.

Mr. Westfield managed a patient tone like a teacher explaining an assignment in logic for the tenth time. "You wouldn't have fallen in, or at least not very far. Maybe fifteen feet. Furthermore, you can see that wells can't be too close together—there isn't room, so we know that since there was a well right here, there can't have been one anywhere else close. All you have to do is fill in this hole." He paused, glancing at Margaret, whose face beneath her sunbonnet had paled. "Tell you what. I'll have it filled in tomorrow. Just for you, Miz Sanders." He bowed.

Dutch almost believed him, he wanted this place so bad. "So it's good it happened, Margaret. It happened once; therefore, it won't happen again. Now we know we'll be safe."

"What kind of logic is that? Are you crazy, Dutch? You've got house fever, that's all."

That did it. They'd take the house regardless of the burrs, patches of hardened oil, and even the hole in the earth. But Dutch didn't want her to accuse him of being domineering. He managed to ask, "What do you think?"

She sighed. "If you like it. Despite all this." She waved a hand to include the house and yard. Then she brightened. "Maybe we should get Eve's opinion. And the Johnsons' too."

"By all means," Mr. Westfield said. "They'll tell you houses are almost impossible to find."

Dutch was amazed that Mr. Westfield agreed. Surely someone local would recognize this for the hazard it was.

"And you have to imagine how nice it will look with your furniture."

"We didn't bring any," Margaret said.

"My wife and I could scare up some. It's good for the town to have upstanding young folks settle here."

When he put it like that, Dutch wasn't sure he wanted to move. He didn't much cotton to the word "settle." Deep down—never mind the existence of his wife and child—wasn't he a free spirit? Margaret stared at the ground, refusing to meet his eyes. He couldn't see her face under the bonnet, but he sensed her resentment radiating toward him like heat from a pine torch.

They stood in silence. Mr. Westfield shrugged, as if to say he'd done his best. Children of various ages watched from the back door of the other half of the house. Mr. Westfield raised his hat to the woman who appeared behind them. "Evening, Miz McNeill. These are your new neighbors." He glanced at Margaret. "Maybe." He turned to Dutch. "Mrs. McNeill grew up here." Dutch studied her. If the harsh climate had affected her, it had only made her more stolid, a bulwark against trouble and the weather. Every part of her large frame—from her thick brown hair brushed into a bun on top of her head to her round arms—suggested comfort and security.

Margaret smiled at Mrs. McNeill, took off her bonnet, and raised her face toward Dutch. "If you want it so bad. And if the Johnsons and Eve approve."

With relief Dutch wiped his sweaty palm on his overalls and shook hands with Mr. Westfield before Margaret could change her mind. "Good," Mr. Westfield said. "Bring your friends tomorrow evening. I'll have the furniture here."

Maybe he was gloating about the deal he'd pulled off with these newcomers, but Dutch would fix this place up. He'd plant roses and honeysuckle and a victory garden like at home.

17

Whistling as they walked back to the boarding house, Dutch put his arm around Margaret's waist, which even after having Beth was as slim as ever, so small his outstretched palms could almost encircle it. Imagine, living in a house so soon. He'd missed the privacy and freedom. He could ask Margaret's mother—his own mother would scoff—to mail him some pine saplings. Beth could grow up here. He pictured her in a few years, straight and delicate as a young tree, with her mama's brown eyes and his dark hair. He had thought Margaret would be delighted at the prospect of a house, but she walked beside him without speaking, eyes down, hidden in that poke bonnet all the women wore. He ventured, "I can build a fence in the back so Beth will have a place to play, away from the hole, I mean, and we can plant grass and flowers."

"That's nice." She sounded abstracted.

Might as well have it out. He girded himself for an argument. He'd forgotten how stubborn Margaret could be. "What's wrong, sure enough?"

"I like the idea of a house, but not this one. It's a dump. And even if it were nice, I've gotten used to living at Eve's." She must have had all the reasons planned out. "I like the company of the boarders. I'm never bored. Eve and the men appreciate my help. I like having my own money. Eve's a friend, almost a big sister. Beth likes her. Eve'll miss us."

Dutch had anticipated that last argument, which for him was a reason to move. "You can still see Eve. It's less than two blocks from her."

"I know."

"So what is it then?"

"I dread telling her we're leaving. She'll take it hard. She doesn't have any family. Her fiancé married some girl in France. She hasn't heard from him in over a year."

"Everybody has troubles, Margaret. You can't solve them all." There. He'd said his say, and he would wait and see what happened. It wouldn't hurt to maintain some distance from Eve. In spite of

Margaret's presence, he couldn't help but notice Eve's long legs and thick auburn hair. And he didn't know whether he could trust Eve not to tell Margaret he was the Frank she'd been seeing before Margaret came. Now Margaret had her tail over the dashboard, walking sedately by him almost as if he weren't here at all. He knew that she recognized the house as unsafe and that she had made a place for herself at Eve's, but she didn't understand that he envisioned the house as an opportunity to fix something nice for themselves. Mr. Westfield told him that wild flowers grew everywhere in the spring: primroses, bluebonnets, Indian paint brushes blanketing the land in pink, blue, and red orange. On the edge of town, they had a view of the river and could enjoy the breeze better than in town. The racket of the wells and the steam boilers wasn't so bad here either.

At the boarding house Eve had already gone to the Red Onion. Dutch was glad, but Margaret lamented, "I haven't seen Eve much lately, and when I do, she hardly talks. I don't know what's wrong." He kept his mouth shut as they climbed the stairs to their new room. Margaret sat in the rocker while Beth nursed. Dutch felt the peace of this spacious room with the stars peeking through the sycamore. He stretched out in the big bed. What luxury. "This beats that little bed all holler."

"All hollow?" She giggled. "Where'd you hear that?"

"Paul maybe."

"Hollow. That's the way I felt last month. I worried about you, Dutch."

"Everything's good now."

"Do you really want to move?" That was Margaret, wear out a subject.

"Sure. We can have room to ourselves. Don't you want to?"

"I reckon." Margaret sighed. "But we'll see what the Johnsons and Eve say tomorrow."

After work they all walked to the half house. Mrs. Johnson insisted on carrying Beth. "You remember babies love me." Margaret didn't seem to mind Mrs. Johnson's cattiness but chattered with her as if they were old friends. No accounting for tastes.

At the house Mr. Westfield shook hands with everybody and ushered them through. "I took the liberty of bringing a little furniture. I hope you like it." He pointed to a studio couch and two wingback chairs in the living room, a double bed and a dresser, and in the kitchen a round pedestal oak table and four chairs with spindled backs.

"It's everything we need. Thank you, Sir." Dutch was delighted, and Margaret smiled. The furniture minimized the shabbiness sure enough.

"Take it before someone else snaps it up," Eve said.

"You don't realize how hard houses are to get. Why, six druggists had to share a house this size for a year before they found anything else," Mr. Johnson said.

"This is a real find." Mrs. Johnson nodded.

Dutch was amazed but gratified that for some reason they weren't bothered by the oil patches or the hole in the backyard.

Mr. Westfield shook hands with Dutch. "It's yours."

"Let's celebrate. Come to our place," Mrs. Johnson said. "I baked a lemon cake."

"You'll love it," Mr. Johnson said.

Dutch admired Mrs. Johnson's ingenuity in finding the ingredients, especially because everybody had been limited to two pounds of flour a month since July. Mrs. Johnson might be nosy, but she was resourceful.

The Johnson's frame house was crowded with furniture, china, and her collection of doll houses. The house was immaculate, starched lace doilies on the backs of chairs and runners on the table and buffet, although Mrs. Johnson apologized for the dust as she showed Margaret her whatnot cabinet with a collection of china hens.

Moving was easy. They had only Dutch's suitcase, the clothes Eve had given Margaret, two quilts, a cradle, and a rug from Eve. Being surrounded by Eve's things was still worrisome, but before long they'd have their own. They made quite a procession. Mrs. Johnson brought towels and dishrags made from flour sacks. Mr. Boyd delivered their new blue willow dishes and a mattress, with all white-cotton stuffing, no seeds at all.

Pleased, Dutch sat in the living room. It looked fair to middling. Margaret made coffee, which they drank from their four new cups.

"Where's Eve?" Mrs. Johnson said. "I thought she'd want to help you move."

Dutch shrugged his shoulders, relieved she hadn't come.

"I guess she's busy. I didn't see her today after school except to pick up Beth." Margaret sounded puzzled.

After the Johnsons left and Beth was asleep in the cradle, Dutch ached to have Margaret all to himself. But the new Margaret insisted on washing the cups, chattering about cooking salt pork and navy beans for him the next night. "I haven't cooked for you in a spell."

"Come to bed now."

First she had to look out the back door. "Dutch, quick."

Dutch ran. His footsteps shook the house. "What's wrong?"

"Look at that moon."

"I thought it was another cave-in." He put his arm around her shoulder. The harvest moon was rising heavy and yellow over the river. It was a sight, he had to admit, silver beams on slow flowing dark water, sand bleached in the moonlight. Margaret leaned her head against him. She smelled of lavender.

"What are you thinking about, Dutch?"

"Maybe there are scorpions or rattlesnakes in our backyard. But it's ours, Margaret. Our back yard, our house, yours and mine. What about you?"

"I'll get up early. Maybe I can find some blue bells and put them on the breakfast table for you."

He should've known. That's what he got for marrying a romantic.

18

"**I**'ll help Eve today. No school." Margaret stretched as she finished her coffee. She could see the deep blue autumn sky through the window. Sunshine poured onto Beth's high chair, making her dark hair shine. "While you're at work."

"Why?" Dutch grunted as he pulled on his boots.

"I haven't seen her much since we moved." Margaret shoveled oatmeal into Beth's mouth, wide open like a baby bird's.

"You see her when you take Beth in the mornings and when you pick her up."

"I don't have time to visit. And she seems distant sometimes."

"What do you mean?" Dutch stood, ready to go.

"She doesn't talk much."

"Leave it. She's tired. You are too. It's Saturday."

"Maybe. But I miss her. I don't want to lose touch."

"Have fun then, doing whatever you girls do." Dutch grinned and kissed her. "You taste good. Save some energy for me." He kissed the top of Beth's head, avoiding the smears of oatmeal. "You're a mess, Beth."

She grinned.

Loading a tray with dirty plates when Margaret walked in, Eve nodded to Margaret. Her face broke into a smile when she saw Beth. "Hello, Baby." She poured coffee, and she and Margaret sat at the table with the men.

"Did you hear about the new gusher west of town?" Mr. Willis said. "Supposed to be as good as the Fowler."

"I haven't read the papers much lately," Margaret said.

"Tell Dutch howdy for me."

"And for me too." Mr. Smith stood up. "It's been quiet around here since you moved."

After the men left, Margaret said, "I've missed seeing you, Eve. I like the house more than I thought, but I miss all this, the hustle and bustle. It was fun, this past summer."

"For me too. Especially having somebody to talk to. But I like keeping Beth in the mornings."

"I came to see if I could help today."

"You must be joking."

They made fast work of the dishes. Her hands in the dishwater, Eve said, "I wonder about one thing, Margaret."

Margaret looked up.

"Why do you call your husband 'Dutch' when his name is 'Frank'? I never know what to call him."

Margaret laughed. "It's confusing. I've heard people here call him 'Frank.' Maybe he thinks it's high time people called him by his real name. He's named after his father, a sailor from Holland. He and a buddy jumped ship off the Florida Keys and paddled to shore on a plank. Neither one could swim. Then he named his first son 'Frank,' but instead of calling him 'Frank Junior,' his family called him 'Dutch' when he was a baby, and it stuck, even though his dad's the Dutchman."

"I understand," Eve said.

"No reason, really."

Over the noise of the wells, Margaret heard a low, prolonged roll. "Was that thunder?"

"Ignore it." Eve waved a soapy hand. "It means nothing."

They heard a louder rumble and then a crash. Eve dried her hands on a flour sack and stepped onto the back porch. "If that doesn't beat all. Look."

Black thunderclouds taller than derricks covered the sun, and what sky was left uncovered had turned to charcoal. A breeze, almost cool, washed over them from the north. They could feel the temperature drop.

"I declare, this may be the rain we've been waiting for."

The sky darkened. Margaret chewed her bottom lip. "I'd better go. Dutch might come home early."

"Hurry. Take this for your heads." Eve tossed Margaret a flour sack.

Exhilarated, Margaret ran down the block. Beth laughed as she bounced up and down. By the time Margaret reached the house, the thunder rumbled every few seconds, but the wind had stopped, and the air, which had taken on a green tinge, felt heavy.

"Don't worry, Beth," she said. Once their kitchen tent at home on Caddo Lake had been hit by lightning, and the tent had burned. They'd had all they could do to save the house. She looked across the river, where dark clouds shouldered their way toward Nesterville.

The calico cat that belonged to the McNeills next door slunk under the house. Beth reached toward it. "Ka-ka."

Margaret paused, delighted. Another word. "Yes–kitty cat." Beth beamed.

A sheet of lightning flashed across the sky, and thunder boomed. Margaret jumped, and Beth clutched her neck, eyes wide. "It's all right, Baby." They watched from the kitchen window as the thunder and lightning, closer and closer together, approached from the northeast over the river. The wind picked up sand from the riverbed and threw it at the house. The sand seeped under the windows and doors. Wave after wave of heavy rain attacked the house. Yellowish-red mud replaced the sand under the back door. In no time the rain transformed the street into a river of mud that would suck down any who dared challenge it. Margaret shivered.

The front door swung open. She ran to shut it so that the mud wouldn't invade the front of the house.

Dutch was wiping his feet on the doormat. "We stopped drilling because of the lightning. Rain at last." He clapped his hands. He rushed through the house and plopped down two buckets and her washtubs by the back steps. "Do we have anything else?"

"What for?"

"We need water, don't we? This is our chance." He was more manic than she'd seen him since the day before Beth was born, when he'd run around the house dusting and mopping every room. He moved the tubs and buckets to the yard, already a sea of sluggish rust-colored mud, and arranged bowls on the steps.

The thunder and lightning stopped, and the pelting rain slacked off, becoming a gentle shower. Dutch yelled, "Come on." He grabbed a bar of homemade lye soap and stripped off his shirt. "We can have a bath."

"Wah-Wah." Beth reached for the rain drops.

"Do you think Beth will get sick?" Margaret said.

"She'll love it."

Margaret handed him Beth, who squirmed, demanding to be put down. Dutch moved the bowls to the ground, and Beth sat on the steps squealing. Margaret stood on the steps and raised her face. The cool rain washed over her, soaking her dress and her hair, which hung in snarls down her back. She felt Dutch watching and smiled, knowing he was admiring the way her thin dress clung to her.

The youngest McNeill girl appeared at their neighbor's back door. "Mama," she shouted. "Can we go out too?"

Mrs. McNeill, the two older children beside her, looked out at the rain. Her tired face softened. "Why not?"

Her children sat with Beth on the steps and kicked their legs.

Margaret surrendered to the warm rain, which cooled her face and shoulders and arms. It didn't take much to make them happy. "This is the most fun we've had since I've been here."

Dutch stroked her hair back from her face. "We've been working too hard."

During the night Margaret woke contented. The drumming of the rain on the tin roof reminded her of home. But by morning, the mud had mixed with oil to form a thick muck that oozed under the front door.

"I've got to shovel it out, Beth. Mud everywhere. All I can see is mud." She started scraping, the mud heavy on the shovel.

When the clouds broke later, she made her way to Eve's. Fourth Street wasn't too muddy; she could walk without her boots disappearing in the oily goo.

The boarding house door was open, and Eve stood on the steps bent over a shovel. Beth's face exploded in a grin. She reached out her arms.

"I can't hold you, Beth. I'm filthy." Eve wiped a smudge of mud off her cheek and looked at Margaret. "What have you been doing?"

"Shoveling mud. What else?"

"My back hurts already." Eve glanced around. "The rain's stopped."

Margaret watched steam rising from the mud. "It's almost pretty."

"Beautiful." Eve threw her an amused glance, but Margaret didn't care. She was new. She had the right to make senseless remarks.

"Let's go downtown while we have a chance," Eve said.

Downtown was not pretty. Horses floundered with their loads, mud to their knees. Some fell and started to sink. Wagoners stopped and, with help from the ever-present spectators, lifted the horses out. Wagons and occasional Model-T's sank to their hubs. Nevertheless, everyone seemed cheerful, grateful for the rain.

"Let's cross down here," Eve said. "I reckon he's already working."

"Who?"

"You'll see." Eve smiled.

In the middle of the main drag, a bear of a man picked up a woman, who settled her skirt around herself. Then he started across the street. The mud sucked as his powerful legs sank.

"Eve, I can't do that, let a strange man carry me."

"Sure you can. You pay him five dollars, and he carries you across."

"Almost a week's meals?"

"Suit yourself. You have the right to sink to your waist if you like."

Accustomed to lines at the stores and the post office, a group of women and some men waited as patiently as the dray horses that struggled through the mud. No question about it: sometimes life moved slowly in this new world. It had to. Daily existence was so hard that folks aged quickly, and the delays brought out an unexpected patience alongside the energy the oil called forth. Even standing in line, men negotiated deals.

"Look." Margaret nudged Eve as the man in front of them pulled out a wad of bills.

"Right. Fat enough to choke a cow. Happens all the time."

Margaret thought it was fortunate that people had money because everything cost a fortune. Even the glass of clean spring water she bought from that enterprising Abbott boy cost ten cents, and she was paying five dollars, one day's pay for Dutch, for the privilege of being carried maybe thirty feet. It took awhile because the bear man good-naturedly stopped to help a sinking wagon.

Nobody complained at the delay.

"Put your left arm around my neck, Miz Sanders, and hold Beth to you with your right." The bear man scooped them up and plowed through the mud.

She'd never seen him before. "How do you know our names?"

"I'm Jimmy Johnson. I know Dutch, and Mom and Dad talk about you all the time. They think you got a good deal on that house."

"That's comforting. It's a wreck."

"You're lucky to find anything."

"I reckon so." She adjusted herself, awkward in the arms of this man not much older than Dutch. She grasped him around the neck and tried not to inhale his acrid smell. "How do you know my husband?"

"The Red Onion maybe."

She frowned. Dutch hadn't taken her, saying it wasn't a fit place. "I didn't know he went there."

"Not very often."

He deposited them on the wooden sidewalk, now covered with several inches of mud and oil.

He turned and lifted his customer for the return trip, Jerry the window peeper, now wearing a coat with his cowboy boots and hat. Gripping his hat, Jerry shouted, "You're fired!" in their direction.

Margaret stewed while Jimmy Johnson strode through the mud with Eve, joking the whole time. As Eve straightened her dress, Margaret asked, "Does Dutch go to the Red Onion?"

Eve raised her eyebrows. "I hardly ever see him anymore. If he goes, it's before I get there. When does he get home?"

"About nine."

"Nothing to worry about. He leaves before it gets rough."

"Why do you play there?"

Eve shrugged. "I told you. I get lonesome."

Margaret brooded, and by the time she met Dutch at the door she had worked herself into a conniption. "Why didn't you tell me you go to the Red Onion after work?"

Dutch frowned. "That's a fine way to greet your husband, after he's worked all day Sunday, snapping and accusing him of who knows what."

She lowered her voice. "I'm not accusing you of anything. I asked you to take me to hear Eve play, and you said it wasn't suitable. That was your very word. But you go there."

"Who told you that?"

"Jimmy Johnson. He carried me across the street today."

"Is that right?" He rubbed his forehead. "I've been maybe two, three times lately. What's wrong with that?"

"Nothing. It's just that I'm so lonely by myself after school, and Beth and I are ready for you to get home."

Dutch unlaced his boots. "Do we have any drinking water?"

"The Abbott boy brought us a gallon today. It cost two dollars."

"Well worth it. I'm tuckered out."

Margaret put fried chicken on the table. "Do you want to wash first?"

"It never does much good, the pump water's so muddy, but I can try."

"I'll heat water for a bath after supper."

He smiled, and she saw the old Dutch beneath the dirt. "Don't bother. I just want to sleep."

She sat across the table from him and, before she could stop herself, blurted out, "But you have time to go to the Red Onion?"

"Come on, Margaret. I'm tired. I worked twelve hours today." He pushed back his plate.

"At least eat your supper. You always like my fried chicken." Her voice rose, taking on the shrill tone she hated when Dutch's mother spoke to his father, as if she welcomed the bickering.

"What's wrong now?" Dutch sounded exhausted.

"Nothing." She sighed. "I'm tired, too, is all."

He touched her hair. "I know you work hard. I'll make it up to you. Someday we'll look back on this and laugh." He glanced around. "Where's Beth?"

"I put her to bed. I thought we could have some time together. By ourselves."

"Margaret, I'm too tired for anything but sleep." He patted her shoulder in a gesture that he probably meant to indicate tenderness but that she interpreted as dismissal. "You know I like to see Beth of an evening."

"She's asleep. Eat your supper and go to bed."

His face flushed; he pushed his chair back from the table. It scraped over the dirt on the floor. He started putting on his boots.

"What are you doing? It's raining again."

"I'm going out so I can have some peace and quiet."

"It's cold tonight. And you always say it's not safe."

"Don't bother your head about it. You need your beauty sleep. Maybe it'll put you in a good humor. Good night." He didn't slam the door, Margaret suspected, only because it was swollen from all the moisture.

19

Dutch stomped along Main Street, not hearing the steam engines and rigs that ran all night. He paused by a dance hall, where somebody played "Down by the Old Mill Stream," one of his favorites. The pianist didn't have Eve's strong touch or her exuberance, which made each note come alive. Stung by Margaret's accusations, he didn't go in but, head down, trudged toward the railroad station. Margaret sounded like his ma, whose temper he could never trust. Once when he was a child, he'd been sweeping, and Ma had walked up to him, shrieked "Can't you do anything right?" and hit him on the ear for no reason. He'd had to take it then, but he didn't have to now. Margaret's gentleness was one quality he'd first loved in her. Where had it gone?

Shivering, Dutch found himself outside the Johnsons' feed store and livery stable. He entered, edging past bags of corn and oats stacked to the ceiling. Jimmy sat bent over a desk in the back. His kerosene lamp cast a shallow circle of light into the darkness. He looked up, startled. "What can I do for you, Dutch?"

"Nothing." Dutch stared at the concrete floor, his sodden clothes adding to the ooze of oil, water, and mud. "I wanted to get out of the rain. If that's all right with you."

"I'm doing the payroll. Sit a spell." Jimmy pointed to a stool by the pot-bellied stove.

"Something stinks."

"Besides you, you mean?" Jimmy guffawed. "It's the cow chips. All we've got. No wood." He returned to his figures, sighing when the numbers wouldn't cooperate. "Help yourself to coffee."

Rubbing his hands before the stove, Dutch felt life returning, though his shirt still dripped. He poured coffee into a tin cup on top of the stove. Old-timers like Jimmy's dad had complained of the drought, the dust piled up in the street, the yellow haze coating skin and clothes. Now they had what they wanted, a rain, but they'd already started to grouse. He did too; the mud and oil mucked up the whole town. No wonder Margaret was testy. Scraping out sludge couldn't be pleasant. He tried to figure how to keep the mud out of their house, but he grew drowsy in the stillness broken only by the horses nearby chewing hay and Jimmy's pen scratching in the ledger. Rats skittered by on light feet like the whispers of old gossip. It was peaceful here with the scent of alfalfa. Even the animal smells reminded him of the barn at home.

Jimmy sat next to him. "I met your wife and baby today. Nice family."

Dutch brightened. Then he remembered their quarrel. "It's hard though, sure enough."

"What isn't?" Jimmy stretched. "Let's go to the Red Onion. I'm through here."

"I should go home. We had an argument, Margaret and I. I don't feel so good."

"Better patch it up."

"Maybe." Never go to bed on a quarrel, Margaret's mother had told him. Margaret would be cleaning up the kitchen now or maybe brushing out her hair, something he often helped her with, but he wasn't in the mood now.

Dutch didn't hear the door open, but Jimmy called, "Pa, is that you?" and added to Dutch, "Sometimes he walks home with me, just to get out, but with this rain I didn't expect him tonight."

"It's not your pa," a muffled voice said.

They turned to face a man with a handkerchief tied around the bottom half of his face. Above the handkerchief Dutch saw narrowed eyes under thick brows.

"Open the safe." His voice was controlled.

"I don't know the combination. Only my dad has it," Jimmy said.

"Open it, son. This is a forty-five. I don't want to have to kill you."

Another man with a handkerchief covering his mouth and nose said, "Better do what he says."

Dutch sat in the shadows without moving, debating whether he could tackle the man with the gun. But the other man also had a pistol, which he pointed at Dutch's chest. "What about you, boy? You open it."

"I don't work here. I just dropped by."

"They all say that." The first man cocked his gun aimed at Jimmy's head. "I'll count to five."

"Jimmy, open it." Dutch's hands trembled as he held the cup, the coffee sloshing onto his hands.

Jimmy stood and turned his bulk toward the safe. Bending, he dived for the man's legs. The gun exploded in the closed room. The horses stamped and neighed. Dutch threw his coffee at the second man's face and butted him in the stomach. The man gasped.

Dutch heard an explosion and then felt pain in his shoulder so intense he couldn't move. From inside the hurt, the last thing he remembered was his screaming that grew and grew until it filled up the room with his suffering.

20

Margaret stared out the kitchen window, though she couldn't see anything. The rain hammered down. She covered Dutch's food and nibbled at her own, which tasted of ashes. She hated this house that would never get clean. She wished she'd never come. What a pointless quarrel. The difficulty of life here affected everything.

Tiptoeing into the front room, she knelt by the cradle and covered Beth with a blanket. Beth's regular breathing and her baby powder smell comforted Margaret. She could hardly remember what her life had been like before Beth or Dutch. A new world had been revealed to her the minute she had met Dutch at the train station when she was fifteen.

She lay awake, loathing the measured chugging of the nearby rigs, which seemed to grow louder as the minutes dragged by. She dozed off but jerked awake thinking that Dutch was home or that the muddy ooze had invaded the bedroom. She picked up Beth, who made only a small sigh of protest, and laid her in the big bed. Beth stirred once, and then her regular breathing resumed. Margaret smoothed the quilt over the baby and, at last, fell asleep.

Before dawn she woke, contented as always in the mornings, but then it all came back: her shrillness, their quarrel, Dutch's leaving in anger. Since they'd married, she felt as if a long gossamer cord, invisible but strong as a chain, always stretched between her and Dutch. Sometimes the cord tightened and sometimes slackened. Looseness could be desirable; sometimes she wanted freedom, sometimes not. Dutch felt the same way. Before she came to Texas, she'd felt a yank and then a slackening of that cord. Sometime during the past night she'd sensed a similar tug followed by looseness. Wanting the reassurance of Dutch's arm around her now so she could fall back asleep, she stretched out her hand. Her fingers touched only coldness. She pushed her hair away from her face and raised her head. Beth slept beside her, but the other side of the bed was empty. Dutch must have slept on the couch. Fully awake, Margaret jumped up, the floor cold and damp, and ran through puddles to the living room: another leak in the roof.

There was no sign of Dutch, and in the kitchen his plate sat untouched on the kitchen table. Margaret pulled a quilt around her shoulders and perched on the couch, her hands clasped around her knees. The minutes dragged. In her mind she pulled on the cord connecting her to Dutch. There was no response. She had to do something.

When she heard Mrs. McNeill stir next door, Margaret wrapped Beth in a quilt. Beth whimpered but slept on as Margaret tapped on the door.

"Margaret, come in." That was Mrs. McNeill, not bothered by Margaret's arrival before dawn.

"Can you watch Beth? She should sleep another hour."

"What's wrong?" Mrs. McNeill lifted Beth from Margaret's shoulder to her own with such practiced gentleness that Beth didn't stir.

"Dutch didn't come home. I have to look for him."

"Let me wake Mr. McNeill."

"I don't have time." Margaret bit her lip to keep from crying. "If I'm not back, will you ask Patsy to tell Mr. Morris I won't be in to teach, that it's an emergency?"

"Of course. At least let me give you a light." Mrs. McNeill took a pine branch with the end cut into slithers and lit it from her wood stove.

"We had torches like that in Louisiana," Margaret said.

"My husband had me bring some. There's nothing like this here."

It was drizzling again. Margaret picked up her skirt and, with the light, hurried west. She struggled through the mud past tents with snores penetrating the canvas, past men fumbling their way to work in the gray light. They stared—a woman alone so early— murmuring "Morning, ma'am."

Eve was taking a pan of biscuits out of the oven. "Margaret, what's wrong? You look sick. Where's Beth?"

"With Mrs. McNeill." She paused, feeling her face redden. "Dutch and I had an argument. It was my fault. He didn't come home. He's never done that before. I'm afraid something's happened. I was hoping you'd seen him."

"Why would I?" Eve sounded sharp. "No, I haven't."

"Would you help me look?"

"I can't. I've got to cook breakfast for the men."

"I forgot." Margaret pushed back her hair.

"Check downtown. Let me know."

On Main Street eight-horse wagons struggled with heavy loads through the mire. Margaret stopped first at the twenty-four hour Corner Drug. Mr. Kelly looked up from mixing two white powders. "I haven't seen him. Check the feed store. Robert Johnson was in a minute ago on his way to the café. He said Jimmy was working on the books last night and didn't come home. Maybe it got late and was raining so hard Dutch stayed with Jimmy."

"Dutch would never stay away unless something was wrong." Margaret kept walking, relieved she didn't have to cross the street. The mudholes looked deeper than the day before.

The door of the feed store was ajar; its hinges squeaked in the wind. Last night's rain had blown inside the store. "Jimmy? Dutch?" No answer. The store was dark except for a few orange embers that glowed and darkened in the stove. She held the torch inside. No one in the front.

Calling again into the silence, Margaret moved past the sacks of feed and bales of hay. She waded through puddles, smelling something acrid above the damp feed. She heard scuttling, and a rat darted past. She jumped. Her torch showered sparks.

In the dim light, the door of the safe hung open. In front of the stove, two stools had been knocked over. Without thinking, she righted them. Something dark spotted the floor. Jimmy lay face down. Near him lay Dutch. Please, God, let him be alive. She knelt by Dutch. His left sleeve was covered with blotches, sticky when she touched them.

Jimmy moaned. "Margaret, help. Where's Dutch?"

"Here, but he won't move." Margaret touched Dutch's arm and then his face. "Wake up."

Jimmy called, "How is he?"

"I can't tell." She put her ear to his chest. "He's breathing, but there's a lot of blood."

"They must've hit me with the stock of the gun. I guess they shot

Dutch."

"Who? What happened?"

"Hijackers. Two of them."

Margaret lifted her torch and glanced around. Maybe they were still in the livery stable hiding, watching her from the darkness. She should check, but she was afraid, and Dutch needed her.

She pushed his hair, matted with mud, back from his blanched face. Without his glasses, he looked vulnerable as a child. He groaned. She whispered, "I'm sorry. Please, let him be all right."

"Margaret, go for the doctor," Jimmy said.

She picked up her skirt and, ignoring the hoots of drivers and pedestrians, sprinted through the mud, which sucked on her boots like hands trying to trap her.

At the drug store Mr. Kelly was waiting on a roughneck, but Margaret burst in. "Where's the doctor? Dutch was shot at the feed store."

"I'll send him, Margaret, the minute he comes in."

The way back seemed interminable, the street crowded, the men surly as she pushed through them.

Jimmy sat leaning against a chair. "I can't get up. My head feels like it's cracking open when I move." He touched a bump above his ear.

Margaret sat with Dutch's head cradled in her lap, smoothing back his hair. She was the reason he was here.

The door creaked. What if the hijackers had returned? Uneven steps approached. "Dr. Miller? Here in the back," Margaret called. She hadn't spoken to him since she'd been kidnapped.

"Let's see your husband." Dr. Miller's low voice sounded calm. His red hair shone in the light of her torch as his long fingers probed Dutch's shoulder. "I have to remove the bullet." He opened his bag.

Nauseated, Margaret sat on a stool with her head between her legs, willing herself not to faint as she'd done before whenever she'd seen blood.

"Are you all right?" The doctor looked at her with concern.

She nodded. "Just tend to Dutch."

"He was shot in the shoulder. I'm not sure how bad. He's lost a lot of blood. They're fortunate you arrived when you did."

Margaret breathed a prayer of thanks. If she hadn't argued with Dutch, he would've been safe at home. She'd send a note to Mr. Morris saying she couldn't teach. She wouldn't budge from the house until Dutch's shoulder healed.

21

For a few days after he was shot, Dutch slept, lulled by morphine. Margaret drew the rocking chair close to the bed, wanting to protect Dutch, to be near and, when he woke, to make amends. She bathed his forehead with a rag. Seeing Dutch defenseless for the first time, Margaret felt unbalanced. Her universe had shifted; Dutch had always been her protector, he and Aut, and then Aut had signed up for the Army, and now she was left without support from either. Sometimes Dutch thrashed around moaning when his shoulder pained him, crying out "Margaret," and then she'd touch his cheek to quiet him. "I'm here, Dutch. Rest." Other times he mumbled something incoherent like "Evie," which made no sense until she remembered that when he was twelve Dutch had a dog named Evie that had been shot by a neighbor. Sometimes he cried out "Ma," and then she was terrified, remembering that before her grandfather died, he kept calling for his own mother.

While Beth played with her doll, Margaret told stories to keep herself awake, although she doubted that Dutch heard her. "I remember, Dutch, when I first saw you. I thought you were a tramp, barefoot and wearing those ragged pants and no shirt, but Aut envied you. He sweated so much in that suit. You were free. Remember? Mama had married Mr. Graham, and we were moving to Oil City."

The pine trees had stood like sentinels on either side of the train, which jerked with the rhythm of the waltz step Ida had taught her. Mr. Graham brought them roses for the wedding in Shreveport, and Aut wove Margaret's into a garland for her hair. The roses drooped in the heat but still smelled as sweet as Mama's perfume. The whole family drooped except Mama, who looked radiant, and she had to have been forty.

Whether Margaret would survive fifteen years to reach forty was doubtful, she felt so exhausted. She yawned and then sighed. "We came to a break in the trees, and there you were at a crossing.

You looked so funny, Dutch, covered with dust and watermelon juice. Your wagon was piled full of watermelons and peaches." She'd wanted a peach so desperately that she could almost taste its sweetness and feel the stickiness of the juice as it would drip down from her chin and onto her new dress. She wouldn't have cared. "I hung out the window to watch you as long as I could." She'd leaned out until the wind blew away her garland of roses, and she cried all afternoon till Mama said to take hers. "I was a spoiled brat." She yawned again and stretched. Fifteen years ago.

"And remember that first day in class in Oil City, Dutch, when Mr. Adams spanked us because I talked to you in arithmetic? We had just figured out you were that boy by the railroad tracks." Dutch stirred. She touched his hand, and he was quiet. "Remember how Mr. Adams bent back my palm? It hurt. That's why I never paddle my students. I was so embarrassed. I'd never been paddled before. But you knew how to cup your hand so the stick wouldn't hurt." She leaned against the back of the rocker. While Beth napped on a pallet by the bed, she'd rest her eyes a minute.

"Mama?" Margaret jerked upright, disoriented. Lands, it must be evening; the shadows stretched toward her from the window, and the light had softened around the derricks. Beth pulled herself up, holding onto her mother's knees, and Margaret set her in her lap and wrapped her arms around her. Beth's hair was straight except for one ringlet in back, already darkening; it would be brown like Dutch's. Beth smelled clean and felt warm as a chicken. Margaret rocked, leaning her head against Beth's.

Dutch's eyelids fluttered. Then his eyes opened. Margaret reached to take his hand. Beth pointed. "Pa-Pa."

Every day Dr. Miller came by to change Dutch's bandage. Margaret wished she didn't need to see him, still remembering the river and the kidnapping, but Dutch liked him. The doctor looked as emaciated as the day he'd helped her off the train, as thin as a pencil, so she always gave him coffee and cake or pie Mrs. Johnson concocted even on the wheatless or sugarless days. Maybe Mrs. Johnson hadn't taken the food pledge. She was a riddle. Margaret had never known anyone so gossipy but at the same time so generous when folks were in trouble.

After two weeks, the doctor said to Margaret, "Dutch is mending. You're the one who looks exhausted." He smiled. "If you're not careful, you'll be my patient, and then what would Dutch and Beth do?"

"I am tired. But I'm so thankful Dutch is alive."

It was true. She hadn't been able to sleep because every night when she crawled into bed, careful not to jostle Dutch, she dreamed of tiptoeing into that dark feed store, smelling the hay and blood, and in the light of the pine torch finding Dutch's crumpled body. Then she jerked awake and lay rigid, afraid she'd disturb him.

She followed Dr. Miller to the door. "I need to pay you."

"Later, when Dutch is better."

Against her better judgment—hadn't she decided to distance herself from this man?—she confided, "I'm not sure what to do. We have money saved from my teaching and Dutch's salary, but it won't last forever."

"Go back to school. They need you."

"I told Mr. Morris I wouldn't be back till Dutch was better."

"He's better now," the doctor said.

"He'll be all right?"

"He may not be able to work in the oilfield. Other than that, he'll be fine."

She stared. Not work in the oilfield? What else could he do? She pulled herself together. "Whatever he does, he might not want me to go back to work."

She wished she hadn't dumped her troubles on Dr. Miller. Mama hadn't raised her to whine. Mama and Mr. Graham had managed, and it couldn't have been easy. But Dr. Miller was accustomed to hearing people's troubles. She shook hands firmly, noticing that his hands remained clean. Even the palms of her chapped hands were threaded with engrained dirt. The minute the doctor left she'd scrub them with the lye soap she'd made before Dutch was shot. Dutch shouldn't be around any more grime than necessary. When he woke, he could see a part of her the way she used to be.

She glanced into the kitchen at the washing, piled almost to the ceiling. Beth moved around in her cradle, playing with the rag doll Mrs. Johnson had made her. Beth and the doll needed a thorough washing. Life seemed too hard. What she wanted was to lie down and not get up for a week.

After the doctor left, she had neither the energy nor the will to tackle the bath or the washing. She watched Dutch sleep, wiping his forehead with a rag she moistened with water whenever he stirred.

His eyes opened, green this time. She never understood what determined when and why they changed from green to blue to gray. "How do you feel?"

"Better. Sore."

"The doctor just left."

"I'd rather see you." He took her hand and stroked it.

She pulled back, self-conscious. "I meant to take a bath and scrub myself. Especially these hands."

"I love your hands. You work hard."

"I want to do everything I can for you, Dutch. I've been thinking a lot while you've been laid up, and the truth is, I've fallen in love with you all over again."

She shrugged, embarrassed. "Sentimental, I know, but it's true." She squeezed his hand. "Anyway, I'm the reason you got shot. Because I quarreled and made you leave."

"Nonsense. We were both exhausted. That's why we argued. Life's hard here. Paul's gone back to Louisiana to see his family. Maybe we should think about going back too."

"Maybe." That was what she'd been thinking, but now that he said it she wasn't sure. "This place does grow on you. And what about buying a rig with Paul? That's what we've been saving for."

"It's not cheap, Margaret. A derrick costs fifteen thousand dollars. Then about twenty thousand to drill. I'm not sure I can work on wells anymore. I don't know what else I can do."

"You can supervise, can't you? Don't think about it while you're sick. The Lord will provide. You know that."

He sighed. "Sometimes I forget."

"Rest. I'll get you some soup. Mrs. Johnson brought it today." She smoothed her apron and walked to the kitchen, clenching her teeth. It was hard to remain cheerful when she felt as energetic as a dishrag and was worried sick about money.

The following day the doctor again dropped by to check on Dutch.

"Why don't you take Beth for a walk while there's a break in the rain?" he suggested.

"Do you mind, Dutch? I would like to."

"The doc can entertain me."

Outside, Margaret felt her body lighten, her exhaustion peel away like a covering of waxed paper as she picked her way through the mud. With each step she distanced herself from injury, pain, and grime. The world looked brighter after the rain, and the air smelled clean, the oil washed out, life full of possibilities. After three blocks she came to Red River, thick as syrup after the rains. Beth on her hip, she stood on a bluff above the river, which had risen, muddy water escaping over its banks, eroding the dunes and carving a new channel. Brown waves crested and, as they broke, sprayed foam like breakers in pictures she'd seen of the ocean. Tree trunks and fence posts jostled each other in the current. A raccoon clung to a log, and Beth reached toward it. Margaret laughed, exhilarated. A sense of familiarity washed over her; as a child she had felt free like this when she'd been allowed outside after an illness, as if she'd been released from an underground dungeon. Sunshine broke through intermittent clouds, dotting the river with moving patterns of light and shade. Dutch would be well soon.

22

"**D**utch, you're on the mend." Dr. Miller sat in the rocking chair drinking coffee while Margaret was out walking.

"I do feel better. Not like I could climb a derrick, but better."

"You may not regain all your strength in that arm."

"I've thought about that." Dutch hadn't thought of much else, but he wouldn't tell the doc, who had a sit-down job.

"It's too soon to know, of course. We'll cross that bridge when—you know." Dr. Miller took a bite of Mrs. Johnson's cake and a sip of the coffee. "Louisiana coffee. Strong." He settled back in the rocker. The doc enjoyed visiting. "Have I ever told you how I got through medical school?"

"No, you haven't."

"I waited tables in a boarding house. Rich kids. Or I thought they were. But the chocolate cake and the lemon pie made up for all the effort."

"Why did you work?"

"I had to. We were dirt poor. I washed my clothes in a bucket in my room."

That made sense. Maybe that's why Dutch liked the doc. He knew what hard work was.

The doc set down his saucer. He looked serious. "I want to talk to you about Margaret. She's worn out, and she's worried sick about money. I told her not to concern herself with my bill." When Dutch started to interrupt, he raised a hand. "We'll tend to it later."

Something didn't sit right with Dutch. He didn't like another man telling him how to take care of his wife, and he didn't like being in debt. He would make sure the doc got paid first thing.

Dr. Miller continued. "But about Margaret: the school could use her back. You might mention it to her."

"My wife work now that I can't?" Dutch felt his face redden, and he struggled to sit up. He wanted to stare at this man eye to eye, tell him to mind his own business. But the world spun as it did after too many beers. He lay back, glaring at the doctor. "She took the teaching job before only because I wasn't here. Now that I am, I will provide for my family."

The doctor remained calm, his voice patient. "Something to think about. She liked it."

Dutch told himself to maintain control. He was grateful to the doc, after all, but he had to explain. The doc didn't have a wife. He couldn't understand any more than Beth how Dutch had to take care of his family. "I appreciate all you've done for us, but my wife is my responsibility. I won't have folks saying I can't support her."

He felt chilled. He stretched his arm for the quilt but couldn't reach it. The doctor pulled it up around his shoulders and tucked it in. Dutch lay quiet, resentful of the doctor's intrusion, frustrated by his own weakness. He wondered what was keeping Margaret.

Dutch stared out the window, Dr. Miller at the floor, until Margaret returned from her walk.

"It's beautiful out, so clean." She and Beth both were smiling, their faces flushed.

Dutch resented her health, her enthusiasm. She set Beth down, straightened as easily as he used to, and asked, "More coffee?" If she noticed that Dutch was frowning or that Dr. Miller was intent on the floor, she didn't say anything.

"I've got to go." The doctor managed a tight smile. He walked out without looking back.

"What was that about?" Margaret said.

"He got lathered up about how I can't take care of you. Some half-baked idea about your job at the school." Dutch watched Margaret with apprehension. She'd been acting strange since they'd been in Nesterville. He'd thought she was tired, but maybe she wasn't happy. Probably Eve's influence. Eve was too independent for her own good. He liked that his wife had quit teaching when he got hurt and didn't want her to go back. "You wouldn't want to teach school again, would you?"

"I'd love to." Margaret's voice and face brightened, her exhaustion erased for a moment. Then she composed herself. "That is, if you don't mind, now that you're better." Her voice trailed away. Disappointment crept into her face, listlessness into her voice.

Dutch felt let down, as if for the first time he hadn't understood what she wanted. It was his responsibility to take care of his family. What kind of man was he otherwise? "I didn't think you'd want to, Margaret. I like having you home. It reassures me, knowing you and Beth are safe."

"I understand. It's how Mr. Graham feels about Mama." Her eyes thoughtful, Margaret sat in the rocker, Beth on her lap. "But it's not what I want. Anyway, I help Eve at the boarding house."

"That's not a real job. Teaching is."

Dutch was as tired as if he'd put in a twelve-hour shift on a drilling rig. This was not the time for discussions. He watched Margaret rock Beth. On her walk Margaret's hair had loosened and hung like a golden cape around Beth, who started playing with a lock of it. Dutch reminded himself of what he kept forgetting: he was a lucky man.

The next day, Dutch got up for breakfast. "I don't feel so bad."

Margaret turned from the stove, pleased, as he moved his injured arm tentatively.

"But I don't feel so good either. I don't think I could waller a bear." He frowned and ran his hand over the wooden table. It felt sticky. "This could use a good scrubbing."

"I haven't had the time." He recognized a note of injured virtue in her voice.

"I'm not saying you should have, Margaret, just that it needs doing. You haven't had a free minute, taking care of Beth and me. I could do it now that I'm better. I'm tired of not doing anything."

"If you feel like it." Sounding curt, she brought their eggs to the table and squashed one for Beth. Beth ate with relish, smearing egg on her face, beaming at them.

Margaret sighed. "Let me wipe your face, Bethie." Laughing with a heartiness that reminded Dutch of Margaret's mother, Beth dodged the napkin in Margaret's hand and smeared egg in her hair. "Beth, no."

"No no no no." Beth grinned.

Dutch was entranced. Surely not all babies were so captivating as Beth. "I've missed a lot, working. I wouldn't take anything for seeing her grow."

"If you saw this all the time, it wouldn't be so wonderful. What a mess." Beth threw her remaining egg on the floor. "Beth, no."

"No no no no."

Margaret lifted Beth out of her highchair and wiped her hands and face. Beth crawled to the back door and pulled herself up, still smiling. She pointed outside. "Wah wah."

He had missed a lot, for sure. Margaret always knew what Beth meant, but he often didn't. "What does she want?"

"To play in the rain, I guess. She doesn't realize it's cold." She handed Beth a tin plate and a spoon and carried the dishes to the sink. "More coffee?"

"It's good. Sit down, Margaret, and talk to me." He hated to admit it, but he was lonely. Even a few weeks without work changed a man.

"I don't have time. I need to iron."

"You're so good to me. You work too hard," he said.

"There's not much choice. Everybody works hard here."

"Everybody besides me." He didn't know what to do. He didn't know how to iron, and he wasn't strong enough to plant a winter garden. "I'm as worthless as tits on a boar."

"You were shot, for heaven's sake. Give yourself a chance." Margaret sounded short again. That wasn't like her. She sat down. "I've thought about the teaching position. It would get me out. I could make more money."

"I didn't think married women could teach."

"Normally they can't, but with the boom they're desperate for teachers. Mr. Morris told me to come back if I could."

Dutch felt his face take on a still look. He was hurt, he couldn't deny it. He didn't want Margaret to know how much he depended on her. "You know I don't want you to work."

"Just for a while, till you're feeling better and can go back," she said.

"Do you really want to?"

"I want to do something worthwhile."

"But you do. You take care of Beth and me and the house." Dutch composed his face and controlled his voice. "It's no picnic living here, first with the dust and now the rain." He stared out at the gray, leaden morning. "And you help Eve too. You already have two jobs. Why would you want another?"

She folded her hands on the table. "Mama wanted me to graduate from high school, especially because none of the others did. You know what trouble it was, how I hated that boarding school. My education was so costly in time and money that I don't want to waste it. Does that make sense?"

He understood that. Margaret's family had sacrificed so she could finish school, and she didn't want to let them down. Ambition wasn't to be sneezed at. Look at the doc, waiting tables in medical school. Dutch himself was ambitious. He yearned for a drilling rig for himself and Paul so much he could taste it. True, he wasn't pleased with Margaret's decision. He'd miss her, but teaching was important to her, and they could use the money. He took in a deep breath and let it out. "If you want it so bad, then do it." Sighing, he watched the mud ooze under the back door, wondering why they had complained so much about the drought. Sometimes people didn't realize how good they had it until everything changed.

23

A week later, Dutch left Beth with Mrs. McNeill and headed downtown in the late morning. He kicked at the leaves and sycamore balls that littered the street. If Margaret were with him instead of teaching, she'd squash the sycamore balls flat or pull the seeds off and send them floating. But whether the seeds would follow their normal routine in this sodden atmosphere was anybody's guess. They used to have battles with sweet gum balls, "spiky balls," Margaret called them.

As he passed Eve's, he paused. Months had gone by, and he still needed to discuss the summer with her. Surely she wouldn't harbor any grudge after all this time.

At the door he knocked. When Eve didn't respond, he went in. The dining room tables were cleared. Eve stood at the kitchen sink, her back to him, washing breakfast dishes. With her sleeves rolled up, she looked strong.

She turned and with a nervous smile nodded toward the stove. He helped himself to some tepid coffee, and, as he set it down, the past hit him with a rush: Eve's sorry coffee, the aroma of chicken frying, the soapy scent of this room where he'd first kissed her. To steady himself, he took a rag and started drying the breakfast dishes. Eve didn't say anything about Beth's not being with him. He liked that about Eve; she never pushed, unlike his mother, who with every breath brought out a question, like a watermelon vine with lengthening tendrils that smothered everything in sight. He couldn't figure out how to apologize or explain about last summer, how he'd felt so lonesome, how her kindness had helped him through a time as rough as a cob.

Dutch would count to the tenth plate he dried, and then he'd say something. Gazing out Eve's window, he braced himself. Only a few sycamore balls remained, swinging in the north wind, which had picked up the minute the rain stopped. Another norther coming. Beside the steps, he noticed a bowl of milk, scarce as it was, that Eve had left for a scrawny kitten, so young it could hardly walk.

Look at its pink tongue lapping the milk. Wasn't that just like Eve, to lose her heart over some helpless creature? Next thing, that kitten would be fattened up and arrogant with a bed behind the stove.

As he dried the ninth plate, Dutch cleared his throat, and Eve turned toward him. "There's something you wish to say?"

Without thinking, he blurted out, "You're a good woman, Eve."

She eyed him skeptically as she handed him a cup to dry. "Why do you say that?"

He fumbled. "I don't know. Margaret said you send every cent you can to an orphanage. You're a good friend to Margaret."

Her throaty laugh bubbled out. "You're such an innocent, Frank—Dutch—Sanders."

"About this past summer. I'm sorry," he said.

"That's what they all say." She laughed with a bitterness he hadn't heard before. "Don't apologize. You were lonely. We don't have to talk about it. Margaret's here now. I haven't said anything to her, and I won't. Forget it."

He had to say something. "You're a good-looking woman."

"You've noticed that?" She chuckled again but narrowed her eyes as she tossed her hair back.

"Come on, Eve. Don't treat me like those drunks at the saloon." Dutch felt as if he were swimming in the murky water in Caddo Lake. He had no idea how deep the water was, only that he was in way over his head.

Eve kept washing cups, her face as red as her hands. "You knew what you were doing. Men. You're all alike. I need a man as much as I need more dirty dishes. I thought you were different, that's all."

"I am different. You don't have to have a conniption." Dutch dried three more glasses. Then he wiped his hands on the dishrag.

He wished he hadn't come, but he still felt drawn to Eve. Without thinking, contrary to what he'd planned, he pulled Eve to him and kissed her full on the mouth. She tasted of peppermint, but her lips were unyielding.

Eve shoved him away with surprising strength. His injured shoulder throbbed. "You're like all the rest. You're worse, because you deceived me, made me think you were single, and then I found out you were married to a wonderful woman. And you don't even know it." She covered her face with her hands and began sobbing with such force that her shoulders shook.

He'd gotten himself in a fix for sure. He was ashamed. He stood with his hands at his sides, making what he hoped were soothing clucks. When she kept blubbering, he placed his hands tentatively on her shoulders. She didn't resist, and he put his arms around her and patted her back like a mother comforting a large child. Eve was so tall that she had to bend to lay her head on his shoulder.

Her hair smelled of gardenias and dishwater. He murmured, "There, there" until she pushed herself back, her face puffy.

She looked so helpless that all he felt was guilt, and he suspected it was merely a taste of what he'd feel later on.

Dutch picked his hat up from the table and jammed it on. He marched to the door and, before he changed his mind, closed it softly behind him.

He stood on Eve's front porch, feeling jumbled—humiliated and angry with himself. He couldn't go home; he felt too dirty. Through the long afternoon he walked, dazed, through town and out to the riverbed, until sunset.

Margaret
October, 1918

24

Eve stopped by just after Dutch had left for work. "Come with me to church. I'm playing the piano."

Margaret looked up from the dishes. "Where's the regular pianist?"

"She's sick today."

The frame Methodist Church, built only two years before, stood out from the tents and shotgun houses. Margaret sat where she could see Eve, who played one of Margaret's favorite hymns her mother had taught her, "O God Our Help in Ages Past." She gave herself up to the peace of the moment. Younger, she'd felt God's presence in the woods, with the sunlight filtering through the pines, insects buzzing above her in the light, and warm pine needles cushioning the forest floor. A church building had seemed stuffy compared to the outdoors. But here the hymns connected her to her family hundreds of miles away. Seated around her, children napped or fidgeted, a man in a blue suit snored until his wife's elbow jostled him awake, and he stared around to check whether he'd been observed. The congregation ranged from businessmen with pale, indoor faces and women in white gloves and dark hats to farmers with sunburned faces and necks and women in calico dresses. She identified oilfield workers from the stains on their hands.

Brother Pound, a tall man with white leonine hair and a bulbous nose, preached on Jeremiah: "Blessed is the man that trusteth in the Lord, and whose hope the Lord is." Brother Pound made faith and trust sound simple, but for most folks, certainly herself, pettiness interfered with resolutions to trust in God. Nevertheless, she could learn. If God is Infinite Love, then He can be trusted. "Blessed" means "fortunate": she was fortunate indeed. Trust, depend, lean, rely, love: easy words, hard applications. Easy to say, hard to do. As she sang the last hymn, "Trust and Obey," another favorite, Margaret sensed a peace she hadn't felt since she'd come to

Nesterville. Perhaps, perhaps, they could have a good life here.

After the service Mrs. Johnson, small teeth gleaming, gushed at Margaret. "I can't tell you how refreshing it is to have you here—a young woman of upstanding family—and this darling baby. There certainly aren't many ladies here." She glanced toward Eve, who nodded. Mrs. Johnson seemed to have determined that Eve was in a middle position between Margaret, a married woman, and the women who worked in the dance halls and the cathouses, whom Mrs. Johnson pretended not to see in the stores. Eve was a single woman whose parents had lived in Nesterville before the boom, who ran a business, and who played the piano and worked in the nursery at church, but she also played in a saloon. So Mrs. Johnson's scheme of the universe was thrown off kilter; she treated Eve sometimes with genuine friendliness and at other times with marginal politeness. It was a shame people could be so closed-minded; they missed so much. And just look at Eve's kindnesses.

Margaret's tranquility dissipated. As they walked home, her annoyance burst out. "How do you ever put up with her, Eve?"

"Who?"

"Mrs. Johnson, who else?" Margaret skirted a mud puddle.

Eve smiled. "I ignore her pettiness and concentrate on her generosity. It's the only way to avoid being bitter."

"Easy to say." The text from the sermon returned.

"You should have come last week. Brother Pound preached on 'All things work together for good to them that love God.' I have to believe that. It's brought me a power of comfort these last two years. Sometimes I think Brother Pound is talking directly to me."

This was another side of Eve Margaret hadn't expected, her strong faith.

"Christianity isn't about being 'good' whatever that means. It's about trusting God's Word," Eve said.

Margaret agreed. Still, living out that belief was what was hard.

The next day at school Margaret leaned against a bare mulberry tree thinking about the sermon and Eve's response as the girls jumped rope at recess. "One, two, three, four." They chanted a new rhyme: "I had a little bird. Its name was Enza. I opened the window, and in-flew-enza."

"Where did you learn that?" Margaret asked Patsy McNeill. Patsy only shrugged.

Where did children get their information? The flu epidemic, according to the papers, was mainly in Europe and in the north.

After school Margaret went to Eve's to help serve dinner and pick up Beth.

"Have you heard about the stolen pipeline?" Mr. Smith said.

"How could anybody steal pipe?" Margaret said.

"They took it during the night."

Mr. Willis nodded. "Did you hear about the house that disappeared in Springtown? Two nights ago. Nobody knows anything about the house, except that it's missing."

Men. Worse than women about gossiping.

"Somebody got shot on Main Street. He made some comment on a crap game."

Crime seemed worse now than when Margaret had arrived. The more wells, the more overcrowding and crime. Or what she had labeled exuberance at first had actually been corruption.

Even Bucky joined in. "What about that Star drilling machine? It was stuck so bad on Main Street that it took eight days to move it four blocks."

"I saw that," Mr. Willis said. "The mud was waist high. They used a power of teams to pull it out. I counted thirty-two. The lead team was more than a block from the rig."

"It's all the rain. Three inches this month. Rigs are down because they can't get the equipment," Mr. Smith said.

Margaret set a bowl of mashed potatoes next to the burly pipeliner who rented the closet room that she still considered hers. The evening they moved, she'd run back inside on a pretext and gazed at the barren room with something like regret. Sentimental again, Ida would say. But her life had shifted like a kaleidoscope with Dutch's arrival. Since then, she'd had more work, less time or energy to sit, gaze out the window, and dream. Why would she want to dream now with her husband here? Life had begun again; the hiatus of being single—even somewhat single—had slipped away. And since Dutch's hijacking, she'd tried to forget all that nonsense with Dr. Miller.

The stout pipeliner said, "What do you think, Mrs. Sanders?"

She stopped, lost, the bowl of potatoes steaming under her nose.

He continued. "About the influenza? Some folks say it's caused by the Germans. That they've come up to the coast and set loose the germ." The pipeliner scratched his bald dome, grimy as his face. "Or maybe the fighting in the trenches causes it somehow."

The table quieted, listening. Then, as if to ward off their fear, they all provided information about this new killer that had appeared spontaneously, eclipsing discussions of the war and even of the oilfield.

"You heard about Mr. Harwell?" a swarthy roughneck said. Margaret pictured the red-faced man at the bank who always doted on Beth. "He keeled over going to work yesterday. Right on Main Street. Jimmy Johnson carried him to the doc. But it was too late. Harwell lay there and died. Two hours later." His low voice assumed the satisfied tone of one who has survived to convey bad news. "You haven't heard, Miz Sanders?"

"I've been so busy lately, with Dutch shot and school and the baby." Margaret gestured at Beth, sitting in a high chair by Mr. Smith, whose wife and five children were still in Louisiana. How one woman could manage five children was beyond Margaret. They were supposed to join him next week if he could find them a place to live.

Mr. Smith sneezed. Conversation stopped, and they all stared. He apologized, wiping his nose with the back of his hand. As talk resumed, Mr. Smith's neighbors leaned away from him, and Margaret pulled Beth out of the high chair. Beth stiffened and hollered in protest. "Hush, Bethie. I don't want you sick."

At home, Margaret said to Dutch, "At Eve's they were talking about people dying here from that flu in Europe. Maybe there's something in the paper."

She shuffled pages of the newspaper and read silently. The flu—the invisible menace, the paper called it—had spread around the world in three months, across America in seven days, killing nearly 200,000 in Boston already in October. No one knew how it started, but it caused death within a few days or even hours. It was called the Spanish influenza because eight million people had died from it in Spain in May. "Listen to this. Four women were playing

cards one evening, and the next morning three of them were dead."
Margaret shuddered.

"What does it say to do?"

"Some people wear masks. Soda fountains have to put in sterilizers or sell only bottled drinks. There's a city ordinance against spitting on the street. The city may close the picture shows and the schools. Stay away from crowds."

"Fat chance around here."

"It might be worse with humidity." She gazed out at the rain, wishing they could isolate themselves and not emerge until this menace was no longer a threat.

"We're perfectly safe for sure," Dutch said.

They heard a knock, and crazy Jerry handed Margaret a note.

"Eve's got a sore throat." Margaret frowned.

"No wonder. She's always around crowds at the boarding house and the saloon," Dutch said.

"She wants us to ask Dr. Miller for some medicine for her when he's here checking on your shoulder." Margaret turned to Jerry. "Dr. Miller hasn't been here lately. Tell her I'll bring her something from the drug store."

Jerry nodded and grinned. As he left, he called out, "You're fired."

Dutch raised his eyebrows. "What was that all about?"

"Just something he says."

Dutch shook his head. "Beth can stay with me. She shouldn't be out."

As Margaret hurried to the drug store, the customary rows of wagons and occasional cars were mired down on Main Street. She'd heard that a horse had drowned in that loblolly by the barber shop. Nothing looked different. Apparently, the flu scare wasn't keeping people away from downtown.

Margaret lined up at the drug store, more crowded than normal. The man in front of her sneezed. She stepped back.

The door burst open, and behind her the men pushed so hard that she almost fell. "Sorry, ma'am." A roughneck stepped aside and removed his hat exposing skin white as a bandage.

He made way for a woman so scrawny that her skin looked pasted over her bones. In her arms she carried a child slightly older than Beth. The baby's face was bluish, and a bloody froth dribbled from her nose and mouth. The woman was sobbing. "Help me!"

Mr. Kelly ran from behind the counter and tried to take the child, but the woman clutched her more tightly. With a gentle hand he wiped the baby's mouth and nose.

Someone in the line called, "Take that kid out of here." He pointed to the doctor's office behind the drug store. Margaret glared.

"The doctor's not in," the woman gasped, sobbing, bent over the baby in her arms. The men stepped back so that she and the pharmacist were alone with the child.

Dr. Miller, thinner than usual, stomped into the store and muttered to Mr. Kelly, "All five of the Abbotts are down with the flu." The doctor took the child, laid her on the counter, and listened for her pulse, bending over her as if she were on an altar, a sacrifice to some child-devouring deity. Murmuring, the crowd moved close.

He took the woman's hand in both of his. "She's already passed on."

"What do you mean?" the woman said. "She was perfectly all right yesterday. I brought her to you. Do something."

"There's nothing I can do. I'm sorry."

The woman collapsed, slipping to the floor by the counter. The crowd parted to make room. The doctor knelt by her. "I'll send someone for your husband."

The woman looked up without expression, bloody froth smeared with mud on her face. "I don't know where he is. He didn't come home from Springtown last night."

When she heard the woman's desperation, Margaret took off her jacket. She noticed the doctor's widened eyes and warning shake of his head but ignored him. She turned toward the woman. "I'll help you."

She wrapped the baby's frail body in her jacket and led the woman outside. The men pushed backward, clearing a path. The woman leaned on Margaret and sobbed so hard she could hardly point out directions. They waded through a low spot; cold water squished around Margaret's boots. Tents without floors were jumbled together. There was no road. The woman's home, a one-room shack probably thrown together at the beginning of the boom from tar paper and scrap lumber, made Margaret's shotgun house look like a mansion. How could this squalor exist beside wells making thousands of dollars a day? Before the woman opened the tow-sack door, she wiped her eyes and nose. A boy, perhaps six years old, his emaciated face solemn, stepped outside. He wore no shoes. Margaret recognized the flaxen-haired boy who'd stood in line at the post office during the summer and who had sporadically attended school in September.

His thin face brightened. "Ma, that there's my teacher." His eyes fell on Margaret's bundle. "Where's Joanne?"

The woman knelt and pulled the boy to her. "She's gone, Jesse. She's in heaven." Her body wracked with coughs, she said to Margaret, "Thank you, ma'am, for coming home with me. We'll be all right."

25

Two days later Margaret woke up feverish, trying to stifle the deep, hoarse coughs that seemed about to tear her apart. How could she teach? She was already late. She struggled without success to sit up, her throat so sore that she couldn't swallow. Her head ached as if someone had lit a fire in her brain and ignited another fire each time she coughed. She clung to Dutch. "I don't want to leave you and Beth. I don't want to die."

Dutch, barely awake, mumbled, "Why would you die?"

Between coughs, she gasped, "I hurt so bad, Dutch." She heard a thump from the living room. "What's that?"

Dutch sat up, prompting new fires in her brain. She turned toward the living room, hearing a "Mama." A hand appeared under the bottom of the curtain that separated the bedroom and living room, and Beth crawled in, her face beaming, her hands smacking the floor. Margaret could only whisper because of the pain in her throat. "She crawled out of her cradle. Don't let her near me."

Dutch scooped Beth up before she reached the bed. "Mama's sick, Bethie."

Beth reached toward Margaret, her hands muddy from the floor. "No no no."

Tears leaked from Margaret's eyes as Dutch carried Beth to the kitchen. She prayed, staring out the window. Some mornings were clear before the rain began. She touched the liquid trickling from her nose. Her finger in the dim light looked dark and smelled of blood. Pain raged inside her head and her throat. She lay still, thinking abut Mr. Harwell, collapsed on his way to work, and the dead baby, its skin blue. Her tears mingled with the dark stream from her nose and dripped onto the pillow.

Dutch bathed her face with a wet rag. Each time he touched her an earthquake erupted in her head and throat, though she knew his hands were gentle. "I took Beth next door. I'm going for the doctor now." He stroked her hair that stuck to her damp forehead.

"Do you have to?" She didn't want those piercing eyes

inspecting her, those capable hands examining her. She hadn't seen Dr. Miller lately except at the drug store when the child died, and he had looked at her only when she volunteered to help.

"I'm freezing." Dutch kissed her forehead and pulled the quilt over her, but a moment later she was perspiring.

"It's probably just a cold." He sounded annoyed but continued, as if he couldn't stop himself. "I don't know why you had to help that woman at the drug store or go to Eve's either. Eve's sick too. You've got to be more careful."

"Now you tell me." Tears oozed out of Margaret's eyes, and she wanted to sob, but it hurt too much to move.

Dutch leaned over the bed and touched her forehead. "I'm worried is all."

Through the wall Margaret heard Mrs. McNeill feeding her children and Beth, who sounded whiny. What if Beth were sick too?

She must have slept. When she opened her eyes, Mrs. McNeill sat beside her holding a bowl. "Can you sit up? I brought you some oatmeal."

"I don't want anything." She closed her eyes to keep out the light.

Dr. Miller stood by the bed, his eyes sliding away as she looked at him in mute appeal, willing him to proclaim that she would survive. When his eyes did meet hers, he made what looked like a conscious effort to speak impersonally. "Let's see what we have here, Mrs. Sanders."

We? "We" don't have anything.

Dutch hovered. "Will she be all right, Doc?"

"We'll have to pray, Dutch." The doctor addressed Margaret, his voice formal. "Drink water, Mrs. Sanders. Aspirin for the pain, but not over two a day because of the bleeding. If it gets worse, don't take more aspirin." He stood up. "Boil her dishes, Dutch, and her sheets. Keep the windows and the doors open. I'll see you tomorrow."

Margaret croaked, "What about Beth?" Pink sputum flecked her handkerchief.

Dr. Miller's gaze remained on Dutch. "Keep Beth out of this room, of course. It seems to attack adults more than children."

Glancing out the window, he indicated Margaret with his hand. "She'll probably be all right." Margaret flinched, hearing herself referred to as "she," as if her existence, flimsy as a curtain, no longer mattered. Dr. Miller looked dog-tired. Through her pain she felt the desire to protect him that had almost been her downfall, but he had referred to her as if they were mere acquaintances. She turned toward the window.

Dutch pulled the rocking chair next to Margaret. The rockers squeaked on the bare floor. "I'll try to take as good care of you as you took of me when I got shot." He took her hand. "You're burning up."

She felt sweaty but freezing. Dutch tucked a quilt around her shoulders, and she was on fire again.

"Dutch, I forgot about school."

"Mrs. McNeill's children will say you're sick. Don't worry. You've got to get well." His voice broke.

While the rain drummed on the roof, Margaret drifted in and out of sleep interrupted by spells of coughing. Her handkerchiefs were flecked with red. Her head and throat flamed scarlet. Her world had narrowed to this room in the shadow of the derricks. When she woke, Dutch bathed her face or raised a cup to her lips. One time he sat next to her, his tears cutting light-colored paths down his gritty face and dropping unheeded in dark polka dots on his shirt. He removed his glasses and wiped his eyes on his sleeve. She yearned to reassure him but couldn't summon the energy.

From the next room, Beth cried. Margaret wanted to ask Dutch what was wrong, but by the time she struggled to the top of her pain, Dr. Miller sat next to her, his long body folded into the rocker, his head in his hands. When she next drifted awake, Dutch dozed in the rocker. Behind him in the shadows stood her mother and her brother and sisters, not as they looked before she moved to Texas but as they were when Mama married Mr. Graham, the day Margaret had first seen Dutch, driving that wagon of watermelons and eating a peach at a railroad crossing. In the shadows of the room, Aut had on that same suit he hated, Rachel wore her first long dress, and Ida a new sailor dress. Mama wore the same big-brimmed hat with roses she wore now. Margaret called, but Mama faded, flimsy as gauze. Margaret felt as empty as when she was lost in the dark woods the year she was six, the pines so thick she could hardly push her way through them, the carpet of pine needles so soft that she gave in to the temptation to sink into them and sleep, and the next morning she walked out, all by herself.

Dutch reached over and took her hand. Margaret realized she must be sobbing.

"What's wrong?"

"I dreamed about Mama. She looked like she did that day I saw you from the train. Remember?"

He leaned close to hear her. "How could I not?"

"I want to see Mama. Will I be all right?"

"Doc said if you made it through a week, he thought you'd be. It's been ten days."

"I've been asleep ten days?" She looked around expecting a transformation in the room.

"Sorta asleep. We gave you water and sometimes aspirin and a little soup. I think you've got it beat. The doc said the flu might go into pneumonia, but he doesn't think it has."

"What about Beth?"

"She stayed with the McNeills when she got bored with me. She's asked about you."

"What?" How could Beth ask anything?

"She does. She says 'Mama okay' and points toward this room. I tell her you'll be all right soon."

"I wish I could see her." Her whole body yearned to feel Beth's soft head against her shoulder.

Dutch's hand, with its characteristic smell of crude oil, felt as cool on her forehead as water from the lake. "Your skin isn't hot. You're not sweating."

Margaret enjoyed her convalescence. The landscape outside her window, with the derricks and even the rain, were objects of unceasing interest, a new world she observed with thankful new eyes. Rabbits crouched in the dead weeds. Skunks marched through the yard. Once a bobcat slunk past. And even in the long nights of rain and ice, a sparrow perched in the mesquite tree outside the window, feathers fluffed against the unremitting wind.

The sense that this was time out of time continued, however. She realized their savings must be about depleted, but with her world circumscribed to this one room, somehow she didn't really care. Dutch told her that not only Eve but Mr. and Mrs. Johnson had been down with the flu, but she couldn't call forth the will to worry about them. She found it difficult to imagine her normal routine, doubting that she'd ever have the strength to take it up again. And she thought about Dutch, picturing him dribbling a basketball in the eighth grade, all grace and fluid motion, the star of the school team the year before he'd had to drop out and go to work. Marriage had turned out to be much more complex than she'd imagined when she was young. She had thought a marriage would run itself. The sole requirement was that she and Dutch would start it, like winding up a clock, and it would proceed with smoothness and precision forever on its own, a perpetual motion machine of romance.

One morning after Margaret had been in bed a month, Dutch brought in a bowl covered with a saucer. "I made this for you. Your favorite breakfast." With a flourish he removed the saucer.

"Grits?" She picked up the spoon, but the smell sickened her. Still, Dutch had made it, so she raised the spoon to her lips. "Maybe you put in a little too much salt."

"Let me get you something else." Dutch looked hollow-eyed.

She stopped him. "You've done more than you need for me." She struggled up in bed, sighing. The pillows were lumpy. Dutch hadn't changed the sheets. Cobwebs hung on the windows.

"I'm doing the best I can, Margaret. You've been pretty sick." He sat in the rocker and watched as she spooned the grits into her mouth. Then his face brightened. "I do have news."

What had happened now? Who else was sick? "Is Eve worse? What about the Johnsons?"

"They're better. The news is about Beth." Dutch grinned. "You remember I told you Beth's been walking holding onto furniture? Yesterday, she let go of the table at Eve's and walked toward me. Two steps by herself."

Margaret's world reeled. It wasn't fair. She, the mother, should be the first to witness her child walking. Beth should've walked to her from Dutch or to Dutch from her, not anybody else, not even her best friend. She had missed a milestone in her daughter's life. Despite her resolutions to be less selfish, to be a good sport, tears spilled down her cheeks.

"What's wrong? I thought you'd be glad."

"I am, but it's a surprise. I wish I could have been there." Dutch's fatigue made him look gaunt, and she'd been too self-centered to notice. "You've done everything right. Look how you've taken care of me. I'm alive thanks to you." She took his hand. "I'll get up. You shouldn't have to wait on me. I'm not an invalid."

She put down her feet as gingerly as if she'd never walked before. She felt nauseated, and the room spun as it had when as a child she used to twirl around until she collapsed, giggling. "I'll sit a minute." One thing at a time.

"What about Beth?" Margaret asked Dr. Miller.

"Why not? You're not running a fever."

Margaret passed a hand through her hair, so matted that she might have to cut it off. What would Dutch say?

Dutch carried in Beth, wriggling with delight. "Beth, let the doc take a look at you."

Dr. Miller smiled at Beth. "There's nothing wrong with this child that a hug from her mama won't cure."

Dutch set Beth down. "Show Mama."

Her fist encircling his index finger, Beth wobbled to the bed and cried "Mama" as she fell laughing against it. Dutch raised her to Margaret's shoulder, and Beth buried her head in Margaret's tangles.

"I'll let myself out," the doctor said, although no one was listening.

Dutch sat on the bed and put his arm around Margaret, who clutched Beth and swayed from side to side. Tears in her eyes, Margaret glanced up to thank the doctor, but he had already closed the door behind him.

"This calls for a celebration." Margaret ignored the dizziness. She tried to stand, but the room whirled, and she lay down again.

Dutch touched her forehead. "Don't overdo it."

"I'm tired of being sick."

"You and Beth are all I have, Margaret. Be patient with yourself."

"I know, I know." She scrunched up her nose and inspected her body. "I'm so skinny." Her breasts were flat. "Dutch, I don't have any milk. I was so sick I didn't even think about Beth having to eat."

"She's been drinking from a bottle. Mrs. McNeill gave me some and showed me how to sterilize them. Beth grabs for glasses when I'm drinking. Mrs. Johnson said she's ready to drink from a cup."

How could so much have changed? She had become unnecessary, useless as an outgrown shoe, in only a month. Disoriented, she gazed at the window etched with frost in delicate patterns that would outdo the most skilled lacemaker.

Beth wore a new sweater. "Where did Beth get that?"

"From Eve."

"It's beautiful. Look at that cable stitch and the embroidery around the collar."

"Yeah, I think she made it herself." Dutch looked away.

Margaret stopped playing with Beth. "What is it?"

"Nothing. Watch this." He swooped Beth up and backed away from the bed. "Call her, Margaret." Perhaps he was changing the subject, but she forgot any suspicions as Beth giggled. When Dutch set her down, Beth held her arms out straight to the side and with concentration took three steps to the bed.

"That's wonderful." Margaret tried to lift Beth above her head and fly her around the way Beth loved, but she didn't have the strength. "I can't pick up Beth any more. What's happened?"

"Give yourself time." Dutch took Beth to the kitchen, their easy laughter blending. Margaret shivered. Alone, she pulled up the covers and closed her eyes. Would she ever be of use to anybody again?

26

Dutch couldn't sleep. Trying not to jostle Margaret, he considered their situation. Now that she was better, he felt cooped up, try as he might to occupy himself. He belonged in the bigger world, making money for her and Beth, who needed new shoes this very minute. He'd promised himself that Beth would never wear shoes that pinched or clothes that were patched, as he had. Beth would have a better life. He needed to be back at work now. Margaret was nearly well. He had thought her sickness must be God's punishment on him for being attracted to Eve. Sometimes he wanted to curse God for allowing Margaret to be sick, Margaret who'd never done anything wrong in her life. He was the one who should be punished.

Maybe God would understand—not approve—how he'd been so lonesome when Margaret was teaching. He had nobody to talk to except Beth, and he couldn't think of much to say to a baby. That's why he visited Eve sometimes in the mornings. She knew how to play with Beth. He would swear on the Bible he was lonesome, that's all. Margaret would understand. What was there to understand? He wished he could tell her. Tell her what? Perhaps the notion was wrong, and he was being punished for that.

From the direction of downtown, one gunshot and then another exploded in the darkness. A bank robbery. Listening, he sat up in bed. Then, above the racket of the wells, car horns honked, the noise swelling until Margaret stirred. "What's that?"

"I don't know." If he strained, he could hear shouts and cheers. "I'm going to see." He grabbed his shirt.

"Dutch, don't." Her fingernails dug into his arm. "It might be dangerous."

"Just a little while." He was already pulling on his overalls.

In the darkness he splashed through puddles on Fourth Street. More people were out than usual. Men on porches rubbed their eyes. He was almost to Main Street when a roughneck grabbed his arm, yelling "It's over. The war's over."

"What?"

"See for yourself." He pointed to a newspaper boy on the corner surrounded by raucous customers, all cheering like kids on the last day of school. Men shot pistols into the air, and drivers leaned on their horns, the noise growing as more people read the Wichita Falls paper, which had already put out an extra.

So it had arrived, the end of the war. Dutch, like most folks, had expected a big offensive next spring or summer. He adjusted his glasses. He'd missed it all, damn these bad eyes. The war had taken Aut and probably Earl too—his folks hadn't heard from him in so long—and Dutch had done nothing. Margaret could talk about how he helped the war effort by producing oil and growing a victory garden, but he felt ashamed every time he saw an injured doughboy shipped home early. That should've been him. Look at Doc. He did his part. But the war was finished now. What would that mean?

He ran back to the house and threw open the door, shouting, "Margaret, the war's over."

Still in bed, she raised an eyebrow, skeptical.

He grinned. "Really. Here's the paper."

She read the headlines: "Sign Terms--War Over." Her eyes filled with tears. "I keep thinking of Aut and Earl. If they could've lasted a few months longer."

"I know," he said. She sat up in bed, and he hugged her.

Later he made another trip downtown. Wichita Falls had put out a second extra: "Draft Now Canceled" and "Armistice Ends the War." The carnival atmosphere grew. Businesses closed; rigs shut down. An impromptu parade formed. Boisterous men joined arms and marched down Main Street. Drivers honked their horns.

As Dutch started home, a roughneck, his breath stinking of liquor, pulled at him. "Come on. We're hanging Kaiser Bill." He handed Dutch a bottle and draped his arm around Dutch's neck.

Curious, Dutch allowed himself to be led toward the train station, where some roughnecks held up an effigy of the kaiser. Everybody booed, waving bottles. Then they raised the effigy and, accompanied by louder cheers, hanged it on a pole by the station. Men threw rocks. Somebody shot at it. A roughneck passed a bottle. Dutch took a swig and handed it back. He wasn't in the celebrating mood. He'd take the newspapers home to Margaret.

27

"Have you heard? The war's over." Dozing, Margaret jerked awake at a loud knock and then a deep voice that she didn't recognize for a minute.

"It's Paul," Dutch called.

"I'll get up." She took her robe from him, Dutch put his arm around her, and they walked into the front room. Still dizzy, she hugged the driller, who felt solid and dependable.

Paul lifted Beth onto his lap. "I hear you've been pretty sick, Margaret. I've been home."

"Why?"

"The rigs here were shut down because of the rain and the flu. My wife and Alice Marian—she's six—had it. They're all right now. I've got to get them here." He held a long package toward her. "Say, I brought you something."

Margaret unwrapped the package and ran her hand over the polished stock of her shotgun, her graduation present from her folks. She and Aut and Dutch carried home squirrels, ducks, and occasional geese for Mama to cook. Margaret had loved to hunt, but now the cold smoothness of the barrel reminded her too much of the violence around here and the war and Aut. She suspected she'd never want to hunt again.

"Mr. Graham took good care of it for me. How are my folks, Paul? I miss them bad."

"They're well. They escaped the flu, I guess because they're in the country. They miss you a lot."

"While you two catch up, I'll make coffee," Dutch said.

Paul stood. "I don't have time, Dutch. I'm going to Springtown. Thought you might come too. I could use you. If your shoulder's healed."

Dutch stretched out his arm where he'd been shot. "I'd like to try. We need the money." He paused. "That is, if Margaret can manage Beth alone."

Margaret smiled. His eyes wide, Dutch looked wistful, like a little boy yearning for his mother's fudge. "I can manage. You've missed the oilfield, I know."

"Oil gets in your blood, all right. As well as your clothes and your skin." Paul reached into his pocket. "I forgot your letter, Margaret."

Dutch pecked Beth's head and Margaret's forehead so quickly that she could barely feel his lips and smell his hair. "You're better, for sure. See you tonight." The door opened, letting in the cold, and he was gone.

Beth drew on the moist windowpane. Margaret unsealed the letter. Out fell a pine twig and two pressed leaves, and she inhaled the outdoors from home. The oaks and sweet gums would be bare among the pines. In the spring, the woods would blossom: the dogwoods, layers of white, and the redbuds, bursts of pink and rose. Mama wrote that Rachel had a third baby just last week, a girl finally, a playmate for Beth. How Margaret missed them all. Maybe she and Dutch could afford to go home or bring Mama to Nesterville. Mr. Graham probably wouldn't come. He wouldn't even go to the church for her and Dutch's wedding, he felt so sad about losing Margaret, so they got married in the garden at home amid his flowers.

She was reading the letter again when she heard a light knock and Eve's voice. Beth crawled to the edge of the couch and, as if she'd been doing it for years, lowered herself feet first to the floor. "Ee-ee," Beth called.

Eve appeared in the door. Beth walked four steps to meet her before she dropped, laughing, on her bottom. "You're a wonder, Beth." Eve hugged her. "And so are you, Margaret. You're up."

"High time." Margaret stood, ignoring the dizziness, shivering as the wind crept between the boards. "This house has holes you could jam your fist through."

"Boomtown real estate. I still say you're lucky to have it. I'd hate to live in a tent. That's where most people die from the flu. It's awful, Margaret. Funerals every day for a lot of people at once. Dutch hasn't told you?"

"I guess he didn't want to upset me."

"Until the war excitement today, downtown's been practically deserted. Most businesses are closed."

They moved into the warmth of the kitchen.

"You've heard about the war?" Eve said.

"Dutch watched the hanging of the kaiser. Then he came home."

"Good thing. It got rough. Somebody started fighting. They always do."

"He and Paul just left. Dutch went back to work finally. While we have time, I wanted to ask you about Beth's birthday in January. What do you think about a party?"

Eve smiled, looking at Beth. "It's a great idea."

"I'd like to have ice cream if Mr. Boyd can get it. Remember how Beth loved it when Mr. Johnson gave her some?"

"She smeared the ice cream all over her hair."

"I've never seen Mr. Johnson laugh so much." Had she ever misjudged him. He seemed nothing like the dirty old man she'd thought him at first.

Beth looked up from the floor, where she was playing with her favorite pan. She fixed solemn brown eyes on Margaret. "Ice?"

Twelve hours later Dutch burst in the door, exhilarated. "I hadn't realized I'd missed work so much. Lots of new wells in Springtown and Nesterville. Some shut down. With all the rain, they couldn't get equipment. And then so many people had the flu. But the rigs are starting up again." He was more enthusiastic than Margaret had seen him since he proposed or maybe since Beth was born. He walked around the room picking up objects—her volume of Longfellow, her Bible—and putting them down as he hummed "Onward Christian Soldiers."

Margaret smiled. "What's going on?"

"Nothing. Why?" Grinning, he stopped pacing and picked up the doily from the couch. "If you feel like it, Paul said he'd carry us around in his new car, and we can show you how the town's changed." He set the doily down. "It's good to be home."

With deliberation Beth took four steps toward Dutch and sat down, her back straight as Margaret's broomstick. Then she crawled to him, hands slapping the floor, and pulled herself up his leg. It was still faster to crawl than walk. "Wait, Beth. I've got to wash. Margaret, help."

"Come on, Beth. Let's heat some water for Papa." Margaret tried to pick Beth up, but she was too weak, so she offered her index finger. Beth gripped it and toddled to the kitchen with her.

Margaret put on water to heat. She fed Beth, who took a bite of mashed potatoes and then bit the spoon, pleased with herself. She grinned around the spoon clenched in her mouth so tightly that Margaret couldn't give her another bite. It was one of Beth's favorite games. It seemed a miracle how she and Dutch, both serious about life, had produced a child who made a game of everything.

"I've written down the people I'd like to invite to Beth's party, Dutch."

"Her birthday party? When?"

"Almost two months from now. The list got long, but so many people have been nice to us." She pulled out his chair, and when he sat at the table she stood reading over his shoulder, her arms around his neck, her chin against his hair. "Can you think of anybody I've forgotten?"

"It's fine." He scanned the list. "What about Dr. Miller? He's not here."

Margaret pushed back her hair. "Do we need him?" She still felt uncomfortable around the doctor; she thought about his tall thinness, his limp that made him appear vulnerable, and most of all his voice like Aut's.

"He's been a friend, sure enough. When I was shot. Your flu," Dutch said.

"He probably can't come."

Dutch frowned. "Why not?"

"He's so busy."

"Invite him. He doesn't have to come. I haven't seen him much since you've been better." Dutch handed her the list.

"Eve and I were talking about the party. We're going to try to get some ice cream."

"Do you think we see too much of Eve? She's always coming over."

"She's my best friend, and she's your friend too."

"Whatever you say." He sounded brusque. The light from the bare electric bulb above the table reflected off his glasses so that she couldn't see his eyes. Normally, his glasses gave him a scholarly look she found surprising. He was a doer, not a thinker. Still, there were depths in Frank Sanders that she had not even suspected. She couldn't figure out what was going on now.

When she placed stew and cornbread on the table, Dutch's mood improved. "You must be feeling better to fix all this."

Margaret assumed a demure expression. She didn't tell him that Mrs. Johnson had brought over the cornbread and Eve had bought the vegetables for the stew.

Dutch still seemed preoccupied, glancing around the room, not responding when she mentioned the war. After he wiped his plate with cornbread, he pushed back his chair. "Margaret, how much money do we have in the bank?"

"About four hundred dollars. Why?"

"No reason." He stood up. "You remember we're going out with Paul next week to look around?" She nodded. He sat down again. "Did you want to talk about Beth's party now?"

28

Margaret woke early and, shivering in the dark, walked into the kitchen on the cold floor, started a fire, and dressed in its heat. The sky brightened, revealing a new smoothness outside the house: the first snow of the year. As the sun rose, the snow turned pink and then sparkled. By tomorrow the mud might lie exposed, but now the landscape looked pristine. She made coffee, humming, and carried it to Dutch. With the snow surely they couldn't go out. She'd enjoy staying with Dutch at home. When she was little, they all sat by the fireplace on bad days, made popcorn, and told stories.

The front door slammed. "I don't want to waste any heat." His face ruddy from the cold, Paul stomped snow off his boots.

Margaret touched Paul's overcoat. "I love your coat. Is it new?"

Paul grinned. "Wouldn't you like to know? Get a move on. I left the car running so it'll be warm."

"We're going? In this weather?"

"At least we won't get stuck in the mud." Paul didn't seem concerned. "Bundle up. We can't have you sick again."

She hesitated. "Maybe I'd better stay."

"You'll enjoy it, Margaret." Dutch started out the door but turned back. "Take a quilt to cover up."

"Is it safe?"

"Sure, let's go." Paul winked at Dutch, who chuckled. Something was going on. Maybe Paul wanted to show off his new five-passenger Model-T sedan, which Dutch told her cost over six hundred dollars, three hundred more than the least expensive model.

Margaret had not ridden in a car since the bank president carried her back to Eve's after she'd been taken hostage. That had been an open model, and she was grateful that Paul's was closed. She admired its silk window curtains and the wood dashboard while she gripped Beth with one hand and the door with the other. The car jerked over frozen streets as bumpy as corduroy roads. Even though it was early, cars and wagons had already left gashes of red mud in the snow.

"Bridgetown first." Paul twisted around and grinned at Dutch, sitting behind him. Dutch punched Paul on the shoulder, as pleased as a schoolboy playing hooky.

"There are twelve oilfield settlements around Nesterville now, Margaret, and Bridgetown's the fanciest one." Paul sounded like a tour guide for the rich investors who came on special trains from Fort Worth. He and Dutch exchanged winks as Paul pointed out a two-story hotel with twenty rooms. He eased the car past a wagon and parked in front of the hotel.

"What are you doing?"

"No questions, my Lady." Dutch touched her lips with his index finger. "It's a surprise." He took Beth from Margaret and, whistling, hustled her inside.

For a boomtown hotel, it was luxurious, the floors carpeted, the windows covered by lace curtains. Margaret smoothed her hair and wished she had worn a Sunday dress. But in the dining room there were no other women except the waitress, a girl who looked barely old enough to be out of school. She wore a plain dress like Margaret's under a pink flour sack apron, and most of the men had on grimy overalls or khaki shirts and pants. The tables were covered with oilcloth stained by only a few spots.

"I haven't seen you two in a spell." The waitress smiled at Dutch and Paul. She nodded in a friendly way at Margaret as she seated them at a table by the window. The river was flowing outside its banks, quadrupled in size since the summer. Now it churned and roiled, occasional chunks of ice bobbing along in the rust-colored water.

Paul rubbed his hands together. "Say, Margaret, you're probably wondering why we brought you here." He and Dutch chuckled.

They were pleased with their surprise. Smiling, she sat back, watching their enjoyment. Dutch took her hand. "I'll order for us."

"Champagne and steaks, the best you've got." Dutch gave the waitress his most charming smile.

"Dutch, we can't afford this." Margaret bit her bottom lip.

"Wait." He lifted his glass. "To our future."

Margaret did not understand, but she raised her glass and

watched the bubbles rise, popping, to the surface. She took a sip. The champagne tasted as light as a day on the lake in May. She took another sip. Dutch and Paul chuckled throughout the meal, and after a glass of champagne, Margaret found herself giggling too.

Dutch called the waitress. "What's for dessert?"

"I can't finish this," Margaret said.

"Leave it. We'll have pecan pie."

"I'm stuffed, I swear. We shouldn't waste all this. You know how scarce meat and sugar are."

"It's a celebration. Anyway, the war's over." Dutch consulted a gold pocket watch, which glinted in the light from the window. Margaret had never seen it before.

She reached for the watch and inspected the embossed designs. "Dutch, where did you get this?"

"At the getting place. Don't worry, Margaret." He dismissed her concern with a wave. "Enjoy yourself."

Still grinning, Dutch helped her into her coat. "This isn't very warm. You need a new coat," he murmured through her hair. "Wait here."

Paul and Dutch went to start the car while Margaret stood in the lobby. Beth whined. Smiling, the waitress approached. "Say, is that fella your husband?" Margaret nodded. "Tell him thanks for the swell tip." Margaret added that to her list of Dutch's surprises. She waited, mystified by all the extravagance: the meal, Paul's overcoat, Dutch's watch.

A roughneck covered with oil ran in. "Have you seen Mr. Sanders?"

Mr. Sanders? "Dutch? In the parking lot."

The man rushed outside, and a minute later Dutch appeared. "Let's go. Quick."

"Dutch, Beth needs a nap."

"No time now."

Pressing her lips together, Margaret climbed into Paul's car.

The roughneck said, "We're down sixteen hundred feet."

Dutch pecked her on the cheek. "See you later."

"What's this all about?"

"Can't explain now." He jumped into the car driven by the roughneck.

Paul and Margaret followed in Paul's car. The snow sparkled so that Margaret had to squint, although low clouds gathered to the east. Tired of the suspense, she was ready to go home, but Paul was concentrating so intently on the icy road that she said nothing.

They approached a settlement composed, as far as Margaret could tell, almost entirely of tents lined up on each side of the road.

"Why, this is Springtown," she said.

"Right. Where Dutch and I boarded last summer about the time you got here." Paul hollered above the wind, which was blowing snow across the road.

It started to sleet. Only the blur of tents and behind them derricks could be distinguished through the particles of ice that slammed against the car. The derricks and tents had multiplied since she and Eve had been here in August searching for Dutch.

It had been madness to go out in this weather. Margaret wriggled her feet but couldn't feel her toes. She covered Beth with the quilt.

"Just a few more minutes," Paul shouted as they crept along the icy mud. After the last tent, Paul stopped near a derrick at the edge of a cotton field. Scraggly unpicked cotton poked through the snow.

Dutch ran up. "Stay here a minute." He covered her lap with a blanket, and he and Paul rushed over to a roughneck, who waved his hat at her. Seeing his oily bald spot, Margaret recognized Mr. Smith from Eve's. He, Paul, and Dutch huddled with several other men, inspecting something in their hands, raised it to their noses and nodded. She shivered in the car.

Dutch ran back. "It looks like oil sand, Margaret. This might be what we're waiting for." He glanced at the derrick. "I have to stay."

"But your good clothes—"

"I'll get more later." He and Paul were all business.

"What's going on?"

"I can't talk now. It won't be long."

Margaret caught his arm. "I want to go home."

"No time. This is happening sooner than we thought. Be patient."

Margaret frowned. "What does this have to do with me? Why did you bring Beth and me here?"

Without answering, Dutch returned to the rig to huddle with Mr. Smith and Paul. The steam drifted away from the boiler used to power the rig, mixed with the blowing snow, and made the whole scene appear unreal: the men scurrying, the drill pipe rising out of the hole, and the derrick appearing and disappearing. The temperature dropped, and the sleet increased.

She'd had enough of being shifted like an object from one place to another. Shivering, she joined the circle of men by the rig.

"Miz Sanders, smell this." Mr. Smith thrust under her nose several gravel-sized pieces of brownish sandstone with the pungent odor of Dutch's work clothes. She didn't understand what she was supposed to inspect. It looked like ordinary gravel.

Mr. Smith pointed. "See the dark pieces? A lot of them. Smell them. Oil sand. About the richest in Texas. Last summer one operator told me he could take some sample sand and let it stand in the sun a week, and then he could squeeze oil out of it." He held up his hand as if to swear on the Bible. "God's truth."

Margaret smiled. Next to fishermen, oilmen must be the biggest liars of all.

Dutch grinned. "It's true, Margaret." He gestured toward a makeshift shelter near the drilling rig. "You're shivering. You can stay in the shack. Lay Beth down for a nap."

"In the mud?" She raised her eyebrows.

"Go see. It'll be warmer."

So chilled and damp she was willing to try, Margaret stepped across frozen rows of cotton to a shelter that had three walls but was partially open on the side facing the rig.

A roughneck warmed his hands over a pot-bellied stove. He gave her a respectful nod and smiled at Beth. "Cute baby." Margaret laid her quilt on the ground. Every few minutes a roughneck eased over to the stove. Shyer than the men at Eve's, they nodded at Margaret. She patted Beth's back and hummed "Trust and Obey." Dutch was right. In the shack she felt warm.

Mr. Smith, his face blackened with oil, stepped inside and held his hands near the fire. When he noticed Margaret, he broke out in a smile. "We may be able to set pipe dreckly, but if the pressure of the gas is too much it may blow." Like the rest, he spoke with enthusiasm, his face alert. "You never can tell." He pointed toward the derrick. "See—we've got eight tanks set up. That should hold it if anything will."

"Hold what? Mr. Smith, I don't understand."

Dutch came in to warm his hands. "This is our lease, Margaret."

"Whose?" She pushed back her hair.

"Ours and a lot of other investors' too, of course."

"Why didn't you tell me?"

"I wanted to surprise you."

"Where did you get the money?"

Dutch looked uneasy."I just took out two hundred dollars. I've saved all I could. And Paul and I are contributing our work."

"You mean you took half our money without talking to me?"

"Don't worry. Tomorrow we'll be rich for sure."

"You're not being paid?"

"I'm working for us, you see."

Margaret couldn't share his optimism. Too many men lost their savings on schemes like this or made fortunes one week and lost them the next. Oil fever, that's what it was, an addiction. Maybe Dutch hadn't told her because he knew she'd raise a fuss, as she should. She could hardly believe they were almost broke. What would they do?

But near the warm stove, she grew drowsy. The men's exhilaration caught her and carried her along despite her objections. Staring at the fire, she crossed her arms on her knees and laid down her head, drifting, envisioning an easier future when Dutch wouldn't have to work twelve hours a day.

She heard a low roll like thunder. More rain coming soon. But there was usually no thunder in winter. The rolling emanated from the earth. It was followed by a louder rumble and shouts. The shack and the ground trembled. A roughneck extinguished the fire in the stove. She stood as Dutch and Paul and the roughnecks pounded each other on the back, whooping and laughing.

A stream of oil shot high above the derrick, poised one long instant, and then fell, coating everything almost up to the shack with a viscous brownish-black fluid. She'd never seen a gusher up close. The men shouted, but she stood silent, mesmerized by this power that roared up from the earth.

Covered with oil, Dutch hollered, "We're rich, Margaret." He picked her up and swung her around. "What do you think of your roughneck husband now?"

Her face was squashed against his neck, drenched with sticky oil. The smell overwhelmed her, but she reckoned she could grow to like it before long.

29

Still sending high a dark plume that danced against low clouds, the well flowed into the evening. Beside it, the empty wooden tanks waited, reminders of human inability to regulate this force. Like a living creature, when the oil was ready to rest from streaming into the sky, it would. Only then would it allow the men to tame it, to divert it into the tanks. In the meantime, all their scurrying and shouting notwithstanding, they were as ineffectual as ants, slaves of the power they had unleashed practically by accident.

Near dusk, the light fading, Margaret could barely see the fountain of oil. Its height decreased, signaling that it soon would allow the men to have their way with it.

Jimmy Johnson, always the first to hear any news, arrived by dark. "Margaret, I brought food. You'd better get some before the men."

She smiled, warmed by his heartiness. "How did you know we were here?"

"Word spreads fast about a gusher as big as this one."

"Is this big?"

"Look at it. You're set for life. When you're living in New York or Paris, remember you knew me when," he said.

"Very funny." She gestured toward the oil overflowing the slush pit. "Why don't they do something about all that wasted oil?"

"It's a help, actually. By flowing, the well cleans out the mud left in the hole."

None of this seemed real to Margaret. In a theoretical way, she was pleased, of course, but she was exhausted, the cold ground felt clammy, and Beth was whining. Jimmy handed her a tin cup of coffee. Inhaling its aroma and warming her chapped hands, she didn't mind that the metal burned her fingers. With the coffee, her mood improved. Perhaps, after all, this was real. Beth sat up yawning, her flushed cheek indented by the quilt, her hair tangled.

Dutch walked over, beaming.

Jimmy pounded him on the back. "This is it. No more work for you. You can lead a life of leisure."

Dutch grinned.

"Have some chicken," Jimmy said.

Dutch glanced at his hands. "I'm too filthy. But leave it here." He watched the diminishing stream of oil. "It's about time. We'll be able to connect the well to the pipeline before long." He signaled to Paul, who was standing with Mr. McNeill. "I may be here all night, Margaret. You can go to town with Jimmy."

Walking to Jimmy's wagon, Margaret looked back. In the dusk, the derrick stood stark against the horizon like a huge wooden tower. A crowd of well-wishers had materialized. Chattering, laughing, they seemed as exhilarated as if it were their well. But Margaret didn't see the Johnsons. "Where are your folks, Jimmy? Did they get over the flu?"

"They're better, but they don't get out in the cold. Concerned about a relapse. I'm surprised you're here."

"I didn't plan it. Dutch surprised me."

"You didn't know about the lease?"

"Not a thing."

Jimmy laughed. "I wish somebody would surprise me like that."

"I still don't understand how they raised all the money. Wells cost more than two hundred dollars."

"Banks are eager to lend the money. Also, promoters advertise stock sales in the newspapers. Even in New York. Investors buy shares for fifty or a hundred dollars, and then they get some of the profits when the well comes in."

So that's what Dutch meant about a lot of other people owning the lease.

Jimmy's delivery wagon, which also served as the town's ambulance and hearse, made for an even rougher ride than Paul's car. Beth fretted, and Margaret felt numb from the cold and the strangeness of the day.

When they passed the Red Onion, Margaret heard the piano. "Maybe I should tell Eve."

"I wouldn't." Jimmy indicated four women by the entrance. "The local temperance league." The women were on their knees praying loudly. "You didn't know? I keep forgetting you've been sick. They're campaigning to close the saloon. They want a town vote."

"Eve hasn't mentioned it."

"She didn't want to alarm you. She's been worried."

"Why hasn't somebody from church said anything?"

"Same thing. You've been sick. You haven't been to church lately. We've had a lot of preaching against drinking. I wouldn't be surprised if they close it down." Jimmy shrugged. "It won't make much difference. You can already get bootleg whiskey just about anywhere."

"I didn't realize that."

"I know a couple of fellas who make it. One's in a dugout in the riverbed. Two dollars a pint. Ask Dutch."

As she climbed down from the wagon, Margaret's hips and legs ached from sitting on the damp ground. She dreaded entering the cold, silent house. There were advantages to living at Eve's, light and heat among them. Carrying Beth on one arm that protested against her daughter's increasing weight, Margaret groped through the dark to the kitchen, found the string, and turned on the light. The bare bulb illuminated their apple-crate cabinet and the oak table with the chairs newly repaired by Dutch. Already feeling better in the familiar surroundings, she started a fire to heat water. Exhausted or not, she had to bathe Beth, grimy as a mud pie.

Later, washing her own arms, Margaret realized how skinny she'd become. Her mother would cry if she could see her now. She sighed as she inspected her cracked hands, rough as tree bark. She doubted her skin would ever be smooth again. She placed a careful dab of cream on her hands and face, and then, remembering their new prosperity, slathered it on her arms and legs. From now on, they'd be strolling through green fields in the sunshine. In bed, she closed her eyes and floated to a softer, warmer place.

Margaret slept as hard as a child, waking to a new world. She felt she had just fallen asleep when she sensed movement in the room and, alarmed, opened her eyes to pale morning light.

Dutch stood next to the bed in clean khakis, his damp hair slicked back, stray curls popping up as his hair dried. He handed Margaret coffee. "Sleeping Beauty, I thought you'd never wake up." She smiled. He'd said those very words in her daydream in the summer.

"You smell good. How did you get so clean?" she asked.

"I took a bath at the barber shop. It's swell that they're open all night." Dutch was all smiles, pleased with the world.

"What happened after I left?"

He sat on the bed and caressed her arm. "Last night the well kept flowing. Then we sent the oil into the tanks. By the time I left, it had overflowed the tanks and was running through the cotton patch."

"What can you do?"

"We ordered more tanks. They should be delivered this morning. I hope. There's a shortage of everything because of all the drilling." He rubbed his forehead. "I've got to go back before long."

"You just got home."

"I wanted to see you. I wanted this well to be a present for you. How does it feel to own a gusher? Part of a gusher, actually. People have already been selling out at two hundred shares to one."

"It's hard to believe. I feel dazed. What about you?"

"This is what I've always wanted. To have something of my own. To be somebody." He stood straighter than she'd ever seen him. With his gold-rimmed glasses he looked dignified as a bank president. Margaret pictured him in perhaps five years, distinguished, in a pin-striped suit and vest.

She nodded toward her hairbrush on their apple-crate bedside table. "Last night I was too tired to do my hair. Do you have time to brush it?"

"It's been a while. Since before you got sick."

She turned toward the window, her back to Dutch, who sat on the bed. As he brushed her hair, his large hands were so gentle that their touch always surprised her. He began with the ends, working up the strands that extended to her waist. Then he laid the brush on the floor, and she leaned against him. He wrapped his arms around her and pressed his cheek against her hair. Quiet, they looked out at the snow.

Dutch slept a couple of hours. Margaret pulled herself out of bed when she heard Beth chant in her own language. All Margaret could understand was a "Mama" interspersed with "no-no-no." In her cradle in the living room, Beth bounced the stuffed monkey

Margaret's mother had created from a sock. With "no" the monkey crashed down; with "Mama" it rose over Beth's head, the rhythm steady as a metronome. Perhaps Beth would be a musician.

Beth's chant grew demanding, the no's more adamant. When Margaret pushed open the curtain to the living room, Beth had already climbed out of her cradle. Seeing Margaret, she grinned, her wide smile transforming her into a miniature Dutch.

Margaret fried bacon and then fried eggs in the grease. What a relief that the porkless Tuesdays and Saturdays and much of the scrimping of the war was over. She smiled. She wouldn't mind having money. She would buy an armoire for their bedroom from the Sears catalogue, burled walnut with curved doors and legs.

Dutch lifted Margaret's hair and kissed the nape of her neck. "You know what I'd like?" He sat at the table, bouncing Beth on his lap. "A Model-T."

"You can't drive."

"I can learn, sure enough. You too. How hard can it be?"

"Can we afford a car?" Margaret wrinkled her nose.

"You forget. We're rich. And six hundred dollars is cheap, Margaret. I saw a driller yesterday who'd bought a car for over four thousand dollars."

"I wish you'd wait. The well might not be any good."

"You know it is." Dutch clapped his hands. "We've always been as poor as Job's turkey. You have to learn to think rich."

"I think we should wait."

"That's a given. You haven't seen anything like the work I have to do now." He laced his boots. "I'll be late. Don't wait up."

30

Margaret stuffed Beth into her snowsuit and ventured outside. Yesterday the snow had melted, and in the night the slush had frozen. The wind whipped around them, stinging Margaret's eyes and nose. From her vantage point on Margaret's shoulder, Beth pulled the quilt off her head. Her dark eyes reminded Margaret of a baby bird. Beth wriggled, wanting down.

"No, Beth, it's dangerous." Margaret slid along. What if she got sick again? There'd been over six thousand deaths in Texas from the flu in October, and now after a respite more cases were reported as the flu turned into pneumonia. Many houses had posted the required sign announcing that a resident had the flu, and people were still encouraged not to congregate on the streets, although the quarantine had been lifted, and the school had reopened. She pulled her scarf tight around her ears and, despite Beth's complaints, covered her head with the quilt.

Margaret opened Eve's front door and called. Beth echoed, "Ee-ee."

The dining room looked normal, plates and cups abandoned. The smell of bacon lingered.

Hearing no response, she opened the swinging door into the kitchen. "Eve?"

Eve sat at the table with her head on her arms, her shoulders shaking.

Margaret touched her hair. "What's wrong?"

Eve jerked upright. Her eyes were swollen, her face blotchy. "Nothing. Everything. Just the blues." Wiping her eyes with her apron, she stood, hugged Margaret, and took Beth. "How's the big girl?"

"She walks all the time. She doesn't like me to carry her."

"If that doesn't beat all." Eve pointed. "Beth, see the cat?" Eve dragged some yarn along the floor. The kitten, sleek and doubled in size, pounced from behind the stove. Beth tried on unsteady legs to grab the cat, but it jumped onto the counter.

"Beth. Here." Eve gave her a pan and a spoon.

"What's going on?"

"Mrs. Johnson came this morning. That old biddy loves to cause trouble. I haven't even started the dishes."

Margaret raised her eyebrows. "Didn't you tell me that Mrs. Johnson means well? Look at how she brought food to you and me when we had the flu."

Eve grimaced. "Hold your horses. I know all that. But this morning was too much. She said that because public sentiment— that's how she put it—disapproves of the Red Onion and because it's going to be closed down, I shouldn't play there because it's immoral and disreputable, and surely I wouldn't want to be seen associating with the trash who frequent it." Eve tossed back her braid. "As if I care what the good women of Nesterville think."

"I swear, they're not worth your time. I saw four of them last night. They looked like they'd swallowed dill pickles. If they have nothing to do but criticize other people, you should feel sorry for them." Margaret was surprised that Eve would take Mrs. Johnson's meddling so hard. She would've expected Eve to laugh it off, to point out that everyone had faults.

"There's more." Eve wiped her eyes with a dishrag. "To change the subject, I told Mrs. Johnson what happened with the Salvation Army. She said they made the right decision about the adoption."

"What adoption?"

"I forgot you were sick so long." Eve sighed. "Last week when I felt better, I heard about a baby girl, eleven months old. Her mother died from the flu, and her father couldn't be located. The Salvation Army asked for someone to adopt her. I applied."

Margaret smiled. Lucky child, to be reared by somebody as kind as Eve.

Eve's eyes filled with tears. "They said they already had twenty-five applications, and they wouldn't consider mine because I wasn't married."

"Sanctimonious, hypocritical do-gooders." Margaret laid her hand on Eve's, searching for words of consolation. "That baby couldn't have a better home than with you."

"Then I wrote the orphanage. My little girl hasn't been adopted.

I don't know whether to be sad or happy about that."

They watched Beth at play on the floor. When she noticed them staring at her, she wobbled to Margaret and pulled herself up. Sit in Eve's lap, she needs you, Margaret willed Beth, but Beth didn't receive the message. Margaret lifted her up.

"Now you know why I'm down. But I can't feel sorry for myself all day." Eve mopped her eyes again.

Margaret looked around the dirty kitchen. "You're exhausted because you've been sick. This is too much work for you anyway. I don't see how you do it. I can help a little." She pushed up her sleeves and collected plates with the hardened remains of eggs and cups with coffee grounds stuck to the bottoms.

They stood at the sink scraping dishes and piling them in the water to soak. She'd felt close to Eve before, but as with Dutch she was discovering in Eve new layers of unknowns. Maybe that's what love meant: learning more and accepting what she found.

"So you're considering getting your daughter back?"

"Maybe." Eve frowned. She turned to Margaret. "I forgot to congratulate you about the well."

"I forgot too, and that's what I came to tell you. How did you already know?"

Eve said, "Red Onion. The best source of news in town. Paul and Dutch came in late last night."

"Dutch? But he worked all night."

"He had to have supper."

"I would've fixed it for him, even if it was late."

"He didn't want to wake you, Margaret. You've been really sick. We all thought you weren't going to make it. Believe me, my case of the flu was nothing compared to yours."

"You don't have to defend him." Margaret pushed back her hair with a damp hand as the steam rose from the dishwater and into her face. "Something else, Eve. I had no idea Dutch was going to withdraw half our money from the bank. If I'd known, I swear, I would've thrown a fit."

"Sometimes you have to take chances, Margaret. Dutch asked me what I thought. I said to do it."

"He asked you? Not me?"

"You were really sick, and he wanted to surprise you. He thinks he's not intelligent because he didn't finish school, and you did."

Margaret said, "That's ridiculous. His family needed money. He was the oldest, so he went to work when he was fourteen."

"Exactly. He's a good husband. You know that."

Margaret remained unconvinced. They were partners, she and Dutch, weren't they, complementing halves? "I still wish he'd told me he was planning to use our savings."

When Dutch arrived home late, Margaret warmed up salt pork, navy beans, and cornbread. Taking off his boots, he announced, "We got the tanks set up. Now we start drilling the next well."

"So soon?"

"We have to. The oil's in a pool underground. If we don't get it out, somebody else will."

"Do we have the money?"

"Margaret, we're rich. You don't have to worry about money ever again." He cupped her chin in his hand, the smell of oil masked by the odor of lye soap. "I did it for you and Beth."

She nodded. But it was more complicated than that. He did it for himself, to show that he mattered.

"If we're already rich, why do we want to drill more?" she said.

"What else would we do?"

"Go home. People do. After they get some wells, they sell out. That's what Eve told me the first day I was here."

"So why doesn't she leave?"

"She said it's her home."

"It's not time to think about selling out yet, Margaret. Paul and I were thinking about giving our friends here a chance to invest in a well, sell shares. What do you think?"

Margaret bit her bottom lip and then smiled. "It's a swell idea. Who?"

"Jimmy. His parents. The McNeills."

"Eve?"

Dutch frowned. "If you like."

"Why are you hostile toward Eve?"

"I'm not." Dutch rubbed his glasses on his sleeve. "She has enough to do as it is."

"The Red Onion may shut down with all the temperance

sentiment around. Mrs. Johnson came to see her about how it was not upstanding to play there. Eve got upset."

"She shouldn't listen to meddlesome people like Mrs. Johnson," Dutch said.

"Exactly what I told her."

"She still has the boarding house. That's a full-time job."

"I think we should ask her if she wants to buy some shares, Dutch."

"I don't feel right about using a maiden lady's savings."

Margaret raised her eyebrows. "Eve—a maiden lady?"

"Does she have enough money?"

Margaret thought about Eve's sending money to the orphanage and shrugged. "I think so."

Dutch turned back to the list. "Invite her in if you like. What about Dr. Miller?"

"It's up to you. You know how much backing you need."

"We owe him a lot."

"Ask him then." Margaret was relieved that she hadn't seen him since she'd recovered from the flu. She hoped she wouldn't for a while.

Dutch was still unsure. "So you think it's a good idea? To ask our friends? There's a risk. We've seen people go bust overnight."

"But you and Paul know what you're doing."

31

Dutch arrived home grinning."We did it." He hugged her. "We raised the money."

"Already? In two days?"

"As easy as rhubarb pie." Dutch snapped his fingers. "People begged to buy shares. We already have one good well, and they trust us."

"How much did you get?"

"Twenty thousand."

"Were they hesitant?"

"Not at all. They were grateful to be asked."

Twenty thousand dollars. A fortune. The oil fever seemed to have infected everybody, including those who'd lived here since before the boom.

"Most people put in fifty or a hundred dollars. Let's see." Dutch rubbed his forehead. "The Johnsons and Dr. Miller and Eve put in a thousand each. They thanked me for asking them."

"Imagine." She was pleased their friends trusted Dutch. She stood behind him while he ate and rubbed his shoulders. "I've missed you."

"Why don't you watch the drilling tomorrow?"

"You wouldn't mind?" she said.

"I'd like you to. But it'll be a long day."

When she heard Mrs. McNeill in the kitchen the next morning, Margaret carried over Beth, still asleep and wrapped in a quilt. Mrs. McNeill smiled. "You both deserve this good fortune. A hard-working young man like Dutch. And a sweet girl like you. We're so grateful to you for asking us in."

As Paul's car bounced along the icy street, Margaret felt she was on holiday. She sat beside Paul, who told her what to expect. "You know that when we've worked in other locations, Dutch sharpens the drill bit whenever it gets dull. From cutting through limestone. But he doesn't have to do that here because we're drilling through sandstone. Every two or three hundred feet we stop drilling and change the bit." He glanced at her. "Is this clear?"

She nodded. "I've heard about cable tools."

"Some of the first wells were drilled completely that way. What happens is, a heavy bit is attached to a long steel cable. The cable raises the bit and drops it over and over and punches a hole in the ground. But now people use rotary drilling rigs because they're faster. That's what we've got. We'll keep on until we get to about thirty feet above the oil sand."

"How do you know where the sand is?"

"We guess. Based on the closest wells. Next we cement the casing–"

"What's that?"

"Joints of pipe. Then we switch to the cable tools so we won't drill through the oil sand by mistake."

"Like the cuttings you showed me Sunday?" She remembered the distinctive odor. Dutch and Paul kept explaining. When the cable tool penetrated the oil sand a few feet, it was lifted from the hole, and the well was "brought in." They made it sound like bringing home a baby. The heavy drilling mud was bailed from the well, a process that permitted the oil to flow to the surface aided by natural gas pressure. Sometimes wells were allowed to flow for days in order to clean out the remaining mud and drill cuttings from the hole and also to take photographs to attract prospective stockholders. Next, the oil was directed into tanks or even open pits for storage, and then a pipeline took it to a refinery. The nine refineries in the Nesterville area couldn't keep up with all the production. More pipelines were laid all the time, but bad weather and theft slowed the pipeliners.

Margaret remained in the car as the rising sun stained the sky coral behind the derricks. She watched a wagon at a nearby well. The wagon carried an entire wooden drilling rig, which had been built and then delivered intact to the drilling location. Pulled by eight horses, the wagon had been modified for the oilfield. It had four axles so it could maneuver and turn as easily as a smaller vehicle to place the drilling rig in exactly the right spot.

This second well was so close to the first that the bases of the derricks almost touched. Like everything else, the timber for the derrick had to be shipped in. Dutch and Paul spoke of thousands of dollars as nothing extraordinary, but Margaret found it difficult to shift suddenly to this new way of thinking; eleven cents for a pair of socks still sounded to her like a normal expense.

She realized she was shivering. No sense in remaining alone in the car when she saw a fire in the lease shack. The roughnecks smiled as they made a place for her. Most of them were in their forties, but she noticed a few younger men, apparently former doughboys, probably wounded and already shipped home from France. Despite the early hour, they looked expectant as they passed around coffee, handing her a tin cup with politeness, but she wondered whether they resented a woman's presence.

Drilling was slow. Margaret settled herself on the ground and watched the occasional flurry of activity as roughnecks attached another joint of drill pipe. There was a lot of laughing, hand warming, and coffee drinking. Yesterday on the way to the dry goods store, she'd noticed a cardboard sign tacked over the regular sign; "Easy Street" was scrawled on the cardboard. It wouldn't be half bad, living one block away from Easy Street.

News travels fast. The next day Mr. Boyd in his overcoat and hat swooped on her as soon as Margaret and Eve stepped inside the store. While Margaret was still stomping off the ice, he bowed. "Mrs. Sanders, delighted to see you up after the flu." He nodded. "Eve, too. Of course." He pulled at the hair sprouting from the mole under his nose. "I have to apologize for the low temperature, but since the quarantine we're required to keep all the doors and windows open." He spread his arms wide. "Tell me when you see something you'd like. Maybe oranges. Rare here. I got them yesterday." Bowing again, he held an orange toward her. "I hoped you'd be in today."

Margaret gazed at the orange, glowing like sunshine. "Here, Eve. It smells like Christmas." Mama and Daddy always had a big pine Christmas tree decorated with popcorn. It filled the corner of the front room. The scent of the tree and the popcorn mingled in her mind with the oranges, one for each of them, which Mr. Graham handed out on Christmas Eve. She'd stare at her orange, a foreign globe of light, and rub its uneven exterior. Then she'd slowly peel back the rough skin, savoring its aroma of places so exotic that she couldn't even name them. She dreaded their first Christmas without her folks, though another part of her looked forward to celebrating Christmas on the plains. A salt cedar from the riverbed might make a jam-up Christmas tree, or in a pinch she could decorate a tumbleweed.

She set Beth down. "I'll buy one orange now. For Beth. Even though it's not quite Christmas." She opened her pocketbook. "I forgot to bring money."

Mr. Boyd, still hovering, rocked on his heels. "Mrs. Sanders, you put as much on credit as suits your fancy. Whatever you'd like. Please."

"Should I get a few oranges, Eve? It seems so extravagant." Margaret felt such yearning for her family that she realized she was about to cry. She rummaged through her pocketbook for a handkerchief but remembered they were all dirty. She should be home washing, not buying exotic produce.

"What's wrong?" Eve touched her shoulder.

"Nothing. I swear, I don't know." She wiped her eyes on her sleeve. "I miss home, I miss Mama and Daddy, and I'm so thankful Dutch is alive." She picked Beth up with such energy that Beth stared at her solemn-eyed. "I'll take a dozen, Mr. Boyd." Margaret burst out crying as Eve looked at her with perplexity, but she couldn't stop the sobs. The war was over, they were healthy, and their well was good; what was there to cry about? Eve took Beth, set her down, and folded Margaret in her arms.

"Mrs. Sanders, you must sit down." Mr. Boyd glanced around as if to see whether the other customers had noticed this unseemly display of emotion. His worried expression twisted his thin lips and emphasized his mole. When Margaret's sobs slowed to an occasional hiccup, he indicated his office in the back.

But she had recovered and wanted to giggle as she dismissed his concern. She sniffed and rubbed her nose with her hand. "I wanted to ask about Beth's party. Do you ever have ice cream?"

"For you, we can get some from Wichita Falls. I'll have it delivered," Mr. Boyd said.

Beth, alerted, stared at him. "Eyes?"

"In two weeks, Beth," Margaret said.

32

Eve arrived early to the party. "I brought Beth's present. Is she dressed yet?"

"I wanted to wait until the last minute so she'll be clean a while," Margaret said.

Eve handed Margaret a package. Inside was a long white batiste dress with embroidery and lace on the collar and sleeves.

"I can't let her wear this." Margaret's roughened fingers caught on the intricate handwork. "It's for a princess."

"Beth is a princess. She'll have a castle soon enough, believe me. It wasn't getting any use in the closet."

"You made this?"

"I told you I have many talents."

Margaret bit her lip. "I forgot. You made it for your baby. I won't tell anybody, Eve, not even Dutch."

"Dutch knows already. I told him some time ago."

"He didn't tell me."

Eve shrugged. "I guess he didn't think about it. He's had a lot on his mind these past few months."

For a minute Margaret felt unbalanced, but, as they pulled the new dress over Beth's head, her unease drifted away like riverbed sand in a wind. Beth preened, touching the embroidery and smoothing the dress, which reached to the floor.

"She's all girl." Eve smiled.

When Dutch arrived, Margaret's discomfort resurfaced. She watched him and Eve with new eyes.

"I took off early in honor of the party." He glanced around the living room. "It looks different in here."

"I moved Beth's cradle and her toys into the bedroom," Margaret said.

"I knew it was something."

Eve smiled. "I've never known anyone so observant, Dutch."

He grinned. "How can I help?"

"Raise the temperature forty degrees and stop the snow," Eve said.

Dutch chuckled, rubbing his hands together. "For sure. Other than that?"

Nothing unusual in their joking. That was their way, although sometimes Dutch acted defensive when he talked about Eve. She was their good friend; that was all. "See what Eve brought?" Margaret said.

"What a beautiful dress!" Dutch scooped Beth up and tossed her over his head. "How's the birthday girl?"

Beth squealed with delight.

"I brought you something too, Beth." Dutch stepped outside and returned with a rocking horse. "Mr. Johnson made it." Carved of pine that Mr. Johnson had varnished, the horse shone like sunshine, smiling at them from under its mane of unbraided rope.

Beth toddled over to it. Dutch lifted her on and handed her the reins, made of red yarn. She grasped the reins. When nothing happened, she made a tentative movement. The horse rocked abruptly. Beth's lips pulled down into a pout.

One hand on Beth's shoulder and the other on the horse's mane, Margaret rocked the horse. Beth smiled.

"Next year," Dutch said, "maybe we'll get you a real horsie."

"Forsie." Beth pushed away Margaret's hand. Beaming, she rocked by herself.

Beth loved her party. Holding the hand of the youngest McNeill child, Beth toddled from person to person, sampling steak and fried potatoes.

Mrs. Johnson peeled an orange. "Such an extravagance."

"The best thing I've ever tasted." Mrs. McNeill licked her fingers.

Margaret set Beth in her high chair. Then she brought out a chocolate cake.

"We don't get food like this around here, Margaret. You've outdone yourself." Mr. Johnson pushed up his thick glasses and smiled at her, a kindly owl with a mustache.

Margaret smiled, grateful that they'd made her feel at home in only five months. She prayed that she and Dutch would be able to repay them with this new well.

She put a spoon into Beth's right hand. Beth switched it to her left, clamping her fist around it. She smeared ice cream and chocolate cake all over her face and the bib that covered her dress.

"Beth, you're a one-girl slum." Jimmy Johnson laughed, sitting next to Eve at the table.

Dutch pulled out a jug. "Let's drink to Beth," he said, and passed around glasses. They all drank.

"And to Paul and Dutch," Jimmy added, "who'll make us all millionaires."

"We hope." Dutch raised his glass. They drank again.

"We do too," Mr. Smith called, his bald spot shining.

Dutch handed Margaret a glass. The strong liquor, as bitter as vanilla extract, burned her lips.

Margaret felt Dr. Miller's eyes on her as he raised his glass. When he'd arrived, she thanked him formally for taking such good care of her. He acknowledged her words with a perfunctory nod.

The talk grew louder until she could barely hear Mr. Johnson, who sat next to her. The alcohol, she supposed, but perhaps not altogether. There wasn't much recreation in town, especially for women: an occasional church picnic or box supper, the silent picture show—though the lines, like everywhere else in town, were long–and the rare medicine or vaudeville show, but the jokes were crude, so women didn't often go. They all worked so hard. They needed this. Look at them. She could hardly believe Mrs. Johnson was laughing with Mrs. McNeill, although Mrs. McNeill held a glass of whiskey.

Inclining her head toward Mr. Johnson, Margaret heard, "We're grateful to you and Dutch for remembering us. We're optimistic about the new lease."

"It looks good so far." Margaret nodded, as if she'd spent more than two afternoons on a rig in her entire life.

"We've all gone whole hog on it," Mr. Johnson said.

"I'm pleased that everyone trusts Dutch," she said. Almost all the men and Eve were smoking. The room was heavy with the odor of tobacco, which settled on her head, pressing her down so that she had to escape or sink into the floor. "Excuse me," she said to Mr. Johnson. It was all she could do to rise and push her way out the back door into the night. She sat on the top step and breathed in air so icy it burned her throat. The stars dripped with such brightness that she could make out the dark ribbon of the river. Orion's belt was covered with the thinnest of flat clouds. Through the door floated the buzz of voices, high-pitched, interspersed with loud guffaws.

The door squeaked. Her shawl dropped onto her shoulders.

Dutch sat beside her and put his arm around her. "Is something wrong?"

"Nothing. It's a swell party."

"How come you're out here?"

"It got so smoky." She couldn't explain what she'd felt: the claustrophobia, the nausea. She leaned her head on his shoulder, peaceful again. "You smell good."

"Like oil, you mean. You're the one who smells good. Last summer I missed your lavender water smell."

"I'm almost out," she said.

"We'll get more."

She sighed. "Where? Mr. Boyd and Mr. Kelly don't have any."

"You'll be surprised about what we can get from now on, Margaret. When you have money, there are ways." His lips brushed her hair. "Ready to come inside?"

"Not quite yet."

"Don't relapse." He wrapped her shawl around her.

"I'll be in pretty soon." She laid her head on her arms and rested. She was about to go in when the door squeaked again. "Dutch, I'm on my way," she called.

She turned to see Dr. Miller, his red hair glinting in the kitchen light.

He spoke formally, his words as cold as the air. "Your husband told me you were here. I came to thank you for the opportunity to become a part of your oil company. Also, thank you for including me tonight."

If he could be formal, so could she. "I'm happy you were able to make it."

"I'm returning to Fort Worth in a few weeks. As soon as Dr. Myers arrives."

"Dr. Myers?"

"My replacement."

"You're moving?" Her chest ached. "Why?" In the silence after her words, the sparrow in the mesquite ruffled its feathers. She lowered her voice, shocked at her pleading tone. "Leaving for good?"

"What's here for me?" Resentment broke through his self-control. "Tell me one thing that's here."

She stammered. "Money?"

"Money isn't everything. Don't be trite. You know that."

"But I depend on you. I mean—Dutch and I do."

"That's right. Dutch and you do." He frowned.

She sighed. He wouldn't look at her. It was selfish to wish for more than she had. One husband. Lucky to have him. She extended her hand. "Thank you for coming to Beth's party. She loves the doll you gave her."

"Glad to be of service." He ignored her hand but bowed in mock gallantry. The door slammed shut after him.

Margaret returned to the living room and joined the women discussing their children and husbands, the boundaries of their lives. Mr. Boyd's wife, Lucille, whom Margaret had met only once at her husband's grocery store, was a tall, gaunt woman with faded blond hair and the reddish, raw skin of one who'd grown up in this harsh country. Mrs. Boyd asked about a remedy for coughs, and Mrs. Johnson, who had been nodding off, brightened. "Try coal oil with alcohol." Leaning forward, she hissed, "Speaking of alcohol, have you heard about the Red Onion being closed?"

"Why are you whispering?" Margaret asked.

Mrs. Johnson nodded toward the kitchen. "Eve—you know. She plays there, and she drinks."

"I declare, what would the men do without the Red Onion?" Mrs. McNeill laughed. "I've been there with Josh. And the food's better than at the other greasy spoons here in town."

"It used to be downtown, you know, until a few years ago when we voted to close it down. Then they moved out by Clara. But the liquor—" Mrs. Johnson broke off as the McNeill children ran in, followed by Beth, their energy growing in proportion to the lateness of the hour.

"We're having a parade," the oldest announced.

Mrs. McNeill called, "Keep it down, you hear?"

The closest child paused. "Yes'um."

Two minutes later as they ran through again, Beth tripped and started bawling. Margaret picked her up, saw only a scrape on her knee, and rocked her.

"They're too rambunctious," Mrs. McNeill said.

She took her children home, despite Patsy Ann's protesting, "But Mama, do I have to? I'm six." Their tired whines and their mother's patient murmurs carried through the wall.

Mrs. McNeill rejoined the women in time to hear Mrs. Johnson give her recipe for salt pork and navy beans.

"Land, that sounds good." Mrs. McNeill sat on the couch. "We've all been dirt poor, but that's about to change, thanks to you and Dutch."

Margaret smiled. "I hope so." Everyone here seemed so optimistic that she questioned her own doubts. They had one good well; perhaps the new well would be good too. She gazed down at Beth's perfect skin, damp from the excitement. Beth's eyelashes fluttered open, and she smiled.

Margaret tiptoed into the bedroom. She put Beth down and stood with her hand on Beth's warm back, watching her sleep.

In the kitchen, she found Eve smoking and playing poker. In front of her was a glass of whiskey, but she looked alert. Mr. Johnson slumped in his chair, his eyes glazed.

"I fold." Mr. Boyd's voice was slurred, his movements deliberate as he waved at Margaret. "Hello, Little Lady."

"Hit me," Dutch said to Paul, who was dealing. He tapped the table. "This is my night. I can't lose." He pulled Margaret to him and set her on his lap, his arms fastened around her waist. "Kiss me for luck, Woman."

Margaret tried to get up. She whispered, "Dutch, you're drunk. I hate it when you're like this."

He let go. "Don't get your tail over the dashboard. Are you my woman or not? Let's all drink to my wife."

"I fold." Eve laid her cards down and laughed. "Dutch, you've had enough to drink." She turned to Margaret. "Let's make some coffee."

Dutch collected his matchsticks, adding them to the pile in front of him.

Paul stretched. "If those were pennies, you'd be rich as an oil magnate."

Dutch chuckled. "You forget. I am an oil magnate. And so are you."

Paul nodded to Eve. "Coffee would go down good." He nudged Mr. Smith, sitting with his head in his arms. "Bill and I have to get to work."

"Now? It's midnight," Margaret said.

Dutch pushed himself up from the table. "Wait. I'll go too."

"Why?"

Paul answered. "You know we're drilling, Margaret."

"Can you work like this, Dutch? You're not yourself."

"I can work anytime, Little Girl. Just you watch."

Margaret had never seen Dutch this way before. He moved slowly, with jerks and exaggerated movements like a marionette. She didn't like it, but she only looked on as Dutch gulped the strong coffee and, waving in her general direction, stumbled out into the snow.

33

"**R**eady." Paul's voice rang in the midnight air.

Dutch was afraid his fingers would stick because the crank was coated with ice. He patted his pockets and realized he'd forgotten his gloves, but he wouldn't go back inside. He wrapped a cloth over the crank.

They'd had a good time. Why did Margaret have to nag about his drinking? Maybe he sometimes hit the bottle with too much enthusiasm, but not often. Margaret couldn't forget her Uncle Jep, the drunkard. But she could ease up. You'd think she was the president of the Temperance League. Even Mrs. Johnson, a teetotaler for sure, had sat there as polite as a Bible salesman with Eve, who could drink the best of them under the table. Eve looked swell tonight, with that auburn hair piled on her head, a few curls straggling down her marble neck. Once, as he'd floated on the euphoria of drink, he caught himself leaning toward one of those curls, his whole being concentrated on its plump roundness, craving to bury himself in its warmth. He'd jerked back, embarrassed, but only Jimmy seemed to notice, grinning and raising his glass. Jimmy hung around Eve a lot, like a dog that wanted to jump on a meat wagon. Jimmy was no prize. He was as good as they made 'em, but he lacked ambition.

The engine caught, and the snow crunched under Dutch's boots as he stepped onto the running board. Wet snowflakes plopped down. Away from the smoke and the complications of women, he felt clean.

He pulled a flask out of his pocket and took a slug. "This warms the bones."

Paul threw him a questioning glance. "If I were you, I'd rather be home. I'm going to Louisiana next week to get my wife."

Dutch took another swig as they waited behind a wagon of pipe. Traffic seemed normal for midnight. "I'd like to buy a few things now that we can afford them. A car, first off. Maybe build a house."

"A house?" Paul sounded amazed. "Put down roots? Are you

ready for that?"

"Why not? Margaret and I've always dreamed about a house. Two stories with a porch all around so Margaret can see the sunrise and the sunset both. I'll plant a garden too." He pictured her in a porch swing, waiting for him in one of those frilly dresses, drinking lemonade. There it was again, drinking. Just because her uncle drank like a thirsty man in a desert, she thought a taste of alcohol led straight to eternal damnation. She could nag sometimes, but deep down where it counted, he knew she was right. He'd seen marriages ruined by drink. Look at Diamond Bob and his wife. Bob was a typical driller, a star of the oilfield, a glamorous man who lived fast. But Diamond Bob, whose name came from the three-carat diamond necklace he bought for his wife, stayed drunk most of the time except when he was working. Every day just before noon his toolie drove to Bob's house, and Bob's wife and the toolie carried him out and laid him in the wagon. By the time he reached the rig, he was sober enough to work till midnight when he started drinking and passed out again. Not much of an existence for his wife, but she must like diamonds. At least Margaret wasn't greedy like that.

The wind picked up, blowing snow across the road and smashing it against the fence posts. Paul leaned forward to see. A tumbleweed blew across the road and over a snowbank.

At the rig the drilling had gone well. Paul had hired a new driller, Glen Vaughan from Wichita Falls, a scarecrow of a man, so lean his overalls hung on him as if designed for someone twice his size. He had large eyes above a thin mouth that grinned easily. Dutch mistrusted anyone who smiled all the time, as though he knew something Dutch didn't, but he could find no complaint with Glen's work.

Dutch inspected the sample of gravel from the hole, crunching it between his fingers and holding it beneath his nose. "Smells like money, all right." Before long, they'd hit the oil sand, which in the offset wells was about thirty feet thick. Next they'd switch from rotary to cable tools and then cement the casing. He inspected the waiting wooden tanks and the slush pit. They were ready for the oil.

During lulls in the drilling, the men warmed their hands in the shack.

"Are we on for tonight?" Glen asked Mr. Smith.

"You bet your bloomers. Join us, Dutch. After work at Ruby Pearl's. It's a good place to play cards."

"I'm a novice. You're too high-powered for me," Dutch said.

"Don't worry. We play for small stakes."

"I'm usually too beat to do anything but go home and sleep." Dutch heard himself making excuses.

Glen said, "Where are you staying, Dutch?"

"Nesterville."

"Some of us rent a cot in Springtown. A dollar for eight hours. It's simpler."

"I might do that."

Paul hollered, "We've got work to do." They ran out, pulling on their gloves.

A few hours later, the sun rising behind Springtown emphasized the dirt and stubble on their hollow-eyed faces. Instead of going to Ruby Pearl's, they'd worked all night.

Paul stretched. "I'll leave it with you, Glen." He turned to Dutch. "I'm not ready to go back to Nesterville yet. Let's eat breakfast in Springtown."

"Is there anything there but greasy spoons? I don't want ptomaine poisoning."

"You could try Reba Jo's," Glen said. In the morning sun, his large eyes sparkled.

Reba Jo's was one of the fourteen-by-fourteen Army tents lining the street. In the cold wind that whipped the canvas walls, men with swollen eyes lined up. Inside, long tables were covered with platters of greasy ham and bacon, cold scrambled eggs, and toast.

Compared to Margaret's meals, it wasn't much, but the coffee was strong enough, and Dutch was glad to get out of the wind. He yawned. "I'm ready for some sleep."

"We've got work to do." Paul repeated his words from the night before. Sometimes Paul seemed like a machine.

"It's my lease, Paul. I'll work when I want to."

"It's our lease. We both work when we have to. You know that. You can't go yet," Paul said.

"I'm not fit to work the way I feel now." Dutch stretched his injured arm again. "It doesn't feel right."

"Why don't you rent a cot? Sleep a few hours."

"Maybe I will."

Dutch approached a hefty woman in a dirty apron bringing around coffee. With a lopsided grimace perhaps intended as a smile, the woman took his money for a cot. The fat on her arms jiggled when she indicated the tent next door.

Dutch pushed open the flap and was hit by stale air punctuated by snores of varied loudness. As his eyes adjusted, he could make out cots against the walls, most occupied by unmoving lumps hunkered under Army blankets. One cot was empty, the blanket still rumpled from the previous occupant. He sighed and sat down. The man next to him turned over and groaned. Dutch shivered. Good thing he was exhausted, or he'd never be able to sleep. He pulled up the scratchy blanket that smelled of oil and sweat; his last thoughts before he fell into blackness were of Margaret's warmth and their clean-smelling bed at home.

Then he was sweating, and the light looked different. He stared at a pinprick of brightness over his head. His mouth felt dry. He smelled wet canvas, oil, and liquor from foul breaths. The tent was stuffy from the damp heat radiating from the walls. Dutch felt disoriented, as he always did when he slept during the day. The man in the cot next to him stirred, breaking the rhythm of his snores. Dutch tentatively stretched out his hurt arm. His shoulder felt stiff.

Pushing aside the tent flap, he saw a transformed world; the snow melting in the slanted afternoon sunlight already cast long shadows toward Nesterville. Cars and horse-drawn wagons of pipe struggled through the mud. He trudged back to the well. Paul would see how hard he could work when he put his mind to it. He wondered what Margaret was doing. Perhaps he shouldn't have left her with all the cleaning up after Beth's party.

34

After Dutch and Paul left, the party quieted down, as if everyone had run out of topics to discuss and energy to discuss them. But they all lingered a spell; no one wanted to confront the snow. They sprawled, listless, in the front room chairs or on the floor. The wind picked up, howling. Margaret shivered, feeling empty, as if the wind were forging a place in her heart. She didn't understand why Dutch was annoyed with her, all because she made one comment— only one—about his drinking. Why did he have to be so sensitive and leave before they could talk? She sighed as she gathered cups from the table, put them in the sink, and wiped the table with a vigor she didn't feel. Mrs. Johnson poked her head in. "Don't bother with this. I'll help you later." Tired laughter spilled into the kitchen. Tucking away her fatigue and pasting a smile over her discomfort, Margaret sat by Eve in the front room.

Eve patted Margaret's shoulder. Maybe she had noticed Dutch's brusqueness.

"Great party." Jimmy leaned around Eve.

"I'm happy everyone's having fun. More coffee?"

"I'll get it." Mr. Johnson went into the kitchen.

"My, your husband is kind," Eve said.

"Always has been." Mrs. Johnson smiled, crinkles like ditches at the edge of her faded blue eyes. "Fifty years we've been married."

It was curious about marriages. Look at the Johnsons. Everybody liked Mr. Johnson. Not many people liked Mrs. Johnson. But they seemed as happy together as newlyweds. Maybe happier. And her mother and Mr. Graham. How brave he'd been eleven years ago to take on Mama, a widow with four kids. Mama had written last week that this was the best time of their lives: the kids grown and settled, just her and Mr. Graham on the farm, free. Margaret loved being with Dutch too, but sometimes life interfered. She wanted their marriage to succeed. From now on, she'd remember that Dutch was under pressure because their friends had all invested so heavily. She wished she could fly over to that well. She hoped he wouldn't catch cold, with the wind up.

It was almost three before everybody went home. Jimmy left with Eve, her face open, relaxed. Alone, Margaret checked on Beth, whose back was warm even though she'd kicked off her quilt. Margaret smoothed Beth's hair off her damp forehead. Last year Beth had been twelve hours old, with wrinkled red skin. Now look at her. Too big for her cradle.

Margaret wandered into the living room. Ash trays overflowed. The house reeked of cigarettes and whiskey. Someone had spilled coffee on the couch. The women had offered to clean up, but Margaret had refused. Now she wished she'd accepted. Sighing, she went to work. She'd have the place spotless when Dutch came home for breakfast.

She scrubbed the couch with cold water and then with lye soap, rubbing back and forth and then in a circle the way Mama did but couldn't remove the coffee stain. Exhausted, she leaned against the couch. The wingback chairs loomed above her as if berating her fruitless efforts to create a home in this God-forsaken place. Willing herself to ignore the chaos, she stumbled into the bedroom. Beth stirred. Margaret prayed she would sleep longer. Shivering, she pulled off her best dress, dropped it in a heap onto the floor, and struggled into her cold nightgown. In bed she wrapped the quilts tight around her to simulate Dutch's warmth. Images of the party ran through her mind: her anticipation, the excitement of knowing she looked pretty, the thrill of watching Beth on her rocking horse. If Dutch were home, they'd giggle over Mrs. Johnson's story about how she spilled a bowl of beans onto the lap of her husband's boss when she was a new bride. The window rattled in the wind.

She woke shivering and groped around the cold bed. No Dutch. She pulled on the cord in her mind; it felt secure. She'd finish cleaning. Beth sat in her cradle playing with her new doll. "Mama?" she called. With her customary enthusiasm, she climbed out of the cradle and wobbled to the bed. Margaret pulled back the quilt and made a place for her. Where did Beth find all that energy?

Beth warmed Margaret like a heater. Maybe today she'd accept

Mrs. McNeill's offer to help her make a rag rug. They could start after she cleaned up and Dutch went back to work. In the past, she'd relied on Mama and Ida for domestic chores while she and Aut and later Dutch roamed the woods, hunted, or rode horses. Humming, she picked up her dress, which wasn't too wrinkled, shook it out, and hung it on the nail by the door.

The kerosene stove kept the kitchen warm, so Margaret opened the curtain into the front room. She put water on the stove and emptied ashtrays. Everybody must have smoked two packs apiece last night. No wonder the house reeked.

"Papa?" Beth glanced up from the quilt by the stove.

"He'll be home soon, Bethie. He's working."

Beth turned back to her doll, reassured.

When the water boiled, Margaret made Beth grits. She started the coffee so it would be ready for Dutch. Stacks of plates and cups sat piled in the sink, but nothing compared to Eve's, and she did them twice a day.

Two hours later she'd finished the dishes, but Dutch still hadn't arrived. Margaret opened the back door to air out the house. It had warmed up outside.

"Beth, I'll read to you on the steps. Here's your coat."

She set her coffee beside her. Beth sat in her lap in the thin sun. "See this picture. It's a king's son and his horse."

"Forsie."

"Look. It says, 'Once up a time.'" One benefit of motherhood she hadn't anticipated was enjoying experiences long forgotten until she relived them with Beth. In the fairy tales the youngest son went on adventures, slew the dragon, solved the riddle, and married the king's daughter. What about the youngest daughter? She herself had come to Nesterville. Existing here was an adventure.

Beth climbed down the steps and toddled over the uneven ground, stooping with her back perfectly straight to inspect the yellow grass stubble that poked through the melting snow. Margaret watched a boy and a dog hunting near the riverbed. She used to love to hunt with Aut. Sometimes they caught the cow and milked her for the cats, which they pretended were enchanted princesses. She and Aut had run through the woods barefoot on the pine straw carpet.

Now she wiggled her toes in her boots and closed her eyes, enjoying the winter sun.

A scream rang out, sounding at first more surprised than terrified. The scream stopped abruptly and then continued again, muffled.

Margaret looked around, confused. Beth wasn't in sight. The screams emanated from the middle of the yard, where a hole less than a foot in diameter yawned. Red mud gaped like a wound through melting snow.

Margaret ran. She lay at the edge of the hole, careful not to dislodge additional mud. She peered into the darkness but could spot nothing. "Beth, can you hear me?"

The screams stopped. "Mama?" Beth sounded far away. Margaret heard her terror.

"Beth, listen." Margaret tried to control her voice. She glanced around the yard as if for help. "I'm here. I'll get you out." She had no more idea how to rescue Beth than how to set a broken leg.

She heard herself screaming incoherently.

Echoing her mother's terror, Beth sobbed, "Mama, Mama."

Margaret pressed her lips together to force herself to remain quiet. She couldn't frighten Beth more; she had to think. "Don't cry, Beth. It'll be all right."

A door slammed. Mrs. McNeill ran over. "What happened?"

"Beth." Margaret gestured toward the hole.

"Is she hurt?"

"I don't know. She keeps crying."

"Can you see her?"

"It's too dark," Margaret said.

"Where's Dutch?"

"Springtown."

Mrs. McNeill said, "I'll get the doctor."

"What can he do?"

"Maybe he'll know somebody."

Mrs. McNeill was gone; her large-framed body moved with surprising speed. Margaret talked to Beth, mumbling incoherent words of despair masked as comfort: "You're a big girl now. Be brave. We'll get you out. Papa will be here soon. Remember what a good time you had at your party." Beth stopped sobbing and answered Margaret with only an occasional weak "Mama," as if speech were almost beyond her. Margaret talked and sang nursery rhymes, spirituals, hymns—anything—as she prayed.

A few minutes later Dr. Miller hurried into the yard and lay beside Margaret. He stared down into the hole. "How is she?"

"She's not talking much."

"I think I can see her." He called, "Beth—Beth" loudly and then waited. She didn't answer.

Jimmy Johnson arrived with shovels. "We'll get her. She's not far. Maybe twenty feet down." That twenty feet might as well be the distance to the moon.

Dr. Miller stood. "This sand may not be bad to dig in. It shouldn't take long." The authority of his voice calmed her.

A crowd gathered. About fifteen feet from the caved-in well, the men took turns digging a hole parallel to the one Beth was in but with a circumference large enough for a man's body so that the digger could be lowered on a rope. Although the sand was easy to dig, it was also prone to cave in. Progress was slow. It was twilight before the digger's head disappeared. The earth closed over him and muffled his voice, which remained determinedly cheerful. Margaret sang to Beth, who didn't respond. Townspeople watched. When each man returned to the surface after his turn, he nodded at Margaret: we're doing the best we can, but it may not be enough; it's all in God's hands. The women huddled together as if their collective presence would add more substance to their prayers. As the shadows lengthened and the sky darkened, everyone grew quiet, no longer meeting Margaret's eye. Discouragement grew in proportion to the pile of discarded sand the men hauled up in buckets. Someone set up lights, and the scene took on a bizarre carnival air, the red mud on the men's faces like clown makeup.

The scent of gardenias mixed with the odor of the fresh earth. Eve lay beside her. "I brought you a quilt to lie on. Let me talk to her. You go have some coffee."

Margaret shook her head. "It would be deserting her." She bit back tears with a fierceness that surprised her. "I'll stay here till they reach her. I won't move." She raised up onto her elbows as her eyes searched the crowd. "I wish Dutch would come home."

"Did somebody go for him?"

"I don't know. He's working late."

Eve got up. "Should I send somebody to the lease?"

The preacher knelt on the other side of Margaret. "We're all praying. God will find a way." He took her hand in his, which felt reassuring, dry and warm. She shivered. Beth would be colder.

"Maybe I will have some coffee after all. Can you talk to her, Brother Pound? I don't want her to think we've abandoned her." Margaret pushed her stiff body off the quilt. "Beth, I'll be right back." She wiped her face on her sleeve. "I realize she might be— sleeping—and might not hear us. But I want to keep trying."

"The only thing to do. They'll be down in another hour or so," Brother Pound said.

"It's been so long—six, seven hours?"

"You should eat something."

Margaret allowed Mrs. Johnson to lead her into the house. She washed her face and hands. Mrs. Johnson put some cold chicken and a biscuit before her. The congealed grease on the chicken nauseated her. Beth must be hungry. Margaret nibbled at the biscuit. Tears welled up, spilling down her cheeks, as she remembered the biscuits Mama made. She wished she could lay her head on her mother's shoulder and rest.

Mrs. Johnson set a mug of coffee in front of her. "Don't cry, Margaret. She's in God's hands."

"I'm so scared. What would we do without her?"

Mrs. Johnson's warmth enfolded her. "I know, Dear. I've never told you that we had another child after Jimmy. A little girl. She passed away when she was two. Pneumonia."

"I'm sorry. I didn't know." They had had Beth only a year.

Dr. Miller opened the door, his eyes worried. "They're down. They're going to tunnel across to her."

Outside, the atmosphere had changed. As long as there was something to do, there was hope. A light had been rigged up at the top of the hole.

Margaret knelt by the well shaft. "There she is. Beth, Beth." The tiny form, covered with mud, didn't move. Margaret ached to wipe the dirt from her face.

The preacher knelt beside Margaret. "She may be unconscious.

It was quite a fall. We won't give up hope."

Margaret lay staring at Beth at the bottom of the shaft. She registered conversations about how digging horizontally was slower than digging vertically because the sand might cave in and bury either the digger or Beth. Margaret kept speaking to Beth, although she realized that nothing she said made sense, that she was talking more for herself than for Beth, who might be beyond hearing.

35

Out of breath, Dutch knelt beside Margaret, her eyes red, her face swollen. Sobbing, she buried her head in his coat. Sometimes he yearned for the release of tears, but in his house boys didn't cry.

Margaret wiped her eyes. "A hole opened up in the earth. Like when we looked at the house before we rented it, remember? She fell in. An old well wasn't capped."

"Did she talk to you?"

"At first. A little."

"If anything happens to her—I mean, if she's dead—"

"She's alive. She has to be." Her fingernails bit into his neck.

"Let me finish. If she's—hurt—I'll never forgive myself," Dutch said.

"For what?"

"For her death. I brought you here," he said.

"You didn't bring me. I came to Nesterville on my own. Against your wishes."

"I mean to this house. You didn't want to move here."

"But I didn't watch her today, Dutch. I should've been more alert. I was tired. I closed my eyes for a minute. I swear, that's all."

"I believe you. And you've been—I mean, you are—the best possible mother Beth could have." Margaret's small arms loosened around him. She'd clung to him so tightly he hadn't been able to take a deep breath.

"Where were you?" she said.

"At the well. Eve found me." He turned to Jimmy. "Ready to lower me?"

"You're too big to fit in the tunnel. The thinnest person here has to go. Doc Miller."

"I don't mind." Dr. Miller walked up, his clothes and face smeared with mud, his eyes focused on Margaret. "You know how much I care for you, for all of you."

"No." Dutch cut the air with his hand. The crowd grew quiet. "She's my daughter. My responsibility." The spectators backed away. Dutch felt isolated. For hours, while he'd been sleeping, working, eating, they had shared this trouble without him, consoled his wife, labored to save his daughter. For his own self-respect, he had to do his part. He inspected Dr. Miller's emaciated frame. The doctor appeared far too puny for this job. Dutch lowered his voice. "I appreciate your offer, Doc, but it's my duty to rescue her. She's my child."

Jimmy intervened. "I know you want to help, Dutch. But we were afraid to make the tunnel any wider. It may cave in as it is."

Dutch stared at the ground, seething. He'd arrived eight hours late, and he wasn't allowed to rescue his own daughter.

Arms folded across her chest, Margaret spoke up. "Dutch, I know you're frustrated, but you're wasting time." She was right.

She took his hand, and they watched while Jimmy tied a rope around Dr. Miller's waist and checked the knot.

"Good luck, Doc." Dutch extended his hand.

"I'll do my best." The doctor nodded toward Margaret. "Take care of your wife."

What did he mean by that crack?

"I'll help Jimmy with the rope." Dutch had to do something. He put on his gloves, and he, Jimmy, and Paul, the strongest men there, braced themselves to lower the doctor.

"Here goes." Dr. Miller disappeared into the hole.

They played the rope out slowly. The slippery sand forced the three men to inch backward to keep from being dragged toward the edge of the hole.

The tension on the rope slackened. Dr. Miller's muffled voice rose. "I'm down." A pause. "I'm going over to her. The hole is barely big enough."

Dutch chewed on his lips. He imagined Dr. Miller dropping onto his stomach and squirming through the horizontal tunnel toward Beth. He kept checking his watch. The crowd grew still, as if they had collectively inhaled and were holding their breaths.

Margaret lay intent at the edge of the hole. She gasped. "He's broken through. The tunnel held."

"She's alive," Dr. Miller called up to them.

Some people cheered, others prayed, but Dutch remained silent, watching Margaret. She nodded at him with relief, her face smeared with mud and her hair snarled like a child's.

There was a whine, followed by a cry, the best sounds he'd heard in his entire life. He swallowed, unclenched his fists, and rubbed his white knuckles. Catching Margaret's eye, he allowed himself a half-smile of hope.

Dr. Miller's voice floated up. "She was asleep." A long pause followed. Dutch made patterns in the dirt with his foot.

"Mama?" Beth sounded bewildered.

"Beth, we're here. You'll be all right. Dr. Miller will bring you up." Tears streaked Margaret's face. She didn't move from the edge of the hole until Dr. Miller pulled Beth, screaming, through the horizontal tunnel back to the main shaft of the hole. Margaret glanced at Dutch, her eyes wide.

"She's just scared, poor baby. No wonder," Dutch said.

The doctor called, "I've attached the rope. Haul her up."

Pale and muddy, Margaret stood by Dutch, holding him around the waist. He took the rope from Jimmy and slowly, hand over hand, drew up Beth's slight body, her weight nothing at all compared to Dr. Miller's. All the way her screams reflected her terror. At the top of the shaft, Margaret reached down and lifted her. Beth was sobbing with such force that her entire body trembled. Dutch clutched that mud-covered body and Margaret both to him. Thanks be to God.

Beth's sobs slowed to gasping hiccups. Dutch held her to his shoulder, and Margaret stroked her muddy cheek, her matted hair. Beth looked around wide-eyed and then laid her head back on Dutch's shoulder.

Dr. Miller's voice floated up from the well. "Ready? I'm holding the rope." They'd forgotten him. Dutch gave Beth to Margaret, while he, Paul, and Jimmy braced themselves.

About halfway up, Dr. Miller hollered, "The rope's slipping." The rope went slack, and there was a thud.

Margaret called. "Are you hurt?"

"I twisted my ankle is all. The rope came untied."

Dutch frowned. That was what happened when you relied on a person with a sit-down job. At least he'd sent Beth up safely.

"I'm ready," Dr. Miller said.

The rope slipped again when Dr. Miller was only a few feet from the surface. Dutch transferred the rope to Mr. McNeill, removed his gloves, and extended his hand. "Doc, grab onto me."

The doctor let go of the rope with one hand. Dutch grasped it and, straining, tugged hard. Dr. Miller was not as light as he appeared, and his hand was coated with mud. Feeling him slip, Dutch reached down with his other hand to give one last heave. His injured shoulder screamed as he felt himself dragged into the hole, but his feet were gripped from behind. Eve called, "Jimmy and I have you." Dr. Miller hauled himself onto the ground, where he lay face down, retching. He sat up and took the rag Paul handed him. When he tentatively put weight on his right foot, he winced. Paul offered him a flask, but he refused.

Dutch lay by the hole, his body spent, his head jumbled. He resented Doc Miller's doing what he himself should have done, yet he respected the doctor for having done it. Mostly Dutch suspected he felt resentment because of what he owed the doctor and could never repay, his wife's and, now, his daughter's lives.

Dutch sat up and extended his hand to Dr. Miller, but Margaret was there first. Still clutching Beth, she hugged him. "You saved Beth's life." Despite the mud on her face, Margaret looked more radiant than Dutch had seen her in a long time. The doctor reddened.

Dutch pounded Dr. Miller on the back. "You did it, Doc."

Margaret, with Beth against her shoulder, moved toward the house followed by Dr. Miller, limping more than usual. They all offered Dutch congratulations and passed around bottles of hootch, as if every one of them had descended into that hole and returned alive.

"Come inside. We'll have some coffee," Dutch said.

But, with replies of "We have to work tomorrow," their neighbors dispersed into the night, their tired but cheerful voices lingering.

36

Dutch stood by the hole and wiped the mud off his glasses. In the morning he'd cover the hole. Maybe they should move.

When he went into the house, the doctor had gone. Margaret was heating water. She sat at the table holding Beth, who was drinking milk, her eyes swollen.

Dutch touched Margaret's cheek and then Beth's hair. He dropped into a chair, as drained as if he'd run all the way to Wichita Falls and back. "I didn't think she'd make it."

"I didn't either." Margaret's voice sounded hollow. "And when you weren't here, I didn't think I could go on. Where were you?" She frowned.

"At the well. You know that." He kept his voice level. They were both exhausted.

He pushed himself up. "Is there any coffee?"

"You can heat some from this morning. It'll be strong, but–" She managed a tired smile.

"Right—it's the way I like it." He put the coffee pot on to heat and poured the hot water for Beth's bath. She was almost too big for the sink now.

Margaret stripped off Beth's clothes. Beth's face was coated with mud, but her body appeared paler than normal. "Do you think she's all right, Dutch?"

"Just scared and tired. What did the doc say?"

"Wait and see. He'll be by tomorrow." Margaret, making a face, tossed Beth's clothes onto the floor. "I'm not sure these can be resurrected."

"We can buy her plenty of new ones."

"I keep forgetting. But the money doesn't matter that much, does it?"

"Not at all." Dutch watched Margaret. She was intent on scrubbing Beth, who pushed away her mother's hands. He pumped more water into the bucket and set it on the stove. "I feel awful about not being here when you needed me."

Margaret pushed back a stray hair with a soapy hand. "Forget it." She sounded curt.

All three of them shared the bed. Between sleep and waking much of the night, Dutch kept his hand on Beth or Margaret for reassurance.

He woke early to another gray dawn. The temperature hovered just above freezing; the clouds promised snow, a day that matched his mood. His shoulder ached, and he was dog tired.

Margaret stumbled into the kitchen. Dark smudges under her eyes emphasized the gauntness of her face.

Dutch rubbed the stubble on his chin. "I don't know how much longer the well will take. Sometimes with weather like this, we need ten days to drill. I don't want to leave you and Beth, especially after yesterday, but I want to be close to the rig if there's trouble."

"What trouble?"

"Like if we twist the drill stem in two. That always causes a delay. I guess I need to stay in Springtown till this well comes in."

She wrinkled her nose. "There's nothing there but dumps."

"That wouldn't matter. Most of the time I'd be at the rig. And Springtown's close." He stretched. "Think about it. All our friends have their savings riding on this well. It's a huge responsibility. What if the well's dry?"

"There haven't been any dry holes around here. Right?"

He nodded.

"Anyway," she said, "If it's dry, it'll be dry whether you're there or not."

"We're getting pretty close to the sand, so we'll know soon enough. It's Paul's and my decision about how far into the sand we go. I may have to stay for a few days."

"What if something else happens to Beth?" Margaret said.

He ran a hand embedded with oil through his matted hair. "Keep her inside. We'll move as soon as this well is finished. If, God forbid, something else happens, call in the doc. Just remember that nobody could have handled this emergency better than you." He glanced toward the door. "Paul's here." The chair creaked in protest as he pushed it back. He kissed her neck that smelled of lavender. "Maybe this isn't the best decision, but I feel responsible."

On the way to the rig, Dutch felt freer. Something about home and family drove him away, maybe because his mother was so hard to get along with. His father was bent down by the weight of her temper like a horse that never rebelled against the whip but kept plodding along. His mother was so mean-spirited that she'd start reading a story to his dad, who couldn't read a word, and stop at the most exciting part. Dutch got angry just thinking about her. He wouldn't be beat down like that, not that Margaret was like his mother either.

"Margaret made us biscuits." He handed one to Paul.

"As I may have said before, you're a lucky man, Dutch."

He knew that.

The roughneck on the night crew hadn't shown up, and they'd needed Dutch. It was a good thing he'd told Margaret he wouldn't be home for a spell.

When Glen returned from sleeping only a few hours, he appeared as energetic as if he'd had a full night's rest. He eyed Dutch. "Are you in for tonight?"

"Why not?"

At suppertime Glen suggested they go to Ruby Jo's. "I could eat a horse and a hamper of greens."

"You two go ahead," Paul said. "I'm not hungry." He was working like a machine again.

Dutch paid his dollar to Ruby Jo, who tucked the money inside her greasy bodice. In August a meal had been only four bits, half of today's price, but he wouldn't bellyache. He could afford it. The fried chicken, he was surprised to find, was almost as tender as Margaret's. Glen wolfed down his meal without conversation; his eyes roved the crowded tables of men, all dirty, all exuberant. Dutch overheard somebody say that, together, the wells in the area produced thirty thousand barrels a day. At $2.50 a barrel, that was something. Somebody else said that, in the Nesterville townsite alone, two hundred wells were producing. Such talk was as intoxicating as the bottle of hootch Glen bought from a blind tiger and stowed inside his coat. Dutch wiped the remains of his gravy with light bread that was again available since the war. He pushed back his empty plate. He felt more energetic than since their first well came in.

Glen flashed his nervous smile. "Let's go to Blondie's."

"A whorehouse?"

"Just to play cards." He sounded as if he was issuing a challenge.

Dutch stood. "Let's go."

He opened the tent flap into Blondie's, one large front room with curtains partitioning off the back. Smoke hung heavy in the air. Like almost every other place in Springtown, Blondie's was heated by coal oil. He drew in one last gulp of cold, clean air and stepped inside the overheated room, where he was hit by the odor of tobacco.

Coal-oil lamps illuminated the card players, their shouts and laughter so boisterous Dutch had to bend down to hear a woman direct him to a vacant table. Her perfume, as fresh as magnolia blooms, surprised him. He stared into her blue eyes.

"What's the matter, Roughneck? See something you like?" Her voice was as soft as flowers.

"I just want to play cards."

"You've come to the right place, honey. I see you brought my friend." She reached up and kissed Glen on the lips, leaving a coral smear on his mouth. "Can't you girls leave a fella alone?" Glen kept his arm around her waist.

"Dutch, this is Blondie. She's from Louisiana too."

"Is that right? I'm from Oil City. Near Shreveport."

"I know where it is, shu-gah. I'm from Marion."

"If you two are through catching up on home news, we'd like something to drink." Glen patted her on the rear.

"I thought you were married."

"What difference does that make?" Glen waved at several women. "Are you here to have fun or give a lecture on morality? Loosen up."

They joined a table. Dutch took the drink and the cigarette Blondie gave him. Mr. Smith tossed out two bits. "I'm in."

To his surprise Dutch won the first three hands. He was pleased, though he knew Margaret would disapprove. In her books gambling was almost as bad as drinking.

"Dutch, you in?" Glen dealt with an ease that Dutch admired, the cards slipping with smoothness through his calloused hands.

"You bet your bloomers. Hit me."

"One mop squeezer." Glen slapped a queen in front of Dutch.

Dutch continued to win. At this rate he'd be able to afford that new lease before long. He hadn't confided in anybody yet except Paul, not even Margaret. The lease he wanted was halfway to Wichita Falls, where the land was still cheap. There hadn't been much drilling there, although a few shallow wells, less than a thousand feet, slow producers but steady, had been drilled about ten years ago. Area maps had convinced him that wildcatting was the only way to make big money fast. Nobody had found the mother pool yet, the source that supplied all the smaller pools around. It must be south of the townsite field, waiting for him.

The stakes grew. Dutch kept winning, not every hand but often enough to stay ahead. Finally, his luck turned, and he began losing.

Before he lost everything, he said, "We have to leave."

"Who are you, Cinderella? It's not twelve yet. Hit me," Glen said to the dealer. Blondie leaned over him, rubbing his neck.

"I'm going back to work. Are you ready?"

"I'll be along." Glen flashed his confident smile. His small teeth glittered.

On the way to the well, Dutch glanced around to be sure no one was following him. He'd tucked his meager winnings into his coat pocket. He breathed in the cold. It was a different world in there for sure, glistening but insubstantial as a dream. The lights on their derrick at the edge of Springtown shone like beacons, the steam from the boiler giving them a rosy halo.

At the rig he joined Paul at the fire. "Aren't you hungry?"

"I brought some ham from the boarding house," Paul said. "But I'm dead tired. I think I'll sleep a spell."

"At Reba Jo's?"

"If there's space."

Dutch grinned. "Watch out for the fleas."

Dutch changed the drill bit, and the drilling began again. He drank coffee, rubbing his hand over the stubble on his face. Saturday he'd go home, have a bath, and put his winnings in the bank. He hated to carry money around. Just maybe he could manage that lease. Beth would be asleep by now, and Margaret might be sitting outside. She liked to drink coffee on the back steps after Beth was in bed, even when it was cold. If he teased her about it, she said it was a way of making sense of the day, spreading it out before her to examine.

37

Eve shook loose powder onto a puff and touched Beth's nose with it. Beth sneezed as the powder floated up, smelling of gardenias. "Try some," Eve said to Margaret.

"I couldn't." Had it come to this? Without Dutch, could she find no more worthwhile way to spend her evenings than to watch Eve prepare for the Red Onion? Margaret yawned. In less than a week, she had established a new pattern for their days, staying up late every night. As a consequence, she was exhausted.

Eve's ivory skin looked radiant in her aqua taffeta. No wonder men stared on the street. As Eve dusted power on her shoulders, images of painted women rose up from Margaret's childhood. How Mama's friends had gossiped. She was twelve and Aut was fourteen when those women moved into the old Lancaster house. Mrs. Dupin, who wore red or purple dresses, had inherited the house, and they'd moved from New Orleans, which she pronounced "Nawlins," to try life in a small town. It was a disgrace to have them in Oil City, Mama's friends said, sniffing. They didn't like it one bit. Margaret hadn't either after Aut started visiting the women every day.

"Why do you go there?" she'd asked, but he'd only tickled her under the chin and told her not to worry her pretty head. She didn't call it worrying; she called it helping him avoid disaster. She followed him once, watching as two girls not much older than he fawned over him on the porch. When they kissed him, they left red marks on his face. Giggling, they led him inside the house while Margaret waited with Shep, hidden in the pines and bitten by mosquitoes. The women kissed him again on the porch when he left. He washed off the red smears in the creek.

Margaret hadn't understood who they were, only that she didn't feel right asking him any more questions. She resented losing her brother. Once he began seeing the women, he slept all day, and when he was awake, refused Margaret's invitations to fish or ride their horses through the woods. Mama forbade Aut's going there, but he persuaded Margaret to take a letter to a girl he called Susie. Margaret read the letter and burned it.

Mama never found out who burned down Mrs. Dupin's kitchen tent and ran the whores off. She said it was the irate townspeople, but Margaret noticed her mother sometimes throwing her a suspicious glance. Mama wouldn't have believed her youngest daughter capable of such destruction. And until she lit the kerosene with a pine splinter, Margaret hadn't understood how fire burns, how it eats like a living creature whatever it can reach, licking into all the corners, discovering and destroying everything. From behind a pine, she and Shep watched the young women rush out of their sleeping tent in their housecoats, one of them clutching a kitten. They looked terrified as their kitchen tent went up in flames. Margaret felt ashamed. She never told anybody what she'd done, not even Dutch, and looking back, she was even more appalled.

"Do you?" Eve was staring at her.

"Do I what?"

"Dreaming again. Do you want some powder?"

"Why not?" Margaret dusted powder on her nose and her cheeks, roughened by the constant wind. Eve was right. The powder smoothed out her complexion. She peered into the mirror, pleased. "What do you think?"

Eve inspected her. "You look swell. Wait." Eve rummaged through her top drawer. "Here. This is light enough to go with your hair." She handed Margaret a small box.

Margaret ran her finger over the pink paste. "I couldn't—"

"Just try it."

Margaret dabbed the paste on her chapped lips. "I like it."

"Let's go. Wrap up Beth."

"I can't. Only men go there."

"I go, don't I?"

"But you work there."

"Mrs. McNeill's been. Stay an hour or so." Eve stood. "What else do you have to do?"

"I'm not dressed." Margaret glanced in dismay at her everyday black skirt and white blouse.

"Borrow something."

"It wouldn't help." Margaret looked at her arms. "I'm so skinny since I was sick." But she was tired of staying alone. She pulled on her coat, gave herself a final turn before Eve's mirror, and blotted her darkened lips.

The temperance leaguers knelt outside the Red Onion praying for the salvation of the drunkards inside. Those women must be dedicated to remain in the cold. Why, there was Mrs. Edwards, a dried-up woman with a face on its way to becoming a raisin.

She frowned at Margaret. "Mrs. Sanders, I cannot understand why you would go in there. And with a baby." She sniffed.

Eve pushed Margaret inside.

"Busybodies," Margaret said to Eve. Maybe they meant well, but why couldn't they stay home and tend to their own husbands?

"They're doing what they think is right. Why does it bother you?"

Margaret shrugged. She wasn't sure she should be here. She adjusted a hairpin to secure a straggling curl. She didn't want her hair falling down.

Through the haze, she made out an oak bar with a mirror behind it. Hundreds of bottles of different sizes and shapes shone in the dim light. Men stood in clumps along the bar, their feet on a rail. Others crowded around small tables in a room larger than Margaret's house.

"Mrs. Sanders." Margaret nodded toward the deep voice, which she couldn't recognize until a tall, slack-jawed man tipped his cowboy hat and intoned, "You're fired." Ah, Jerry, the man with no clothes.

Eve pointed to a table next to the upright piano, which must have led a hard life, the ivory yellowed and peeled off some of the keys. That piano had probably been here as long as the saloon itself, years before the boom. Perhaps it had arrived on a covered wagon.

Margaret sat knees together while Beth fidgeted on her lap. Eve began with Scott Joplin. He must be Eve's favorite, and no wonder. His music could cheer up anybody.

A blonde woman placed a soda water in front of Margaret. "Is this all right, Miz Sanders?" She added an extra syllable, sa-yun-ders.

Margaret looked up. How did this young woman know her?

"I saw you at the school before it closed. You taught my little sisters. The twins?"

The braided girls, with straw-colored plaits that reached to their waists.

"How are they? I miss teaching them."

"They passed on from the flu. Ma went a week later."

Margaret hugged Beth to her. "I'm so sorry."

"I'd better get back to work." The young woman sighed. "What do I owe you for the soda water?"

"On the house." The bartender waved at Margaret. "We don't get many ladies in here," she said. Lay-uh-deez. "We've never had a baby here before that I know of." Bay-uh-by. She handed out drinks from a tray so large her slight frame looked top-heavy.

What kind of future did this girl face? She might marry a roughneck and have tow-headed children who would make a game of riding the rod lines, as Margaret used to. She'd balance on the rod, connected at one end to a pumping jack and at the other end to a gas-powered fly wheel that rotated and pulled the rod lines back and forth to run the jacks for all the wells around. Children loved growing up in the oilfield, but women not much older than this one already looked dried out, aged before their time by the sweltering summers and harsh winters. People said there was nothing between Nesterville and the North Pole but a barbed wire fence, and it was down. A stale joke, but Margaret understood.

A chair scraped. Dr. Miller stood above her, eyebrows arched. "What are you doing here?"

"What do you mean?" Some nerve.

"Here. A saloon."

Margaret smoothed her hair. In the lamplight, he probably wouldn't notice her lipstick and powder.

"And with Beth?"

"Why not?"

He shrugged. "May I sit down?"

"Suit yourself." If he could be rude, so could she. He tipped back his chair and gazed around the room. He still looked as skinny as an umbrella. "When are you going back to Fort Worth?" she asked.

"There's a snag. My replacement had a better offer, so I'll stay till my partners find somebody. Nesterville needs at least three more doctors." Dr. Miller drummed his fingers on the table in time with the piano. "Where's Dutch?"

"In Springtown a few days. At the well, I guess."

Dr. Miller raised his eyebrows. "You guess?"

"I mean, he feels responsible because our friends"—she peered at him through the smoky air—"our friends like you have invested their savings in this lease. It's easier to be close to the rig when they need him." Her voice trailed off.

"Bright idea." Dr. Miller looked skeptical. He crossed his eyes for Beth, who crowed and beat with her fists on the table. "Beth looks recovered from her ordeal in the well shaft."

"Thanks to you. We're so very grateful, Dutch and I." Her face tingled as she remembered Dutch's guilt that he hadn't been more help and her resentment that he hadn't arrived sooner. They sat without speaking.

The room grew smokier and the voices more boisterous. At a nearby table, a roughneck and a farmer hurled insults. One dove for the other's knees, and a scuffle began. Men gathered, encouraging the brawlers. Anything for amusement.

Beth whined, struggling to climb out of Margaret's lap. "I'd better go home." Margaret stood, relieved to have an excuse. She leaned toward Eve. "Goodnight."

Eve didn't miss a note. "Not by yourself. Dr. Miller can carry you home in a jitney."

"I'll be fine." Margaret remembered having said those same words to Dr. Miller when she'd first arrived. She didn't feel much more confident now.

"Don't be ridiculous." Eve glanced at Dr. Miller. "See that she gets home."

"It's on my way." He sounded reluctant. Her house was no more on the way to his room than the school was. But she allowed him to lead her through the press of roughnecks. Beth coughed. Margaret wished she hadn't come.

Outside, the temperature had dropped. Some of the temperance ladies were still kneeling, although Mrs. Edwards was gone.

The jitney driver asked, "You hear about the murder in Bradley's Corner yesterday?"

"Which one?" People considered Bradley's Corner the most

wicked place around.

"A man got shot because he had the smallpox. God's truth." Both hands left the steering wheel for emphasis. The car angled to the left and barely missed a wagonload of pipe, but the driver kept talking. "A man with his face marked with the smallpox was sitting by that big dance hall, the one covered with tar paper?" The driver paused, as if to make sure he had their attention. "The dance hall operator told him to move along, and when he wouldn't, the operator hauled off and shot him."

No question about it: life was getting more dangerous. Margaret could relax only when they returned to Nesterville with its wagons, cars, and crowds along Main Street. Compared to the oilfield settlements, it was the center of civilization.

She wondered whether to invite Dr. Miller in for coffee to let him know once and for all that she didn't feel uncomfortable around him. At her front steps, she pushed back her hair. "Would you like some coffee?"

He only smiled and stroked Beth's cheek. "I've got work." Ah, the universal excuse. "Tell Dutch I said good luck on the well." He was gone, whistling "The Maple Street Rag."

Inside, the house radiated emptiness, creaking as she fumbled for the light. It was a treat to go out when and where she pleased, but she missed Dutch. She wanted to tell him about the Red Onion. He was probably already asleep in a tent in Springtown. He'd no doubt bring home lice.

The door slammed. She heard Dr. Miller protesting and then Dutch laughing. He was home.

"Margaret, look who I met. I want him to hear the news." He sounded exultant. "I left early to tell you."

Margaret ran into the front room. Her husband swooped her up and spun her around. Her skirt flew out. What must Dr. Miller think? Dutch set her down as easily as if she weighed no more than Beth.

"Tell everybody to be at the rig tomorrow. We've got the casing cemented. Now we start bailing." Grinning, he pulled from his pocket a handful of cuttings. The aroma of oil filled the room.

She rolled the damp gravel in her palm and held it to her face. "I do like that smell." She stuck her hand under Dr. Miller's nose.

He bent down. "It's oil, all right."

His breath warm on her palm, she pulled back, conscious of his eyes on her.

"Congratulations," he said.

Dutch went to the kitchen and came back with a bottle. "Let's celebrate. It's your well too."

"No," the doctor said, "I really have to leave."

Before Dutch could protest, he was gone. Dutch shrugged and looked at Margaret. "What did you do today?"

"I went with Eve to the Red Onion. I thought you'd be gone tonight." Dutch's mother would accuse her of not tending the home fires.

"I bet that caused a sensation sure enough." Dutch laughed.

"Nobody seemed to mind. Mrs. McNeill's gone there." Odd. Dutch didn't care. A lot of men would get their jib hung. He must trust her.

"Have some champagne. We can celebrate better by ourselves." Pleased with himself, he handed Margaret a jelly glass. She held it under the bottle, but the cork blew like a gusher.

38

The morning dawned almost clear. The thin sun streaked through distant clouds trailing to the east. Margaret fried eggs in bacon grease and watched a coyote in the riverbed pick its way through ice-coated weeds that glistened in the sunshine. Beyond the sand dunes, the river ran silver. The coyote broke into a trot.

After she took Beth to stay with Mrs. McNeill, Margaret and Dutch took a jitney to the rig. "Tomorrow, Margaret, we've got to buy a car," Dutch yelled above the roar of the wind.

"Maybe we should wait."

"Why?

She hated to depend on anything concerning the oil business. They'd be disappointed. "Like you said before, this well could be dry."

"It won't be. There haven't been any dry holes around here. Remember?" Dutch frowned. "Anyway, we've got one good well. Even without anything else, we're set for sure."

"I feel responsible for our friends. I don't want them to lose their shirt."

"They won't. Where's your spirit of adventure? You've always encouraged me."

Margaret didn't know. These days she held back, while he pushed ahead, like with the poker playing and the talk of buying, while she wanted only to save. A successful marriage was like a balanced seesaw. They both couldn't be free spirits. Having Beth had changed her. Still, she missed her old freer self.

At the rig Paul said, "We can drill into the sand soon. We'll go in a few feet and see what happens."

"Come on, I'll show you the rig." Dutch took Margaret onto the derrick platform, where the noise of the engine was so loud she couldn't hear his explanations. She covered her ears, smiled, and nodded. She could understand why many drillers were taciturn. Dutch had told her about drillers that never said a word, only gestured, to the tool dresser or roughneck, who had to guess what they wanted. Dutch claimed he'd worked for a driller who rarely spoke. Once on the way to work, the driller asked, "You know my little dog?" Dutch had leaned over for an answer, but the driller didn't say anything else all day. Then on their way home, the driller said, "Died." Dutch swore the story was true.

He motioned her down from the platform. As soon as she was on the ground, he led her to an empty tank. "You'll like this." He climbed to the top, the wind whipping his hair. He beckoned. "Come on. The view's swell."

"You know I hate ladders," Margaret hollered up to him as she remembered her terror on the bridge with the bank robber.

Dutch extended his hand toward her. "Come on. I'm here." Her heart beat so hard it pounded in her ears.

"Don't worry about me."

She grasped the first rung, her eyes fixed on Dutch, grinning perhaps ten feet above her. As she moved up, she felt more confident. Jubilant, she pulled herself onto the narrow platform at the top. Dutch hugged her.

"You did it." He pointed north and then east. "You can see all the riverbed and past the town."

She clutched Dutch's arm. Spread around her were the tents in Springtown, the houses and the Red Onion in Clara, and beyond them the derricks in Nesterville. In the daytime all the derricks made the town look like a forest of burned-up trees in a miniature town for a child's train set. Dutch was right. It was a magnificent view.

Their friends gathered, their noses red from the icy wind, their faces expectant. A few men crowded onto the derrick platform, partially enclosed with timber to keep out the cold. The rest huddled around the stove in the lease shack, passing around fried chicken and coffee. Margaret warmed her hands while she listened to speculations about their upcoming prosperity.

"What will you do, Jimmy?" Mr. Smith asked.

Jimmy Johnson fixed his gaze on the sky. "Laugh at me if you like, but I saw a house in Dallas advertised in the paper. Three stories. A mansion." He glanced at Eve, who stood beside him.

"I've always wanted to live in Dallas."

Margaret smiled. Everybody had dreams.

In the late afternoon, as the derrick cast a shadow toward Nesterville, Margaret heard a rumble and then a deafening whoosh.

"Put the fire out."

"Wait," Paul shouted. "We're not ready."

Dutch planted himself on top of the last joint of casing. "This might slow it down."

Margaret gasped as the oil forced its way around Dutch's body as if he were no bigger than an ant. She knew that tools sometimes shot out of the hole and injured bystanders. Dutch laughed as the sticky fluid soaked him. "I tried." He wiped his face but only smeared the oil.

The dark fountain shot up so high Margaret had to tip her head back to keep it in view. It rose higher than the seventy-foot derrick before it cascaded down and covered the floor of the derrick platform and the surrounding area.

Mr. Johnson placed himself in the path of the descending oil. "I've always wanted to do this."

Glen passed around a bottle.

"Never too early to celebrate." Mr. Johnson put his oil-drenched arm around his wife's shoulders. She recoiled from the sticky goo. Laughing so hard her shoulders shook, she took a sip of Glen's liquor.

She stuck out her tongue. "Land, that's strong."

Jimmy clapped his mother on the back. "You're a sport, Ma." They all hugged and laughed, as manic as children at a birthday party, this well the biggest, the best present of all.

Dutch changed behind the shack into a clean khaki shirt and pants, but traces of oil remained on his face. He grinned when he held out his oil-soaked clothes toward Margaret.

"You take care of them." She scrunched up her nose. "They're filthy. I'll never get them clean."

"Don't worry. We can afford new clothes now." Dutch put his arm around her and then turned to Paul. "Are you ready?"

Paul eyed the gusher. "It may take hours for it to settle down." He punched Dutch on the shoulder and shrugged. "Why not? I can afford to replace a suit now if I have to. I'll do it." Paul ducked into the shack.

Margaret knew that controlling the well could be dangerous. Surely it wasn't time for Paul to begin his usual ritual when a well came in, changing into a new suit, but Paul liked drama. When he rejoined them, he wore a waist-seamed and double-breasted suit, the most fashionable style.

Then he paid the men, who lined up, drinking from bottles of bootleg whiskey. Last, Paul threw his overalls, as was his custom, to the youngest roughneck. They all cheered. Five years ago, at the first well they'd worked on together, Dutch had caught Paul's overalls. He and Paul had discovered right off that they shared the ambition to keep them striving until they owned their own rig and wells. And now they did.

They celebrated at the Red Onion, watched by hollow-eyed roughnecks slumped over the bar, waiting to go to their rented cots. Dutch pulled tables together and ordered champagne.

When they were seated to his satisfaction, Dutch stood. His grin touched each of them in turn and lingered on Margaret. How poised he'd become. "We've seen what may be the biggest gusher of them all. Who knows? It could produce more than the Fowler."

Eve, sitting next to Jimmy, raised her glass. "I'll drink to that."

They all cheered. Dutch loathed speaking in public, blushing and stammering whenever he had to address a group. Maybe prosperity changed a man. Margaret found herself looking at him with new eyes. Here it came again, falling in love with the same man once more.

He held up a hand to silence them. "I have a proposal for all you stockholders in"—like a professional speaker he paused for effect, his eyes on Margaret's— "the Margaret Oil Company."

She smiled, her face warm. "I'm honored."

They clapped. Jimmy whistled.

Dutch wasn't finished. "We have a winner." His expression became serious. "But we also have a lease too small to allow us to drill any more wells." His eyes again moved around the table. "I propose that we don't stop here, that we have the vision to look to the future. I haven't even told Margaret." His dark eyes caught hers. "I wanted to surprise you."

The room felt chillier. She pulled her coat around her shoulders. A Dutch who could make speeches was admirable, but, please, no more chances.

Dutch raised his eyes to the group. "I found some land to lease south of Nesterville, close to the Daniels' farm. Nobody's drilled near there, so we can get it cheap. The mother pool hasn't been found. It has to be right there. We can wildcat, all of us together. Paul and I will volunteer our rig, as we did on this lease." He glanced at Paul, who nodded. "We want to offer all of you the opportunity to channel your profits into another project. We can drill for twenty thousand dollars." He looked around, his hands outspread. "We can't lose. What do you say?"

Margaret tried not to show her dismay. When she had thought the insecurity of their lives was over, it returned, more threatening than before. With his new-found speaking ability, Dutch made it sound easy, but drilling was as risky as gambling.

They were all subdued, their eyes on the table. Mr. and Mrs. Johnson glanced at each other.

Margaret waited as the silence grew heavy.

Mr. Johnson pushed back his chair. "Dutch, I am grateful—as everyone else is—for what you've done for us. We can never thank you enough for this opportunity. I can't speak for anyone else"— his eyes went round the table—"but Eula May and I are too old to risk anything else. A wildcat's a long shot."

They all nodded. Nobody looked at Dutch. Nobody spoke. Margaret stewed in silence. Surely someone would support her husband. She might not want risks, but neither did she want other people to doubt his judgment. He and Paul knew oil.

Dr. Miller cleared his throat. He, if anybody, would understand the business angle to Dutch's idea and would set them straight. "I agree with Mr. Johnson. Most of us can't afford more risk. Maybe later...." Feeling betrayed, Margaret glared at him. He wouldn't meet her eyes.

One by one, they drifted out. Their unfinished drinks sat in damp rings on the table. Even Eve left, nodding at Paul and Dutch. "I'm sorry."

The waitress placed a bill between Paul and Dutch. Dutch ran his hand over his chin. "What do you think, Margaret? Am I crazy?"

"Certainly not. You and Paul did something wonderful. You made them rich. You helped them fulfill their dreams. They're little people. They have no sense of the future. All they can say is 'thank you, but no thanks.'" She took Dutch's hand, lying palm up, vulnerable, in both of hers. She squeezed it hard, feeling the calluses. "We'll manage. If they don't want to do this, you and Paul can do it alone."

"I guess we'll have to." He pushed back his chair and stood. "Let's go home."

Dutch couldn't rest. He prowled. Drumming his fingers, he bent over maps that covered the table. "I've studied these, Margaret, until I'm blue in the face. There's a pattern. The mother pool has to be right here." He jabbed his forefinger at a bare spot. "That's where our new lease will be. Yours and mine and Paul's, since nobody else wants to invest in it." He stood and started pacing through the house, occasionally smacking his hands together.

Margaret sat and watched. "Dutch, I'm jittery looking at you, and I'm exhausted." She yawned. "Why don't you take a bath?"

"I can't relax. I keep wondering if the well's still flowing or if Paul's been able to get the oil into the tanks."

"Come here. I'll rub your back."

He smiled.

39

Before dawn, Dutch eased out of bed and with his lips touched Margaret's hair, jumbled over her face as she slept. She didn't stir.

As always first thing on his way to the rig, Dutch checked the sky. It wasn't snowing, although the usual flat clouds hung low.

The well was still flowing, and Paul still appeared alert although he'd worked all night.

Dutch glanced around. There was always the risk of theft. Tools, pipeline, tanks disappeared overnight. "Any trouble?"

"Nothing. A few drifters, but that's all."

"Good thing we've got the slush pit." Dutch and Paul stood on the edge of the pool, almost full from the overflow.

"I wish we'd made it bigger," Paul said.

While they watched, the crude reached the top of the pit and overflowed. It trickled through the cotton field, cutting a path toward Springtown.

"At least two tanks were delivered last night, I see," Dutch said.

"We could use more. Have you heard when the new pipeline will be finished?"

"Any day now."

"That's what they've said for a month." Rubbing his eyes, Paul yawned. "I'll sleep a few hours."

"Sure," Dutch said.

Gradually the flow subsided so the crew could divert it to an eight-hundred-barrel tank. In three hours, that tank was full. The well was producing even more than they'd anticipated.

Rested, Paul returned in the late afternoon. "We have to lease that land near the Daniels' farm before somebody snatches it up."

"I found out that Mister Daniels is in Dallas till tomorrow." Dutch stretched, exhausted but not relaxed enough to go home. He called to Glen, who was ending his shift. "Let's see if we can find a friendly game."

"I'm your man."

Paul grinned. "Don't spend it all."

"No danger of that," Dutch said. Paul was an ideal partner, not cowardly like the others.

Two hours later, Dutch surveyed his winnings, chips stacked in front of him like tumbleweeds against a fence. Maybe anger at his friends' lack of nerve caused him to play aggressively. Maybe it was luck, like the story, probably untrue, about how Burke Burnett won his ranch with four sixes in a poker game. He and Paul might have almost enough to drill with what he'd won tonight. These men were high bidders.

"Better stop while I'm ahead." Dutch gathered up his chips.

Glen looked up. "Don't leave now. Give us a chance to get some of that back. The party's just starting."

"I need to get home."

"Missing the little woman? I would too if my old lady looked like Margaret."

Glen was jealous. The more Dutch protested, the louder Glen's objections became. Dutch shrugged and shoved his winnings into his coat pocket. He'd go home tonight. Tomorrow morning, first thing, he'd deposit all the money in the bank, and if nobody wanted to go in with Paul and him, they'd wildcat themselves. He jammed on his hat.

As Dutch stood, Glen stared at him, his eyes narrowed. Dutch didn't care. He was sick of Glen's envy disguised as joking. Dutch walked outside.

The drizzle had become a downpour. The street was clogged with men and wagons. He was glad to be going home. Margaret would probably be cooking, her face flushed, the kitchen warm. He'd sit by the stove and read a fairy tale to Beth. In front of the saloon, he avoided the mudhole so deep that last week a mule had drowned in it. Looking for a jitney was probably as pointless as trying to stay dry, but he tried. Tomorrow after he went to the bank, he and Margaret would buy a Model-T. They could take an early train to Wichita Falls. Getting there by train was easier than driving. There'd been talk of fixing the road since he'd been here, but with the flu epidemic and the rain nothing had been done.

From behind him came a voice that sounded familiar. "Hey, fella, got a light?"

Dutch turned in the downpour to face a man whose scrawniness reminded him of Glen, but with his coat collar up and his hat pulled over his eyes, Dutch couldn't tell. For a minute, the man didn't say anything, just stood there, drenched, with one hand inside his coat.

When he pulled out his hand, he held a blackjack. "Hand over your money. All of it."

"Glen?" Images of the night last fall when he and Jimmy Johnson had been hijacked ran through Dutch's mind. It had been raining then too.

"Let's have the money. Now." The man's voice was louder, as if the hijacker—it must be Glen, sure enough—were building up his courage.

"You must be joking." Dutch swung at the man's stomach, but for someone who looked too out of shape to fight a field mouse, the man was strong. Dutch was aware of a head-splitting pain by his temple and then only the stench and cold wetness of oily slime on his face.

40

Margaret waited for the iron to heat on the stove. She sprinkled the clean clothes with water, rolling them tightly, so that a neat row awaited her. If only life could be that orderly. The unexpected upset any equilibrium they achieved. Now that she'd recovered from the flu and they had a jam-up well, she had hoped for a moment of security, even peace. Then Dutch's hankering to wildcat emerged. But that decision couldn't be responsible for her unease now. She felt a yank on the intangible cord that bound her to Dutch. The cord slackened. In her mind she tugged again but felt no response. Perhaps she'd better carry Dutch some chicken-fried steak. He'd like it, and she'd be reassured.

But in town, the crowds were, if anything, thicker than in the fall. She couldn't find a free jitney. At the livery stable Jimmy Johnson was hitching his horses to the ambulance wagon that doubled as a hearse.

She petted the bay mare, the white star on its forehead standing out, its muzzle soft as velvet. The mare whinnied. Margaret stepped back, laughing. She missed having horses. Maybe they could buy a couple, and Jimmy could board them. Or they could buy some pasture in the country, and in a few years, Beth could ride by herself. "Jimmy, I need to go to Springtown."

"I'm fixing to go there myself," he said. "Somebody's hurt. I'd be pleased to have your company. Where's that young'un?"

"Eve wanted to keep her."

"Eve's good with kids all right." He glanced at her basket of food and threw her a hang-dog look. "My, that smells good."

"Have some. I made plenty. Jimmy, you need a wife of your own."

He grinned, not the least embarrassed at her meddling. Probably he heard so much of it from his mother that he'd become immune. "No wife. You and Dutch have a good marriage, but it's not for me. Too much work."

Margaret agreed. Marriage did require work, but for her, the trust more than compensated for the effort. However, that argument wouldn't convince as entrenched a bachelor as Jimmy.

"Anyway, why do I need a wife when I can have your good food?" Jimmy grinned again as he took a chunk of steak. He knew he was a charmer.

The road was crowded. The drizzle began again. She pulled her hat down. Sheets of lightning flashed. The horses flattened their ears.

Jimmy indicated the massing piles of dark clouds. "I don't like this."

"Me either." Lightning and thunder made Margaret want to crawl under a pile of quilts and hide her head.

"Nothing like the twisters, though."

Margaret peered at the black thunderheads, which had commenced rumbling. "Tornadoes?"

"Not this time of year. Mainly in the spring. The sky turns green and then black. The wind roars like a train."

"Something else to look forward to."

The drizzle stopped, but the air felt heavy, waiting. The sky flashed behind the derricks, and lightning zigzagged toward the earth.

Jimmy patted the horses and murmured soothing words. Her heart beat fast. In the wagon they were a perfect target for lightning.

A crack louder than a hundred guns cut the still air, and, on the far western edge of Springtown, an explosion of flames leapt into the sky. Margaret gasped.

Jimmy slowed the wagon. Wide-eyed with fear, the horses stamped. "Lightning struck a tank. It's happened twice before. The town'll burn up this time."

Margaret brought her hand to her mouth. "Dutch is over there. The lightning hit where our wells are."

"We can't go much farther."

"Dutch is at the well. He might be hurt. I have to find him."

As they reached Springtown, they watched oil pour out of the exploded tank and follow the ruts in the street, rivulets of rainwater thick with mud. Explosions accompanied waves of fire that raced down the street like a blazing river. The heat hit them like a wall. Flames and black clouds of smoke leapt higher than the derricks.

All around them, cries were mixed with the crackle of flames that devoured tents on both sides of the street.

"It's all going. I'll try behind the town. Maybe we can get to the west side." Jimmy's voice softened. "I don't know what else to do." He had given up.

"Dutch is alive, Jimmy. I feel it." She prayed for a miracle, even though their wells, the tanks, the slush pits for the overflow—everything was to the west.

The roaring conflagration devoured tents nearer them.

"I don't dare go any closer." The horses tried to bolt. Jimmy pulled up near a group of men, standing like pale specters in the glare of the flames.

"I'm going on, Jimmy."

"What can you do? You'll get yourself killed."

"Is that all you can say?" Fed up, she jumped from the wagon. She turned her ankle as she landed, but she limped on despite the pain.

"Come back. You can't help Dutch now."

Jimmy's voice died away in the roar of the fire and the chaos in the street, and she seemed alone, her isolation broken only by screams and crashes.

A moment before the fiery canvas next to her exploded, she plunged behind the tents, staggering through hot air permeated with the acrid scent of burning cloth mixed with oil. She tripped on the charred body of a man as she watched another man run, his clothes aflame. Beyond the brightness a group of men huddled.

"Help me find my husband."

Their faces bleak with loss, they stood without responding. She limped past them, stumbling across what until a few months ago were rows of cotton. She refused to succumb to her terror, but repeated, "I won't give up. I'll find Dutch."

Past the tents, she looked back toward the main street of the town. The fire would suck up everything. All lost, all of it. Her ankle throbbed. She longed to sit in the mud and rest, but the slackness of the cord in her mind impelled her to continue limping behind the wall of flames. She had no notion of how long she wandered, searching.

On the far side of the town, the fire was sputtering out, although a few tongues of flames still burned, leaving charred timbers that had been derricks and tanks. The ground felt hot through the soles of her boots. Steam rose from the blackened ground, which sizzled in the rain. The air reeked of oil and a sickening sweet smell.

She approached another group of men. "I'm looking for my husband. He was at a well near here." She pointed west. "Dutch Sanders?"

A lean man covered with soot rubbed his eyes. He looked dazed. "Lady, no telling how many people are dead. You'd best go home and wait."

She continued toward the blackened remains of their tanks and slush pits, which were still burning. Standing in the mud, she kicked a piece of charred timber probably from their derrick. The hot air was thick with ashes. Her energy dissipated. She slumped to the ruined earth. She hated this place. If Dutch hadn't been infected with the oil fever, they'd never have come. All this destruction resulted from greed. She searched in the mud until she found a rock. Its heat burned her hand, but she threw it at a smoking beam, and it bounced with a satisfying thud and a shower of sparks.

She yearned to lie down and sleep and never get up. It would be easy. She sat shivering as the rain splattered and sizzled on the hot ground and mingled with her tears.

From the curtain of ashes around her, Jimmy's bass voice called her name. She ignored him; he would only tell her he'd found Dutch's body. A spirit materializing from the murky air, he squatted beside her. His face was streaked with soot, his eyes red.

"He's gone, Jimmy. He won't ever come back."

"Margaret, Dutch is alive."

"He can't be. You see all this." She gestured to the half-burned timbers, all that remained of their derrick, their dreams.

Jimmy put his hands on her shoulders, speaking as he would to a child. "Listen. Dutch is not dead."

She shook off his hands. "Where is he?"

"In the wagon. It's where you jumped down. He's hurt. I met Paul. He'd found Dutch. We've been looking for you."

"Dutch is alive?" Margaret stood. "Show me."

He pointed.

She ignored the shrieking of her ankle and hobbled over the uneven earth.

Paul motioned toward the bed of Jimmy's wagon. She saw a still form with a lump by his temple caked with blood and mire. Sobbing, she knelt and with her skirt dabbed at his face, coated with mud like a mask. Under the mud, he looked defenseless without his glasses.

On their way to the clinic in Nesterville, they picked up four wounded men, their cracked skin blackened.

"Can't we go faster?" Margaret braced herself against the side of the wagon and eased Dutch's head onto her lap, trying to soften the jolting. She stroked his matted hair and willed the wagon to fly like a hawk across the plains.

As they drove east surrounded by other wagons and cars, Margaret overheard snatches of Jimmy's and Paul's conversation.

"It's all gone. Everything. I put all my savings in y'all's lease." Jimmy sounded bitter.

Paul shrugged. "We all did."

Fire was inevitable in the oilfield. Everybody knew that. Nothing but the hand of God could have stopped it. And wells could be recovered. Not everything was lost—the derricks, the tanks, and the pipe line—but the oil was still there.

The wagon bounced. The other men moaned, but Dutch lay still. She remembered when she'd run into him at the train station in Oil City, four years after she'd last seen him in school. She recognized him as one of the big boys who played with Aut, but she couldn't remember his name, so she called him "Albert" the whole ride to Shreveport, where he was working and she was in her last year at the Catholic school. At the station he'd lingered, his hazel eyes admiring her, and she'd preened, basking in her new power. He'd agreed to come fishing at the lake. As he turned away, he said, "By the way, my name's not Albert. It's Frank." She remembered how humiliated she'd felt, but he had shown up at the lake on Sunday carrying a fishing pole and wearing his best suit.

Dutch groaned and opened his eyes. He stared. "Margaret, why are we in the hearse? I'm not dead. Don't let them bury me."

"You're not dead. You're hurt bad."

"They'll bury me for sure." He tried to raise himself.

"This wagon's the ambulance, too, remember? Jimmy's carrying you to the doctor. Paul's here."

But Dutch kept squinting. He reached for Margaret's hand. "Keep me with you."

"I will. But you're not dead. I thought you were though. What happened?"

He gripped her hand. "I can't remember. I left the well. I think I played poker. I was in the mud. Paul said he found me wandering around in the fire." He touched the lump on his head and grimaced. "Now there's this."

"You don't know how you got it?" She peered at the bump matted with blood.

At the clinic, Jimmy helped Paul ease Dutch out of the wagon. Margaret hovered behind them. The examining rooms were already full, so they laid the men on sheets on the floor. Margaret sat with Dutch's head in her lap. How long must they wait?

Jimmy left with a perfunctory nod.

"What's eating him?" Margaret said to Paul.

"He's upset about losing his money. He blames Dutch and me."

"What did you do? You gave everybody an opportunity. They knew it was a risk. Anyway, you and Dutch and I lost two wells and our rig, everything we had. And the wells can be recovered, can't they?"

"That takes money." Paul shrugged. "People want a scapegoat when things don't work out."

"Doesn't Jimmy care what happens to Dutch? Or them?" She indicated the burned men on the floor and in the hall. "They probably won't pull through. At least Jimmy's not hurt."

"It happens all the time, blaming other people."

That didn't make it right, she wanted to tell Paul, but he leaned against the wall, his eyes closed, his face covered with soot, exhausted. She'd been chattering and had forgotten that if it weren't for Paul, Dutch would have burned up in the fire. She touched Paul's shoulder. "I can't thank you enough."

He opened his eyes. "He's my friend. Remember last year when I fell off the derrick, and Dutch carried me to the doctor? Three miles through the woods. The doctor said I wouldn't have made it if Dutch hadn't brought me in. Today all I did was find him walking around confused and took him to the wagon. I did all I could. It may not be enough."

"He has to get well." She couldn't lose him now. This had reminded her how much she cherished him. "I wish the doctor would hurry." Dutch had slipped into unconsciousness again, his face pale. Maybe oblivion was a blessing.

The nurse, a placid woman with a Scottish accent, crouched beside them. She stroked Dutch's tangled hair back from his face. "We'll take your husband next, Mrs. Sanders."

"How do you know me?"

"Dr. Miller talks about you. Everybody knows about you and Mr. Sanders and Mr. McKnight here. What you did for your friends. Giving them the opportunity to profit from the boom. It was a verra noble thing."

"Everything was lost in the fire."

"I know, but you tried." With a cool hand, she patted Margaret's arm. "That's what counts."

Margaret didn't agree. What good was the effort if it failed?

Dr. Miller bent beside her. He probed Dutch's head and instructed the nurse to wash the wound.

"It doesn't look good, Margaret," he said. "We'll have to wait and see. He has a concussion. Watch him. Try to keep him awake." He touched Dutch's shoulder. "Dutch, can you hear me?"

Dutch opened his eyes. Margaret pleaded with him.

"You have to stay awake, the doctor said."

Dutch smiled at her and closed his eyes.

She sighed. "Dutch, wake up."

His eyes still shut, he said, "I don't want to."

"You have to."

His eyes flickered open, and he touched his head. "That smarts."

Paul went to look for a jitney to take them home.

41

Dutch drifted in and out of consciousness, sometimes aware of Margaret, sometimes lost in pain. He dreamed he climbed a cypress tree above Caddo Lake. Willing himself not to look down, not to succumb to dizziness, he placed his foot on the next branch the way Margaret had shown him. The bark scraped his skin. He pulled himself toward her, her brother, and her sister, all lined up on a limb waiting. They were ready to jump. He couldn't let on that he was terrified, not in front of Aut and Rachel. He couldn't lose face in front of Margaret, who though she was the youngest scrunched up her eyes, pinched her nose, and plunged into that opaque water. She didn't surface for so long that he always wanted to rescue her, but Aut had told him Margaret liked to swim underwater. He reached the branch where they waited, smirking, savoring his fear and their superiority. He slid onto the limb with both hands, his legs dangling. One by one they pushed themselves off the limb. He willed himself not to scream as he fell toward the lake and down into its coldness. His foot touched something squishy. He pushed toward the light at the surface, a ceiling miles above him. But the longer he kicked, the farther the ceiling receded. He could never reach it; he was about to drown. He felt no terror, no dread, only surprise and comfort as he slipped into darkness that no longer brought fear, only rest, and he floated as easily as a leaf or a feather. The dark became light, and he found himself wafted up into brightness and color, drifting and spinning, all ease, all lightness, enveloped in peace.

Dutch opened his eyes. Sunlight from the window fell on Margaret, who sat next to him, sleeping. Her gaunt cheeks were streaked with tears.

"Margaret?"

Her head jerked up. She turned to him with a smile so dazzling that he had no regrets about leaving the dream. He belonged here.

Her touch on his forehead was cool. "Here we are again."

"What do you mean?"

"Like in the fall. When you were hijacked before," she said.

"I can't remember." It was bewildering, not having any notion of what he'd done, as if his mind had been swept clean of all the recent past.

She took his hand. "You said you woke in a mudhole outside the saloon. It's a wonder you didn't drown. Paul found you. He said you were wandering around, dazed. He saved your life. Lightning hit a tank, probably one of ours. I've never seen anything like it. Oil boiled out of the tank and ran down the street. It looked like a wall of flame coming at us. And the heat and the smell, like—things—cooking. It was awful."

"Is everything gone?"

She nodded. "The whole town burned up."

"We lost both wells? The rig too? Everything?"

"Except your life. We have to remember that." Both her hands, soft and small, encircled his.

He frowned. "It still isn't clear. I'm not burned. I went to play poker with Glen. I think I won a lot of money. Did you check my pockets?"

"Why?"

"It seems like I had almost enough to wildcat on that lease south of town."

Margaret searched his jacket. "Nothing there."

Dutch rubbed his forehead, concentrating. The pain intensified when he moved. "Where's Beth?"

"Playing with her dolls."

"Papa." Beth toddled to the bed. He touched her silky hair.

Beth climbed beside him, her brown eyes solemn as she inspected the bandage above his ear.

Dutch tried to smile but could only grimace.

"Beth, don't shake the bed," Margaret said.

"She's fine, aren't you, Bethie?" Dutch tried to ignore the pain each time he moved.

"Papa." She touched his face with warm fingers. Then she climbed down.

"I guess that means I'm cured. I wish she'd tell my head that."

"It hurts bad?"

"I wouldn't want to climb a derrick." Dutch tried to laugh, but the effort shook his brain. He couldn't think what it all meant. First, he'd try to remember.

Paul walked in, his blue eyes hard. "I can't find Glen."

"Do you have my money?" Dutch tried to sit up, but his head screamed.

"What money?"

"I think I won a lot. Before the fire. I hoped you'd found it in my pocket."

"I didn't find anything," Paul said.

"I guess I lost it."

Paul scowled. "Stolen, more than likely."

"By that hijacker?"

"Whoever gave you that lump and left you to die in the mud." Paul's lips set in a line. He sounded grim.

42

Margaret didn't care about the money. If—when—Dutch recovered, they could go live on Caddo Lake with Mama and Daddy while he recuperated. She'd had enough of boomtown life, though she'd miss all their friends. Dr. Miller planned to escape to Fort Worth as soon as his replacement arrived. She'd miss him, but she'd be relieved not to have him around as a reminder of her foolishness. She'd miss Eve most; she'd never felt so close to a friend before. Living in these spartan conditions, people had to depend on each other. Maybe it was like living through a war, Nesterville besieged by a malevolent black liquid of infinite power. Sometimes the oil seemed like a viscous river of malign intent, flooding their town, their homes, their dreams until it submerged them all. Other times it seemed like a fire with its power to seek out and consume everything in–or near–its path. River or fire, it was a presence–Presence?–never to be ignored. They should go home. She yearned for the softness of the pines, the coolness of the lake.

Humming, Margaret carried coffee into the bedroom. Dutch had raised himself in bed. Paul and he bent over a map.

"What about here?" Paul pointed to a blank spot.

"Perfect." Dutch nodded.

Margaret raised her eyebrows. "You're supposed to be convalescing."

Dutch smiled. "We've found the mother pool. We can't miss."

Would this oil fever never end? They were as naïve as boys. "We don't have any money," she said.

Paul dismissed her objection. "That's the least of our worries. We'll raise money the same way we did before. That's what banks are for. We'll recover our two wells in Springtown, and then—"

"You mean drill them again? Get new tanks?"

"Right, the whole thing." Dutch frowned. "I know it's a lot, Margaret, but we have to. The wells belonged to our friends too, not just us. You do understand?"

She nodded.

"After that, Paul and I want to wildcat here. And here." He bent over the map and pointed.

So their plans to wildcat were only postponed, not changed. Money was a trifle, made or lost overnight. Margaret bit her bottom lip. Now was not the right time to mention returning to Caddo Lake.

Dutch slept, exhausted from all the planning. Margaret sat next to him, praying and rocking Beth. She'd sat here after Dutch had been hijacked the first time, and Dutch had sat here when she'd had the flu. Their lives circled, returning to where they began, or perhaps they swung like the pendulum on their clock in the front room, which had just begun to chime. Beth napped, heavy on her shoulder, but Margaret couldn't relax. The rocking chair creaked in a monotonous pattern, but for the life of her, she couldn't make out what it said.

"I thought you could use a little help." Eve said. "I brought soup."

Beth, shouting "EE," toddled to her and clung to her long skirt.

"How did you find out so fast?"

"Same as always. Jimmy came to the saloon to take me home. He's decided it's not safe for me to be out alone at night."

"Hmmm."

"Leave it, Margaret. It wouldn't work. I'm not the marrying kind. Neither is he. We talked about it, but the truth is, his mother's pampered him so long he'll never leave home." Eve raised Beth, giggling, above her head. "Actually, I do have news. I'm going to pick up Samantha next week."

"Samantha?"

"My daughter."

"In the orphanage?"

"Isn't it wonderful? I wanted to tell you first because you suggested I bring her home."

Margaret hugged her.

"I had no idea I could do it. I think seeing you with Beth changed my mind."

"She and Beth will be friends."

"I forgot why I came, I guess because I'm so happy. How's Dutch?"

"Better." Margaret twisted her lips. "But it's strange. Jimmy's bound to have told his mother. You'd think she would've been here. Or the McNeills. I heard them, but they haven't come over. Dutch is not contagious. Don't they care that he almost died?"

"They're busy, I reckon." Eve shrugged. "I can stay with Dutch and Beth a spell if you want to get out."

At Boyd's, Margaret lined up. She wanted to buy oranges for Dutch, although they had to watch every penny. She tried to catch Mr. Boyd's eye as he bustled around Mrs. Edwards. Margaret smiled, but Mrs. Edwards's eyes flitted over Margaret as if she were empty space. The wind whipped into the store. Margaret shivered.

"Two oranges please," she said

Mr. Boyd was polite. "Two dollars."

Margaret gasped. "So much?" She wavered. They were expensive, but Dutch was sick, and he'd loved the oranges at Beth's party. "I'll put them on our bill."

"Cash only." Mr. Boyd surveyed the line behind her while he pulled at the hair sprouting from the mole under his nose.

Margaret frowned. "Last week I had an account."

"Not anymore." Mr. Boyd shrugged and rocked on his heels as the women behind her fidgeted, pretending not to eavesdrop. "Do you want the oranges?"

Margaret handed them back. "I'll wait." She hunched her shoulders. She felt as vulnerable as if she'd been seen in her chemise.

"Next, please," Mr. Boyd barked. Margaret pulled her coat tight and walked into the cold.

At the pharmacy she lined up, her eyes on the ground. She didn't want to risk more rebuffs.

"May I help you?" Mr. Kelly's voice was impersonal.

"Aspirin, please." She fumbled in her purse for her last two bits. She studied Mr. Kelly's face to determine whether his attitude was cooler than usual, but he'd never been effusive. Maybe she was paranoid, expecting rejection.

Outside, she saw Mr. Johnson. He could explain what, if anything, was going on. Since that first day, he'd treated her with nothing but kindness. She called. He looked straight at her and turned away. With his weak eyes, he probably didn't recognize her. She ran to catch him. Panting, she touched his shoulder to attract his attention. He jumped, shying like a spooked horse.

"Have you heard about Dutch? He was hijacked."

"Jimmy told me. Sorry to hear it." His words were kind, but his tone was formal. Margaret had never seen him so skittish. Stroking his mustache, he stood before her trembling, glanced around, and then backed away. "Excuse me. I have to join my wife."

Mrs. Johnson met him at the corner. He inclined his head in Margaret's direction. Margaret waved, and Mrs. Johnson nodded. Perhaps still sensitized by Mr. Boyd's rudeness, she was imagining their unfriendliness. They turned and walked away. Not the Johnsons too. She was hurt more by their scorn than anyone else's.

Margaret was relieved to meet no one else she knew. She needed time to adjust to her new role of pariah or, at best, nodding acquaintance. In the front room she threw her coat on the chair. Mr. Boyd—and maybe Mr. Kelly, the Johnsons, and the McNeills— acted as if the fire in Springtown had been ignited and fanned by Dutch and Paul themselves. Some friends.

She tiptoed into the bedroom. Dutch slept, one arm outflung. She touched his pale forehead. He felt hot, and the lump on his head looked as swollen as before.

In the kitchen Eve was telling Beth a story: "So the mother rabbit went to look for the baby rabbit all over. She looked in the riverbed, but the baby wasn't there. She looked in the house, but it wasn't there. Do you know where the baby was?" Eve paused. Margaret pictured Beth with her eyes and mouth wide. "It was right there under the back step. And do you know what they did when the mother rabbit found the baby? They ate their favorite food. Carrots."

Maybe Eve had persuaded Beth to eat vegetables. Margaret peeked into the kitchen; Beth sat in her high chair with her lips clamped shut. Noticing Margaret, Beth banged her spoon on the high chair and called, "Mama."

Eve turned smiling toward her. "I do enjoy Beth."

Margaret sat at the table and reached for the bowl of carrots.

"Beth, open your mouth. Now." Her troubles returned, flying in the window and sitting heavy on her shoulder like crows.

"What's wrong?"

"They all acted like I was trash, Eve." She listed them on her fingers: "Mr. Boyd, Mr. Kelly, Mrs. Johnson, even Mr. Johnson."

"If that doesn't beat all." Eve paused. "It's true that sometimes people are treated differently when they have money and when they don't. You know that." She glanced at Margaret, who nodded. "That's part of it. If they're angry with you, it must be because of the fire. They invested so much in the lease, and now it's lost."

"I didn't cause the fire. Neither did Dutch."

"They have to blame somebody."

"Don't they know everything's a gamble in the oilfield?" Margaret said.

"They forgot. Now they're embarrassed."

Margaret wrinkled her nose. "I don't buy that."

"Think about it. Deep down, they're not angry with Dutch or you or Paul. They're mad at themselves. They see money flashed around. The newspapers have been filled with it for six months, even during the war and the flu epidemic. You've seen it. Oil fever. It infects everybody."

"Maybe." Margaret remembered the euphoria she'd sensed everywhere when she arrived. Eve, for all her common sense, had succumbed to the oil fever too, investing her savings along with everybody else. And Margaret herself had felt similarly, as if the money and the drilling weren't reality but a fascinating never-ending game, with fountains of black liquid as the prize.

"People love to gamble, and it could be that for a little while they allowed themselves to forget a truth they all know: in an oil boom most people don't become millionaires. They go bust."

Margaret understood. They had been carried away, her mother would say, had allowed themselves to hope for something better than their grubby existences.

She sighed. "The other problem—the real problem—is that we don't have any money. We used our savings on the leases. The quarantine for the flu's over, and the school's open again, but I don't want to teach while Dutch is hurt."

"What about working more at the boarding house, like last

summer, until Dutch gets better and you can teach again?"

Margaret nodded. She had one friend left.

"You can start as soon as Dutch can stay by himself."

When Dr. Miller came to see Dutch, Margaret told him how she'd been treated rudely or ignored. "It's not surprising, Margaret. They have to blame somebody. There's nothing like trouble to show you who your real friends are."

She knew that.

"I'm relieved to be going back to a city where there may be some sanity left." Smiling, he met her eyes. She smiled back. "How's the patient?"

"Much better, thanks to your help. See for yourself."

After supper, the wind diminished. Margaret wrapped a quilt around her shoulders and sat on the back steps. The days were noticeably longer and warmer now.

"Beth, look." She blew a soap bubble as big as Beth's head. Beth chased the bubble, a puff of iridescence, in the calm evening air.

The door creaked. She raised her head. "Dutch, it's cool out here. What are you doing up?"

"I heard you and Beth laughing."

Margaret scooted over, Dutch sat, and she pulled the quilt around them both.

"I feel strong enough to wrestle a bull."

"Right." She laughed.

Beth toddled after the bubbles, her hair bright. Past Beth, tumbleweeds piled against barbed-wire fences. The fields of winter wheat glowed green; delicate shoots poked through the mud.

Without warning, as she looked toward the river, a feeling of serenity and peace descended on Margaret, a gift unasked for. It would no doubt dissipate as quickly as it had arrived, but for now it brought her comfort and hope.

The long whistle of the southbound train cut into the stillness. Tomorrow, the train would be in Shreveport. So would the muddy water in Red River. She wanted to tell Dutch how she'd stay here or return to Louisiana with him, whatever he wanted. But the words faltered in the pale silver light, slipped, and floated away unspoken.

Bibliography

Benton, Minnie King. *Boomtown: A Portrait of Burkburnett.* Quanah, Texas: Nortex Press, 1972.

Crowder, Dorothy. *Tales of the Red River Valley.* Burkburnett, Texas: n.p., 1988.

Harries, Meirion and Susie. *The Last Days of Innocence: America at War, 1917 - 1918.* New York: Random House, 1997.

Landrum, Jeff. *Reflections of a Boomtown: A Photographic Essay of the Burkburnett Oil Boom, 1912 - 1982.* Wichita Falls, Texas: Humphrey Printing Company, 1982.

Sullivan, Mark. *Our Times: 1900 - 1925.* V. *Over Here, 1914 - 1918.* New York: Charles Scribner's Sons, 1936.